THE BROKEN AND THE BOLD

The De Veres, Book 3

Leslie Vollard

ARE YOU SIGNED UP FOR DRAGONBLADE'S BLOG?

You'll get the latest news and information on exclusive giveaways, exclusive excerpts, coming releases, sales, free books, cover reveals and more.

Check out our complete list of authors, too!

No spam, no junk. That's a promise!

Sign Up Here

www.dragonbladepublishing.com

Dearest Reader;

Thank you for your support of a small press. At Dragonblade Publishing, we strive to bring you the highest quality Historical Romance from some of the best authors in the business. Without your support, there is no 'us', so we sincerely hope you adore these stories and find some new favorite authors along the way.

Happy Reading!

CEO, Dragonblade Publishing

**Additional Dragonblade books by
Author Leslie Vollard**

The De Veres Series
The Skull and the Lute (Book 1)
The Sword and the Damsel (Book 2)
The Broken and the Bold (Book 3)

CHAPTER ONE

July 1176 AD
Off the coast of Ireland

FIONOLA BALANCED ON the railing of her ship in the pale moonlight, one hand gripping the rigging, as she hurled a clay pot of pulverized lime across the water and onto the stern deck of the *Midas*. She smiled as a cloud of stinging, blinding dust enveloped the few of the other ship's crew that were awake at this late hour.

In a few short minutes, she might see her brother. Black Stephen would pay for what he'd done to him. But she couldn't get ahead of herself. First, she had to take this ship.

She signaled Colm and Seamus, who threw more pots, ensuring the cloud of lime covered the entire length of the ship's deck. Hearing their crewmates' howls of pain, sailors on the *Midas* swarmed up from belowdecks, only to be blinded themselves by the fine billowing dust. Within minutes, there was no more movement, as the entire crew of the *Midas* sat weeping uncontrollably, coughing and wheezing on deck.

With a swipe of her finger, Fionola signaled to Aidan, Ronan, and Thomas to throw the grappling hooks, which made satisfying thunks as they dug into wood. Rope ladders stretched across the water. Masked and veiled to keep from breathing the lime, she and her crew climbed out over the water and up onto the swaying deck of the other ship. Her men made short work of tying up the crew, and she wrenched a key ring from one of their belts before descending below.

Pulling a candle and flint from the pouch on her belt, she raised a quavering light and climbed down the hatch. Could Liam be here? Had she found him at last?

Navigating around piled crates and sacks of goods that had been plundered from her homeland by Black Stephen, she picked a path to the cabins in the bow of the ship. Opening one door, she was greeted with nothing but a straw pallet and a wooden sea chest. The next one was empty as well, and the next. But when she opened the fourth, an acrid stink of sweat and excrement hit her like a punch. Moving her candle, she peered into the cramped space. Haunted eyes stared up from three gaunt male faces that showed expressions beyond both hope and fear.

Her heart sank. No Liam.

But these, they still deserved to be saved, just as she had saved so many others from Black Stephen's clutches.

The slaves' heads were roughly shaved to prevent lice. Their shackled bodies bulged with muscles, but their sunken eyes and hollow cheeks attested to their meager diet, just enough to fuel their forced labor on the ship and stave off starvation. They wore nothing but filthy rags tied around their waists, and sores and scars from whips covered their backs. These men likely had some value to Black Stephen. Most of his slaves labored on land, but he liked to keep his hostages at sea to prevent any chance of rescue.

The men blinked at her from the shadows.

She knew what they saw—a short, bearded pirate in leather armor, face covered, only the eyes visible, with a thin blade at his side. Another master to serve, another man to abuse them and work them to death. In a low alto voice that passed for a man's, she asked in Gaelic, "Do ye know a man named Liam MacMurrough from Wexford?"

There was no answer. Her nails bit into her palm. She had

been so sure this time.

She tried again in English, then French.

When she had almost given up hope, one of the men cleared his throat. "I knew a man named Liam MacMurrough from Wexford," he said in English between wracking coughs.

An Englishman, and an aristocrat by the sound of it. Was he friend or foe? She would have to take the chance. If there was even a chance he knew where Liam was, she needed to take him with her. Besides, Black Stephen had imprisoned him. The enemy of her enemy was her friend, at least for now.

"We were trapped on this ship together for..." The man closed his eyes as if doing a difficult calculation. "Two years," he finished, opening his eyes. "They moved him to another ship two weeks ago."

Two bleedin' weeks! If only she'd been quicker. But still, it might not have been him. "Did he tell you anything about himself, any details that might confirm he's the man I'm looking for?"

"What are you going to do to him?" The man's dull eyes still held a tiny spark of defiance. He would not betray his friend. She smiled beneath her scarf despite herself.

Reaching a decision, she lifted up the key ring.

"Save him, like I'm going to save your sorry hide, ya bucket of snots. Wait one moment."

She approached the man who knew her brother, unlocking his shackles. He stared down at the raw flesh of his ankle, covered with festering sores, then back up at her. He didn't move.

Turning to the other two men, she continued unlocking. They both kept their heads down and refused to speak. Only the Englishman was bold enough to meet her gaze.

"Liam had a twin sister named Fionola." the Englishman said at last.

He said her name correctly. *Fin-OH-lah.* Her grip tightened on her candle. She'd found the right ship at long last, but she'd arrived too late. She clenched her teeth to hold back a howl.

"Is there anything ye can tell me that might help me track him down?"

The man fell into a coughing fit and spat something viscous on the floor. "The captain that took him was one of Black Stephen's men, and he was headed to the port of Honfleur. I'd recognize him if I saw him. That's all I know." The man stifled another cough. "Take me with you. I can help you find him."

Yes, he was coming with her whether he wanted to or not, even if she was wary of Englishmen after what Black Stephen had put her family through. If only her own bleedin' grandfather hadn't invited the buggers into Ireland. This husk of a man was the best lead she had. Of course, she would interrogate the crew, but they might not cooperate and tell her what she needed.

"What's your name?"

"Charles."

"And you two manky bollocks?" she asked, turning to the others.

They remained still and resolutely silent.

"Can you stand, Charles?"

"Yes." With one hand against the bulkhead, he staggered to standing.

She gave a brisk nod. "Good. Ye're free to move about the ship," she said to the two silent men. "As for you," she said to Charles, "we have work to do."

CHARLES'S HANDS SHOOK as he followed the pirate captain toward the ladder up to the deck of the *Midas*, wondering why the man kept his face hidden when all the others had removed their scarves when the lime dust was washed overboard. Was he hiding some injury or deformity, or was he wary of being seen by strangers?

Charles turned from the pirate captain and looked around at

what was once his ship, back when it was the *Wind Song*, and he was the son of a baron. But all of that had changed when he accidentally overheard Lord Stephen de Burgh plotting to kill Lord Pembroke, his liege lord, and then make himself high king of Ireland. When Charles confronted Lord Stephen, the man had stolen everything he had, handing him over to Captain Edward as a slave. Like the ship, Charles was now tainted beyond all recognition.

Was he dreaming this? It hardly seemed real. If he were free of Captain Edward, shouldn't he be ecstatic? Instead, he felt numb, hollow.

Sean staggered after him, half-carrying Niall, who was too sick to move.

Charles took over when Sean faltered at the base of the ladder.

As he climbed through the hatch, supporting his friend, he saw that most of the deck was covered in lime dust. A man he didn't recognize was washing it away with bucket after bucket of seawater. The air had a hint of something that stung his lungs, but he didn't care. The moon and stars above brought tears to his eyes. It had been so long.

Niall bent double, coughing, and Charles eased him down to the deck. "Thank you, Charles," Niall whispered in Gaelic between coughs.

Niall grabbed his arm. "If you ever go to Kilkenny, please let my father and sister know I died happy and free."

"You're not going to die, Niall."

Shaking his head with a sad smile, Niall laid back on the deck and closed his eyes. He looked peaceful despite the horrible rattle coming from his chest.

At that moment, someone yelled, "Charles," and his head snapped up. It was the masked man that freed him—a pirate by the looks of him. He was standing at the bow, directing the movement of cargo from one ship to the other. Charles didn't trust him an inch, but anything had to be better than being Black

Stephen's slave. And that Gaelic lilt was so like Liam's. Perhaps they grew up together near Wexford?

He stood up and looked down at Niall for a moment, saying a silent prayer to Saint Raphael for healing, then walked over to the man that called him.

"Your friend is in poor health," the man observed. Charles nodded. "My men will care for him. Do not fear."

Charles could do nothing but stare. He was beyond fear. Death would be a relief after the hell they had endured.

"My crew will take him to safety," the man continued. "But you are coming with me." He nodded toward the ship tethered to the side of the *Midas*. The man had an unusual voice, slightly higher than one would expect, but resonant and commanding.

Charles didn't move. "To find Liam?"

"Aye."

Charles looked at Niall as he opened his eyes and blinked in the moonlight. Did he dare trust a pirate's word? But then what choice did he have? He was utterly at the man's mercy, and he could not stand to spend another minute aboard this ship.

"Am I your prisoner now?"

The man pondered for a moment before responding, "Guest."

Charles didn't believe that for a moment, but anything was better than life on the *Midas*, worked to the bone, always on the verge of starvation, the captain's ever-present whip flaying open his back at the least excuse. He nodded warily.

"Are you strong enough to climb across on the ropes?"

"I think so," he said.

"Say your goodbyes and go," the man ordered. "We leave shortly."

Charles had no choice but to comply. He looked around as the man walked away, trying to decide what he might say to the two men who had shared his humiliation. It was painful to look at them. They were almost wraithlike in the moonlight.

"Goodbye, Niall. I have to go," Charles said, gently squeezing

Niall's hand.

Niall nodded and closed his eyes.

Standing, Charles made his way over to Sean, who was leaning on the rail, staring at the other ship. He took a position beside him, looking out.

Sean spat on the deck. "Pirates."

"Can't be worse than Captain Edward," Charles said, hoping it was true.

"I suppose not. That man was the very devil," said Sean. "But be careful. I don't like the look of that captain."

Charles took a deep, rattling breath. "You be careful too. Find your way home if you can."

"I will." Sean closed his eyes and crossed himself.

"Time to go," the pirate yelled to Charles from across the deck.

"Goodbye, my friend," said Sean.

"Goodbye."

Charles made his way across the deck and climbed up onto the ropes, shimmying across as best he could. He could only hope that what awaited him wasn't worse than what came before.

CHAPTER TWO

FIONOLA REMOVED HER polished metal helm, throwing it in the armor chest under the aftercastle with unnecessary force. Her unruly curls sprung free, and she tied them back in a queue with a leather thong. The evening breeze began to cool the battle heat still raging within her. Heart still pounding, she joined Uncle Colm at the tiller as they steered away from the *Midas*. She pulled a knife from the sheath concealed in her left gauntlet and stabbed it into the top of the barrel beside her.

How could she have been so close and still missed? God only knew what Black Stephen's lackeys were doing to Liam on board that ship.

"No luck again?" Her uncle stroked his beard. White steaks in the red bristles gleamed in the pale silver light of a quarter-moon. The enormous, rectangular sail of the *Draconis* blotted out half the stars in the sky.

"No." Fionola let out a string of mumbled expletives and plucked her knife out of the barrel and stabbed it again.

"The price on your head will go up."

She shrugged. No amount of money would tempt her crew to make a deal with that devil. They all knew too well what a double-crossing viper he was. Most were former slaves of his that she'd rescued. Just like that poor man huddled by the aftercastle. He sat on the deck, his back resting against a crate, staring at the sky as though he'd never seen it before. Little did he know that all her hopes rested in his trembling hands.

"We were close. Yer man," she said, pointing, "knew Liam. He says Liam was transferred to another of Black Stephen's ships just two weeks ago."

Colm closed his eyes and shook his head.

She clutched her sword with a death grip. "Next time we won't miss."

Silence stretched between them, interrupted only by the creaking of wood and the endless lapping of water against the sides of the ship.

"Fi—" Uncle Colm began.

"Captain," she snapped.

"Aye, *Captain*. I only wanted to say that we'll find him. I have faith in you. We won't fail. No matter how high a price he places on your head, we'll bring that bastard down."

If only she had faith in herself. She'd failed too many times. Five years now she'd been trying to find her brother, and what did she have to show for it? An ever-increasing bounty for Captain O'Bannon.

"We won't fail," she agreed, pulling the knife out and stabbing it down again. "Why Granda trusted that man to help restore the glory of Leinster, I'll never understand. Black Stephen is nothing but a gobshite in fancy clothes. Granda should have known better."

"At least you escaped before your grandfather forced you to marry him."

A shiver ran down her spine at the thought. It had been a close thing. She'd only been fourteen at the time. Fortunately, she'd been able to escape on Uncle Colm's trading vessel with a handful of friends and family who were loyal to her.

"Your grandfather deserves a special place in hell for what he did to you and your brother," her uncle said, patting her shoulder.

"Aye. Father always protected us, but when he died in battle, Granda was free to do with us as he pleased. At least Liam is still alive, which is more than I can say for the other kin Granda gave away as hostages to seal alliances."

"At least the old bastard is dead."

Aye, Granda Dermott, deposed king of Leinster, was dead and buried, but the alliance with King Henry lived on. And Fionola and Liam would never truly be free of their grandfather's cruelty until they escaped the clutches of Black Stephen. She had no desire to antagonize King Henry. Her family had sworn loyalty to him, and she honored the oath, but what he was allowing to happen in his name in Ireland was shameful.

Pulling the knife out again, she began carving little divots into the lid.

"What did that barrel of salted venison ever do to you?"

She stopped, narrowed her eyes, and stabbed the knife down into the lid again.

"Better the barrel than that dryshite we took captive," she grumbled, looking at the object of her hatred, tied to the mast.

"True," her uncle said, following her gaze. "He may know more about your brother. Whether he'll share it, though…"

"He'll talk, or I'll gut him like a fish and feed him to the krakens."

"Perhaps you'd best wait until morning," her uncle suggested gently.

He had a point, damn it all. If she questioned the *Midas*'s captain in her current mood, she'd likely skewer him within minutes, and what good would that do? Best to cool off a little and come at it fresh in the morning.

"Perhaps I should," she mumbled, grabbing her knife again and resuming making little divots.

Uncle Colm looked at the knife and then at her. "You're very much like your father, ya know."

She knew. That was the trouble, wasn't it? If only she had a bit more of her mother's grace and patience. But then, if she behaved as she ought, there'd be no one to rescue her brother.

Her mother wanted nothing more than for her to marry a

chieftain or perhaps even a king. She lived in terror that Fionola would turn out to be wild and rebellious like her youngest sister who fell for a rogue and found herself carrying a child out of wedlock. Both her sister and the child died in childbirth, and Mother believed it was God's retribution. How many times had she made Fionola swear that no man, but her husband would touch her?

Even on her deathbed, sick with fever, she made Fionola repeat her promise. Not that it mattered now that she was disguised as a man. No one would dare touch her as Captain O'Bannon. Even Seamus, who had proposed more than once, wouldn't dare take liberties. He knew how many knives she carried.

"He'd be so proud of you," said Uncle Colm, bringing her back to the present.

She let out a bitter laugh. "That I've become a pirate?"

"That you've become a warrior and that you'll turn over heaven and hell to do right by your family."

"No, he wanted a *son* to do those things. It was only because Liam was not the son he expected that he encouraged me in my wild ways. If Liam had been the warrior and I had been the gentle one—"

"Aye, but that's not how it was. You were a firebrand from the start. It's a wonder you survived your childhood, some of the shenanigans you got up to. You thought you were Queen Boudica reborn. And maybe you are. Your father certainly thought so."

She smiled ruefully beneath her scarf. "I failed him. Liam and I both did. Even if I succeed in this mad quest, I'll never be the son and heir he truly wanted. Not that Liam will be either, gentle soul that he is."

Uncle Colm shook his head. "Your father loved you both. He had the children he wanted."

"Aye, but in the wrong bodies."

How many times had they had this conversation over the last

five years? It didn't matter. It never solved a thing.

"Fi—"

"Captain."

"Captain," Uncle Colm said gently. "I'll remind you of what you've told the countless slaves you've rescued from Black Stephen's clutches. It doesn't matter who you are or what has passed. All that matters is what you do from this moment forward." He put a calloused hand on her shoulder and squeezed. "Your father isn't here, and neither is Liam. Thanks to your grandfather, the MacMurrough clan's fiercest warriors lie dead on the field of battle, and what few remain are following Black Stephen around like so many trained dogs. It was clear from your earliest days that you were your father's true heir in all ways but one. You're a born leader, and we need you. Only you can save Liam."

She gripped the pommel of her sword all the tighter as he spoke. Not a day went by when she didn't question herself in private. Could she truly carry this weight? Was she leading them all astray? She was just a twenty-year-old girl with an unnatural penchant for sword play. What right did she have to risk men's lives as if she were a clan chieftain like her father or a king like Granda Dermott?

"We need you, Captain," Uncle Colm said, squeezing her shoulder again. He was the humblest of her uncles, but also far and away her favorite. Thank heavens Auntie Maeve fell in love with a kindly merchant instead of some bloodthirsty warrior.

She nodded stiffly. "I won't let you down."

And she wouldn't. Too much was at stake. Her uncle wasn't wrong. She was better suited to lead than anyone else. With her father gone and Liam captured, there was no other choice. Not that she'd ever wanted to play the docile daughter.

The truth was, she liked being Captain O'Bannon. When she took to sea in this disguise, it was out of necessity, but slipping into men's clothes and a man's role felt as natural as breathing. She'd always felt like a fraud in a skirt, and it was a relief to live in a way that felt honest. Funny how honesty required a false beard.

"I should go talk to Seamus."

"Well, go on then," her uncle said, waving her away.

She grabbed her knife, slid it into the scabbard in her gauntlet, and headed down the ladder to the main deck. Giving the man tied to the mast a wide berth, she headed toward the bulky shadow of her first mate who was securing the last of the boarding party's armor beneath the forecastle.

Spotting her, Seamus paused in his work and shooed away the other men milling around.

"Captain, congratulations on your success!"

"Success? You call this success?" she grumbled in a low voice.

"I do," Seamus said, gathering his bulk and standing to his full height. He towered over her, but it didn't intimidate her. She knew she could take him in a fight. And had on more than one occasion. "We captured an enemy ship, won some excellent booty, and brought a prisoner on board who can tell us where to look next. Don't tell me you're upset about it."

By way of answer, she growled.

"I see," Seamus said carefully. "And to what do we owe this foul mood after a rousing victory?"

Of course, he didn't understand. This was never his quest. Seamus was a good man, and he hated Black Stephen as much as any of them, but he wasn't part of the MacMurrough clan. This wasn't his fight.

"We missed Liam by two weeks. Two bleedin' weeks!" Reflexively, she pulled out the blade in her gauntlet. Seamus took a hasty step back and put his hands up. Seeing the alarm in his eyes, she sheathed it again. "Apologies. It's not you I'm angry at."

Lowering his hands slowly, he took a wary step back towards her. "Perhaps it's best if you don't question the prisoner tonight."

She gave him a level look. "That's what Colm said."

"And he was right. He'll be no use to us if you carve him up into stew meat."

"I wasn't going to carve him into stew meat. I'm not an eejit."

She reached for her knife again, realized what she was doing, and stopped.

Seamus' eyes narrowed. "No one on this ship would dare to call you an eejit, Captain, least of all me."

It was no good taking this out on Seamus. It was hardly his fault. She sighed.

There was a softness around Seamus' eyes that worried her. He wasn't gearing up for another proposal of marriage, was he? It had been blessed months since he last asked. He was a sweet man underneath all his bluster, but she wasn't interested in him that way. Besides, how could she consider marriage before she completed her quest? She had to keep up the ruse of Captain O'Bannon at all costs.

"Do you think you still have room in there for my breast-plate?" she asked, nodding toward the enormous storage chest, and hoping the change of subject would put an end to his maudlin looks.

"Aye," Seamus said carefully.

She nodded and began unbuckling the heavy, boiled-leather garment. Her breasts strained painfully against their binding as she shrugged out of her armor. The pain was a small price to pay for the freedom of living as a man. And everything depended on her maintaining her disguise. As a woman, Fionola had no hope of rescuing her brother.

"The men are happy with tonight's takings?" she asked as he stowed her breastplate.

"Quite pleased, Captain."

She nodded. "Open a keg of ale. Let them celebrate. I'm going below to have a chat with Thomas."

"Aye, Captain."

Leaving Seamus behind to stow the last of the arms and ar-mor, she headed for the hatch. On the way, she noticed that the man she'd liberated had fallen sound asleep against a crate.

"David," she called out to her skinny, weedy-looking cabin boy. No matter how much she fed him, he was thin as a twig.

"Go below and get a blanket for our guest."

David went scurrying. Moments later he returned with a length of thick woven wool. Fionola took it and looked down at the sleeping man. Something in her heart tore at the sight. Would her brother look so frail and down beaten when they finally found him? But there was a strength in this man she admired. Despite everything, he'd stood up for his friend. Even to her. It was a promising start.

She crouched down and tucked the blanket around him, careful not to wake him. He clutched it close in his sleep. The moonlight washed over his features. He was a handsome man, this prisoner of hers, gaunt as he was. He had high cheekbones and a firm jaw. She felt an inexplicable urge to trace his jawline with a gentle finger.

Shaking herself, she stood up abruptly. That would not do. That would not do at all.

"Captain, are you all right?"

She whirled around to see Thomas's warm, familiar face.

"Seamus mentioned you wanted to speak to me," he said. Divested of his armor, her dear friend looked almost like the priest he had once been, tall and lean and all too understanding in his rough-spun tunic and hose.

"Yes," she answered. "Let's go below. I wanted to discuss what we should do with our prisoner."

"Aye, Captain."

"Come."

Turning away from the sleeping man, she headed for the hatch. Her guest was a problem for the morning, just like her prisoner. That mad moment of wanting to touch him was something she would worry about some other time. For now, she had work to do.

CHAPTER THREE

THE SUN BLAZED overhead, penetrating Charles's closed eyelids and waking him with a red glow. He was the perfect temperature as warm air was tempered by a salty sea breeze. Keeping his eyes closed, he tried to remember where he was. How was he lying in the sun? They were only brought up to the deck to work. And where were his chains? He felt oddly buoyant from the absence of their weight. He was covered in a cloth, as if someone cared for his comfort. From the gentle rolling of the waves and creaking of wood and ropes, he knew he was still on a ship, but it smelled clean. The eye-watering stink of the brig where he and his fellow prisoners were held was gone.

He opened his eyes to a slit, determined to observe further before showing he was awake. The bare feet of sailors traversed the deck. He could make out the bow in the distance. This boat, unlike the *Midas*, had a crenellated forecastle. A hooded silhouette he recognized stood tall, looking out over the water. No, not tall, he revised as he saw another sailor stand beside the man in the hood. Straight, proud, and commanding, but not tall.

With a jolt, the memories of being rescued from the *Midas* came back to him. After two years of being a slave, receiving worse treatment than the lowliest animal, his fervent prayers had finally been answered. He was free of one hell. Had he entered another?

Opening his eyes slightly wider, he looked for any familiar faces, either of his fellow prisoners or the crew of the *Midas*. With a start, he saw Captain Edward blindfolded with arms and legs tied around the mast. His empty stomach clenched at the sight. For a moment, everything disappeared from his vision, and he was unable to shut out the memory of being strapped to the mast of the *Midas* with Captain Edward's whip biting into him again and again in a brutal rhythm.

Breathing deeply, he forced himself to return to the present. As far as he could tell, no one else from the *Midas* was here, at least not on deck. It made sense that the captain was bound, but why was he himself left free? He hardly dared hope his captivity was at an end, but perhaps he had found a kinder captain who might treat him with a modicum of humanity.

High hopes for a pirate, but then, so far, this pirate had been nothing but decent to him and was likely his only means of finding Liam. Why was this pirate so interested in Liam? What, exactly, were his intentions?

When Charles stirred and blinked his eyes fully open, he was nearly blinded by the full force of the bright, midday sun, and multiple shadows approached. He cringed away involuntarily as one of the shadows crouched right beside him, but a gentle hand touched his shoulder. Vivid memories of Liam sprang up at that touch. How many times had Liam comforted him, calming the maelstrom in exactly this way? He closed his eyes, and tears leaked from their corners.

The soft pressure on his shoulder stayed, but the shadow moved, blocking the sun so that he could open his eyes without being blinded. "I won't hurt you, Englishman," the man said softly.

It took great effort to hold back the wracking sobs he felt building in his chest. He looked into the enigmatic eyes of his hooded rescuer, reading wariness, but also kindness and concern. The captain kept his nose and mouth covered with a scarf so that only his green eyes were visible, as well as the twin braids of a thick, red beard that peeked out the bottom of the veil. Charles wondered idly what lay beneath that scarf. What possible cause would a pirate captain have to hide his face from his own crew? This was a man with secrets, even if there was surprising warmth in his gaze. Dare he trust?

"I am Captain O'Bannon of the *Draconis*. You're no longer a slave, and you're under my protection."

Relief and elation washed through him, even though he knew he should stay wary.

"I'm afraid you must remain with me while I complete an urgent mission," the captain continued, "but you're free to move about the ship. My cabin is strictly forbidden to everyone on this ship except me on pain of death, but otherwise you may go where you please. You'll receive the same rations as my crew, and we will do our best to heal you."

So not entirely free yet. That was too much to hope. But at least this captain planned to treat him like a person, which was more than he could say for the last. The man was probably after something, but he couldn't bring himself to care as long as he was breathing clean fresh air, seeing the sky every day, and eating regular meals.

Charles pushed himself to sitting, his body stiff and aching from the unfamiliar luxury of sleeping stretched out instead of dozing chained to a bench. "Thank you, Captain O'Bannon," he said in a croaking voice before falling into a fit of coughing.

"Get him water," the captain ordered one of his men. Moments later, the man handed him a battered metal cup filled with lukewarm fresh water, careful not to spill. He drank it down greedily, and the coughing abated.

"Thank you for rescuing me," he tried again. "I thought I would be in that hellhole until I died." The captain gave his shoulder another gentle squeeze. He remembered the man's query about his friend. "You are looking for Liam."

The captain nodded, and Charles reached a decision. Looking deeply into the mysterious green eyes that faced him, he made his request. "With your permission, I would like to join your crew and help you find him. He was my friend, and I want to see him safe and free."

Something softened in the captain's sharp gaze, and he blinked several times, as if holding back some strong emotion.

"Do you speak any Gaelic?" she asked—in Gaelic.

"I've learned a bit," he answered in the same tongue.

"Do you know anything of sailing?" the captain asked in English again in that familiar Wexford lilt.

Charles cracked a smile. "I grew up by the sea. I've been sailing for as long as I can remember, though I've never seen a ship quite like this." He looked again at the elevated forecastle and then back to the aftercastle, crenellated like a fortress and providing a platform from which to bear down on any enemies at sea. There was a single, rectangular sail with red and white vertical stripes.

The captain's eyes crinkled at the sides, as if he was smiling, though his mouth was still obscured by the scarf. "The *Draconis* is a unique vessel. I took her from another pirate who took her near Calais."

So far, these pirates seemed more humane than the so-called king's men that served Black Stephen. He was in no position to be picky about who rescued him. His father would be horrified, but Winchelsea was a long way away. At the moment, he couldn't afford moral outrage. "I confess, Captain, I never imagined I would turn pirate, but I stand by my offer to join your crew until you find Liam. You saved me, and you seem to be on an honorable mission. And I am a man of my word."

The captain nodded. "Might I ask how you came to be on that ship?" There was a note of caution in the captain's voice. The real question, Charles knew, was what importance he had to Black Stephen. It was well known that he kept hostages enslaved on ships to keep their families from rescuing them.

Charles needed to answer carefully. There was no telling what the pirate might do if he found out Charles was a noble.

Best to pretend to be a simple sailor caught up in the tides of war.

"I came to Wexford with King Henry's men to support Lord Pembroke in his campaign to defeat King Ruaidrí of Connacht and bring peace to Ireland, uniting it under King Henry's rule. Our ship was placed under the command of Lord Stephen de Burgh."

"Black Stephen." Captain O'Bannon grasped his sword.

Yes, Black Stephen, infamous marshal to King Henry, responsible for looking after the king's prostitutes, dismembering malefactors, and enforcing the king's weights and measures. For performing this strange assortment of tasks, he'd gained a barony. His ambition knew no bounds, nor did his disdain for the English nobility who he claimed scorned him for his humble origins. Charles had discovered too late just how duplicitous the man was.

"Our captain got into some kind of trouble with Black Stephen," said Charles. Best not to explain what sort. "I don't know the details, but as punishment Black Stephen imprisoned him, enslaving him aboard one of his so-called merchant ships."

Charles had overheard Black Stephen plotting to overthrow Lord Pembroke and make himself high king of Ireland, not that he could afford to disclose such a dangerous secret. Who knew where this captain's loyalties lay? He seemed to have no love for Lord Stephen, but was his distaste strong enough to outweigh the price that would be on Charles's head the moment it became known he'd escaped?

The captain tilted his head to the side, waiting for him to continue. Enigmatic eyes the vibrant color of new leaves in springtime studied Charles's face as he took a breath and cleared his throat.

"Out of loyalty to our lord, we mounted an unsuccessful rescue attempt, and Black Stephen threw us all in chains and handed us over to Captain Edward. We tried to escape, jumping overboard and swimming for shore, but—"

"You swim?"

"I do." It was a risky admission. Some viewed swimming as a sign of the devil.

"Good. A man of the sea should swim." A sensible captain. *Thank heavens.*

"They sent boats after us and caught us. After that, they split us up onto different ships to keep us from conspiring. What happened next is hardly worth telling. You saw for yourself what it was like in that ship. Two years have passed since then. And now, you've rescued me."

The captain closed his eyes and shivered. "And Liam?"

"We were imprisoned together for two years. I don't know how long he was there before I arrived. Thanks to him, I was able to keep my sanity." *Mostly.*

Gesturing with his head toward Captain Edward, the captain asked, "That pox bottle would know what happened to Liam?"

Charles glanced at the man who had made his life a living hell then squeezed his eyes shut and nodded.

"I'll extract what he knows," the captain said in a matter-of-fact voice that should have shocked him. "There may be…noises."

Thinking of the scars all over his body, the disease he'd endured, and the men he'd watched die, he found he couldn't muster even the slightest sympathy for his former captain. "Whatever you do, it won't be worse than he himself has done." The man was a devil and deserved a long, painful death.

"Seamus," the captain ordered the man standing next to him, "give Charles food and ale and clean clothes, and show him where to find the soap and bucket so that he can clean himself."

"Aye, Captain," Seamus answered before heading away at a brisk walk.

"We'll talk more, Englishman," the captain said, patting his shoulder one last time. "For now, rest and recover. You're safe with us." Captain O'Bannon stood and walked away. There was a strange grace in the way the man moved. For some reason, it made him think of his sister, Carenza. Charles shook himself. He must be very addled if a pirate captain reminded him of his sister.

Seamus returned with an outfit just like the one he had on—a rough linen shirt and breeches, and a sleeveless brown woolen cotte to wear on top, with a wide leather belt to gird it. He also brought a wooden bowl with a hard biscuit, a piece of cheese, some raisins, and a piece of cured venison. After setting down his load, he handed over a pewter tankard of ale. To Charles, it looked like the finest feast he'd ever seen.

"My name is Seamus. Welcome to the crew."

Charles nodded in acknowledgment as he chewed off a tough piece of the venison. His stomach tried to rebel. It was too rich after years of living primarily on thin gruel. But he couldn't stop himself. It was too delicious. He ignored his roiling stomach and washed the venison down with some ale, gritting his teeth to keep it down. "I'm Charles. Pleased to meet you," he managed to say at last.

"Go slowly, Charles. Your stomach will thank you. And so will the crew. They'd rather not clean up your vomit."

Knowing Seamus was right, but unable to slow himself down, he switched to the hard biscuit, which at least would force him to take smaller bites. And hopefully his stomach would be more accepting of something made of grain.

"When you've taken the edge off your hunger, the crew and I would appreciate it if you would clean yourself. No offense, Englishman, but you're manky as a midden heap."

No doubt Seamus was correct. He'd become inured to the smell himself, but he remembered the stink hitting him like a wall his first day imprisoned on board the *Midas* with his fellow unwashed slaves. It took him three days to keep any food down in the stench. Reluctantly, he put down his precious bowl of food.

"Show me to the bucket?" he requested, picking up his clean clothes.

Seamus motioned with his head for Charles to follow and led him aft stopping just in front of the crenellated aftercastle. It was such a luxury to stand and walk freely. It had been so long.

"Here's the bucket and soap," Seamus said, pointing and wrinkling his nose. "There're some rags there you can use to clean yourself. The sooner you throw that shite rag you're wearing in the sea, the better." Seamus turned and hurried away, mumbling, "for all of us" as he went.

Looking down at his "shite rag," Charles decided he agreed and stripped the hated garment off, tossing it in the sea with a sense of profound relief. On a ship full of men, there was no need for modesty, and he relished the feel of the sun on his skin. It was cleansing somehow, and much less painful than the salt water would be.

Washing was going to be agony, he knew. He had sores on his head, back, and legs, and the stinging from the rare wash-downs on the *Midas* always left him with tears in his eyes. At least here, he could bathe at his leisure and choose when the salt water would touch his wounds.

He lowered the bucket over the side and pulled it up full of icy cold seawater. Picking up the soap and wetting a cloth, he set to work, starting with the crusty stubble on his head. As he worked his way down, it felt like he was washing off the entirety of the last two years. Washing his sores wasn't as painful as he feared now that he could choose for himself when and how to do it.

His fortunes were turning at last. Perhaps he could even find a way to go home to Winchelsea once they found Liam. Dare he hope?

But no. Cleaning his skin didn't change the corruption within. His mind wasn't the same now, and he knew it. He couldn't go back to who he'd been, and the new Charles wasn't sound and fit enough to do right by Winchelsea as its baron. Better by far if they all thought him dead and he made his own way whatever way he could in distant lands. Perhaps he would stay a pirate. Why not? Black Stephen would never allow him to go home and tell his tale. The only thing that had kept him alive these last two years was that Black Stephen still didn't know who had been with him that fateful night when he'd overheard Lord Stephen's plotting.

At that moment, a cry of pain from Captain Edward pierced his ears, and he winced. Pirates weren't exactly virtuous either, of course.

There was another cry, and Charles shuddered, feeling the onset of his madness. The sound of men crying out affected him strangely. When he heard it, his mind lost its mooring, and he was filled with a desperate need to escape. Everything else gave way to this overpowering urge.

Stop. Please stop. Make it stop.

Pressing his hands to his ears, he crouched to the deck, hiding his head between his knees. His heart pounded furiously, and he was breathing heavily. He forced himself to focus on breathing in and breathing out…in…out…until at last, the feeling passed, and he returned to his ablutions.

As he rose, he noticed that Captain O'Bannon was looking his way and had seen his pathetic reaction to Edward's cries.

Christ's teeth.

Turning away, Charles sighed. There was nothing to be done. Captain O'Bannon was going to learn about his weakness one way or another. If he hadn't learned now, he would have seen it at some later date. Charles finished cleaning himself as quickly as he could, his skin tingling from the brisk seawater, dressed in the clean clothes Seamus provided, and hurried back to his bowl of food.

Going as slowly as he could manage, he savored each bite. The raisins in particular gave him joy. He'd forgotten that flavors could be so intense. The sweetness was better than the best cakes he could remember eating back in Winchelsea.

Too soon, the bowl was empty. He started coughing again and had to hoist himself up to spit over the side of the ship. Another swig of ale helped calm him, but it also made him drowsy.

Drifting in and out of consciousness, hours passed. Twice

more, he heard Edward's cries and curled up with his hands over his ears, but each time it passed, and he recovered. To while away the time, he studied the crew and listened.

Amongst themselves, they all spoke Gaelic. He knew a fair amount from his time with Liam, Niall, and Sean.

Seamus appeared to be the first mate, though it was hard to tell. There didn't seem to be a strict hierarchy aside from everyone's immediate and unquestioning obedience of the captain. Pirates weren't known for discipline, he supposed. Seamus was boisterous and profane and absolutely devoted to the captain. He took personal offense when someone failed to execute the captain's orders perfectly, though everyone else seemed to take his bluster with a grain of salt, despite his commanding voice and burly physique.

There was a portly man named Colm steering the ship at the moment, patiently watching the sun and using his compass to make minor corrections as they headed northeast. He was dressed in a long white cotton tunic over loose pants of the same fabric. His full red beard and hair were streaked with white. He looked considerably older than the rest of the crew.

There were two young men who seemed to prefer each other's company. From what he gathered, their names were Ronan and Thomas. When they had a break in their work on deck, they sat down together near the aftercastle, and Ronan used a piece of charcoal to draw an exquisite portrait of Thomas on the deck. As soon as he was done, he washed it away, removing every trace.

At one point, a man named Aidan came up from the hold and had a boisterous argument with Seamus over what they would eat at the evening meal. Apparently, Aidan was the cook, though he also wore a long blade at his side, and he looked like he knew how to use it.

As the sun began to set, Captain O'Bannon came over to him again and crouched down to speak. "It only took three toenails to extract what I needed."

Charles laughed looking down at his own toes, more than half with scabs where a nail would normally be. "Not very impressive, given how many he's taken from me."

"He had a grudge against you?"

Exhaling slowly, Charles answered, "Yes, he did."

"Why?" The captain's gaze was penetrating.

Telling the truth wasn't an option. The captain might sell him back to Black Stephen in exchange for Liam. But Charles didn't feel comfortable lying either.

"He didn't like who I was and punished me for it," he answered carefully. He fully expected the captain's next question to be about who exactly he was, but instead the captain nodded.

"Who you were doesn't matter on this ship," the captain explained. "All that matters is what you do."

"Thank you," Charles said, flooded with relief.

"Do you know how to fight?" the captain asked, eyeing him up and down.

"It's been a while, but I was good with a blade and better with a bow before I was captured." He was excellent with a blade and superb with a bow, but who knew how much of that skill remained after all this time?

"I noticed earlier you have trouble when you hear loud noises."

Charles's heart sank. He'd hoped the captain would ignore his sad little episodes, but no. His humiliation was complete. "When I hear men yelling, especially in pain or anguish, it—"

The captain held up a hand to stop him. "Here. I brought you some beeswax for your ears. Use it when you need it." He handed over a small lump and left without another word.

Charles stared after him, speechless. In all his agonizing over his mind's failures, such a simple, practical preventative measure had never even occurred to him. That the captain had both noticed and cared enough to offer help moved him beyond words. Pirate or not, Captain O'Bannon had earned Charles's loyalty.

CHAPTER FOUR

THREE DAYS HAD passed, and Charles still couldn't bring himself to sleep below decks. So far, the crew had largely left him to his own devices. His cough abated significantly, but it was still there. With regular food and exercise, he felt strength returning. His limbs craved activity, even as his lungs urged him to rest.

Every morning, he paced the deck, careful to stay out of the way of the crew as they worked. The summer sun shone on his pale skin, and he drank it in until the welcome heat turned to a burn. Then he sought shade beneath the aftercastle. Part of him wished he could lie in the sun until he blistered, but he knew he had to limit himself until his skin returned to the bronze tone it took on whenever he spent time out in the open.

Throughout the day, he kept an eye out for small tasks he could do without being told—a rope to coil, a barrel to secure, a mess to sweep up. He was careful not to do anything that would attract notice, and he made sure he knew how a thing should be done before he did it. It wouldn't help anyone if he put something in the wrong place. He knew the captain's orders were to rest, but he couldn't bring himself to stay still.

Near dinner time, the captain stopped by for their brief daily conversation. "You have everything you need? The men treat you well?"

"Everyone has been most kind, Captain." Charles coughed, but it was shallower than the day before—a mere tickle compared to the deep rawness before. "I would like to help. Please assign me some tasks so that I can contribute."

The captain turned to meet his eyes. "I appreciate your offer, but I need you healthy first. Rest. Recover. There will be plenty of work soon enough."

"Captain," he called as the captain began to walk away, "I know my strength has limits, but I need to be useful."

The captain paused and nodded. "I understand." He looked Charles up and down and seemed to reach a decision. "I brought you on board to learn what you know of Liam. Tonight, you'll dine with me and tell me what you know. Come."

Charles complied instantly, following the captain belowdecks to where Aidan served them hard biscuits, grilled fish, and pickled carrots. They returned to the deck and seated themselves cross-legged on the planks of the forecastle.

"Tell me what you know," the captain said as soon as they were seated. "Everything."

Charles looked into the intelligent, green eyes of the man across from him. Even to eat, the captain kept the lower half of his face hidden, lifting his scarf only enough to put food in his mouth. What was beneath that scarf? Charles cleared his throat.

"I met Liam when I was captured and brought aboard the *Midas*. We were imprisoned together for two years. He refused to keep track of the days, so I don't know how long he was there before I arrived. He said it was easier not to count, but I couldn't help myself. I had to know. He seemed to accept his fate in a way that I never could."

Pausing, Charles took a bite and looked up at the captain. The expression in those eyes remained unreadable, though it was clear he was paying avid attention to every word Charles said.

"We understood each other's conversations, which was a blessing," he continued. "For a while, I was chained up with a Viking, and we had no language in common." He took a bite and chewed quickly.

"Liam told me about growing up in Wexford with his twin sister," he continued. "He used to joke that their sexes should have been reversed. He was too soft for a man's world, and she was too willful to be content as a woman."

The captain's gaze dropped, and he took a deep breath. "I'm surprised he's survived this long. He's too gentle for his own good."

"He's stronger than you think, Captain. He has a soft heart, but a strong body. He is also less brittle. He didn't resist like I did. When they beat him, he never broke. He was like…" Charles closed his eyes, searching for the right words. "He was like water, giving way when struck, but returning to himself as soon as it was over."

The captain nodded without looking up, his dinner lying abandoned on his dented metal plate.

"I'm sorry, Captain. Have I said something wrong?" It wasn't easy to read the man, but the tension in his body betrayed some strong emotion.

The captain looked up again, the expression in his eyes hardening. "Go on," was all he said in a voice almost too soft to hear.

"Liam was sick a few times, but he always pulled through. He was healthy when he was transferred. I think the man that took him may be related to Captain Edward. There was a striking resemblance between them. I remember the man mentioning that they were on their way to Honfleur. He never said the name of his ship in my presence, though."

"It's the *Gorgon*—another of Black Stephen's ships, and the man is Captain Gregory. In the upper holds, he transports goods like any merchant, but in the lower holds, the bastard transports slaves to sell to the Vikings." The captain turned his gaze northeast, as if he could almost spot the ship on the horizon.

Charles nodded. "Captain Edward told you?"

"He did," the captain said, turning back to Charles.

"And you trust him?"

"Christ, no."

"But you trust me?"

The captain looked at him for a long time in silence. "No, Englishman, I do not trust you. But so far, you've made no attempt to resist or betray me. Show me the value of your word through actions, and you may earn me trust in time."

Charles smiled. "That sounds like something my sister would say. She was always the politician in the family."

"You've a sister?" The captain's gaze sharpened.

"I have *three* sisters, all smarter than me, but especially Carenza. The world would be a better place if she ran it. I've often thought my father would be better off if she was his heir."

The captain's eyebrows shot up. "You've a high opinion of women."

"I have a high opinion of my sisters," he said with a shrug. "I find most women exceedingly dull. It's not necessarily their fault, mind you. Women are what the world allows them to be. But I've always been a troublemaker when it comes to my sisters—teaching them things they shouldn't know, giving them books they shouldn't read. I can only hope in my absence they've continued to defy expectations. It would be tragic if the world's finger shakers got hold of them and crushed their spirits."

Charles clamped his mouth shut, concerned he'd said too much. If he wasn't careful, he'd blurt out that his father was a baron, and no good could come of that.

"Your sisters are lucky," the captain said.

"Fionola was lucky to have Liam, and he was lucky to have her. They were both quite unconventional, but at least they had each other," he said, eager to change the subject. "She must be terribly lonely without him. I know how fiercely he misses her."

The captain closed his eyes and clenched his fists.

"I'm sure he misses you too," Charles added quickly, not sure what to make of the captain's reaction.

"Thank you, Charles," the captain said after taking a deep breath and opening his eyes. "That's enough for now. You're dismissed."

Worried that he offended the captain somehow, Charles hurried away to find somewhere else to finish his dinner. He never should have started blathering on about his sisters. Something about the way the captain looked at him left him unsettled. There were deep currents behind those eyes that Charles couldn't begin to fathom. The captain was a man of few words, but what little he did say was spoken with authority and precision. If he was ever going to earn the captain's trust, he would have to tread more carefully when they spoke.

CHARLES WAS TOO perceptive by half. Did he suspect Fionola's secret? It was one thing for him to mention her but something else entirely for him to say what he did about women and then go on about how much Fionola must miss Liam. He saw altogether too much of her heart. The loneliness was eating her alive. Liam was the only person who ever truly understood and accepted her. Did Charles know her identity, and was he toying with her? She'd had to clench her fists not to pull a knife on him for daring to tread so perilously close to her secret.

He didn't know. He couldn't know. It was a coincidence, and she couldn't afford to let him unsettle her like that.

Where did he pick up such unorthodox ideas? Clearly, he'd grown up wealthy, talking about heirs and books like that. Was there some corner of the world where women were given greater freedom and respect, at least the wealthy ones? Or was he encouraging them simply for the sake of mischief?

But he'd accepted her brother too. He spoke about Liam with respect, recognized his strength despite his softness. Was it possible for a man to be so accepting? And an Englishman at that?

"Captain..." Ronan tapped her shoulder, and she jumped.

"What is it?"

"Our prisoner nearly sawed through his ropes with this." He held up a broken shard of pottery.

"Christ in a cup," she grumbled, turning her eyes to the heavens, searching for patience.

"I tied new ropes and searched the area to ensure there was nothing else he could use. My apologies fer the oversight."

She took a deep breath and shook her head. "You caught it, and you took care of it. That's what matters."

"Thank you, Captain."

He lingered for a moment as if he had something more to say.

"What is it?"

"Why did you jump just now when I came up? You aren't an easy man to startle."

She looked around to make sure no one was in earshot. "I'm worried Charles might suspect," she murmured.

"Suspect what? That you're a lousy archer?"

"That's no secret," she said giving Ronan a look. "You know what I mean."

He smiled sideways and shook his head. "Not possible," he murmured back. "He'll learn soon enough you've bigger balls than anyone else on this ship. What makes you think he suspects?"

"Something he said about his sisters and then a comment he made about how much Fionola must miss Liam."

Ronan chuckled and shook his head. "You worry too much. Every bleedin' member of this crew knows you're a man, including the few of us that know otherwise. If he questions you, challenge him to a duel. He'll be forced to retract or die, and either way, your secret will be safe."

She frowned. "What if I lose?"

Ronan grinned. "When have you ever lost? Even when you were a girl, you had no trouble exacting your revenge on anyone who tried to cross you. D'you remember that time the chieftain of the O'Malley's was visiting your father and his pimply son tried to kiss you? It's a good thing I arrived in time, or you would have slit his throat with that dagger of yours."

"Mama always said to protect my virtue with my very life." And Fionola had. No man had ever laid a hand on her. Not that she didn't wish from time to time she was a little less virtuous. She envied the men on her ship for their freedom to take unvirtuous pleasure when the opportunity presented itself. But she'd promised Mama on her deathbed that no man other than her husband would ever touch her.

"And you do a very good job. Though you're not likely to get many advances as Captain O'Bannon."

She chuckled and shook her head. "Thanks for your advice, Ronan. You're right. I'm overthinking this."

"My pleasure, Captain." He made a mocking little bow and bounded away toward Thomas.

Ronan was right. If Charles uncovered her secret, it would be easy enough to dispatch him. The trouble was that she didn't want to, and not just because killing was wasteful. There was something about him. What he said about his sisters made her smile. She wanted to believe there were men in this world who held such broadminded views about women. And his loyalty to Liam had made her like him from the first, despite his being English. Also, he had nice eyes and a charming smile.

Nice eyes? A charming smile? Where did that come from?

Shaking herself, she decided to head down below to check on Captain Edward. He needed a reminder of his peril. When she opened the hold, she found him squinting in the torchlight and cowering against the bulkhead in his fine wool cotte with gold embroidery. Some sad hairs sprouted from his lip and chin after several days without a shave. The long, thin, limp hairs on his mostly bald head were pasted to his sweaty jowls.

His hands were tied behind his back and his ankles bound together. The foot with the missing toenails was wrapped in a clean bandage. She was a civilized captor, after all. There was a metal chamber pot in one corner. Someone came down to help him with his needs and provide meals three times a day. It was more than he'd offered the men he enslaved. She didn't do it out of kindness. She just didn't want her ship soiled.

"Come to finish me off, you Irish fiend?" His well-padded body quivered as he spoke.

She pursed her lips beneath her scarf and shook her head. This performance almost deserved an eyeroll.

"I'll have my revenge, you know. Just you wait."

She raised an eyebrow. "Oh, aye? Tell me more. I like a good joke."

"I'll carve your heart out, roast it on a stick, and feed it to my dog," he snarled.

At that, Fionola guffawed. "Is that the best you can do, Englishman? Because right now you're the one on a leash." She casually unsheathed a dagger from her belt and began examining it.

"What are you going to do with me?" he asked licking his lips. A bead of sweat trickled down his brow. "I bet you're going to try to ransom me. I'm a friend of Lord Stephen de Burgh. He'll pay any price to ransom me."

That earned another laugh. What a pathetic man. "I haven't decided what to do with you yet, but I'm definitely keeping you until I find Liam."

"No..."

"After that, we'll see. It depends on what Liam tells me about his treatment, though the Englishman you were holding prisoner has already told me a thing or two."

She crouched down next to him, blade in hand, and watched as the man's eyes bulged in terror.

"Charles? What did he say?"

She began cleaning her nails with the tip of her knife.

He shrank back. "Don't believe a word he says. He lies about everything." There was disgust in the man's voice as he spoke.

"Is that so?" she said, examining the point with great attention.

"You'll be sorry you brought him on board. He never does anything without the whip. I've never met a lazier man. Thinks he's too good to work," he said, spitting on the floor. "He claims to be related to the baron of Winchelsea. Can you believe it?"

That piqued her interest. Perhaps Charles was more than the simple sailor he claimed to be. She sat back and crossed her legs, tapping the flat of her blade against her other hand. "Tell me about him."

"He was a bad influence on your friend, Liam." He said the name with a sneer. "The two of them were always whispering and conspiring together. Liam knew better. He only needed a little reminding with the whip to bring him back in line."

Her jaw clenched at the mention of whipping her brother. She stabbed her knife into the deck, and Edward flinched.

"Charles never knew when to surrender," Edward continued. "I had to whip him until my arm hurt, and he still wouldn't break. I injured my shoulder, you know." He looked at his right shoulder as if he thought she would be sympathetic. "Stubborn man caused me more trouble than he was worth. I wish my cousin took him instead of Liam."

So, Charles refused to be cowed. That boded well. She looked forward to seeing him in battle, assuming he knew how to fight. If not, he could be taught. A man who could face fear and pain without flinching was worth his weight in gold on a ship like this.

"The only time I ever saw him work was when Liam was sick. He pulled two men's weight to spare Liam. But then Liam would get better, and Charles would go right back to being a useless turd."

She thought back to the small tasks she spotted Charles doing around the ship when he thought no one was looking and shook her head at Edward.

"Mm. Can't stand a useless turd." She pulled her blade out of the wood and stood up. "Until next time, Turd. I'll let the crew know about your new name."

She took her torch and left him alone, locked in the dark, as she smirked beneath her scarf.

CHAPTER FIVE

C HARLES HAD BEEN on board a full week now as they made their way to northern France in pursuit of Liam, and Fionola couldn't stop looking at him.

After a week of plenty of food and rest, not to mention a proper haircut and shave, Charles was distractingly attractive for an Englishman. She caught sight of him bathing again, completely by accident, but she couldn't tear her eyes away until his glance flitted toward her. She quickly looked off at a point just beyond him, pretending she was really searching for something else.

Half an hour later, though, she could no longer pretend. Charles's naked body still haunted her thoughts. She never should have looked in the first place. There was no privacy on board a ship, but that made it all the more important not to ogle. Nonetheless, her eyes kept coming back to him throughout the day, as surely as a compass needle points north.

Her mind should have been on the hunt for Liam and the information she'd pried from Edward.

Three toenails. Pathetic.

She was so close she could taste it, but instead of plotting her next move, she couldn't stop thinking about Charles's lovely, haunted, deep brown eyes, flecked with gold. Or his powerful physique, honed by relentless, grueling work.

Never before had she reacted like this to a man. She'd lived surrounded by men for five years, seeing them in various states of undress on her ship, and not one of them had jolted her composure like this.

Only Seamus, Thomas, Ronan, and Colm knew her secret. All but Seamus were part of her father's clan—the few loyal friends and family who had helped her escape marriage to Black Stephen. Colm was her uncle, though she never called him that except in private, and Ronan was her second cousin. Despite their presence, it wasn't safe to be a woman alone on a ship full of men, even if she could best any one of them in single combat. It was even less safe to live as Fionola MacMurrough. Black Stephen would love to have her in his clutches to take revenge for the humiliation of her running away. She had no choice but to keep up the ruse so that no one suspected.

Charles couldn't find out, of course, which meant she absolutely had to stop looking at him like a ripe fig she wanted to devour. Not that her virtue was in any danger as long as he thought she was a man and that her name was O'Bannon. But she needed to put an end to this dangerous train of thought.

The poor man was sick and suffering spells. It would get better, she knew. She'd freed enough of Black Stephen's slaves over the last few years to know what was in store for him. His body was healing quickly enough with sunlight, clean air, and adequate food. His mind was another matter. The wounds within would fade with time but never fully heal. It was no use waiting for a full recovery. One had to find practical solutions to keep the demons at bay. Charles wasn't the first man she met who went to pieces when he heard loud noises, nor was he the first she'd given earplugs to. It seemed to help them feel more in control. She could only hope that Charles felt the same.

What a time to lose her mind over an Englishman. And of all men, why the one that was close to her brother? If he shared her brother's proclivities, she might have more luck with him as Captain O'Bannon. After all, they slept side by side in that brig for two years. She should find out. Surely that would put an end to this ridiculous, girlish crush.

Restless and unable to settle down to sleep, she rose from her straw pallet and went up on deck. Charles continued to sleep there rather than below with the rest of the crew. It was a mild, clear summer night, perfect for sleeping under the stars. When he came into view, he was sitting up and looking at the sky. She went and sat cross-legged beside him.

"Checking our navigation?" she asked, picking an innocuous topic that surely couldn't get her into too much trouble.

He smiled at her, and she was glad he couldn't see her blush beneath her scarf. "We're heading almost due south. By my guess, we should be passing Falmouth tomorrow. The wind is coming from the northwest, and we're traveling at eight knots, so we're making reasonable time to Honfleur." So, he was observant and a competent navigator. Good to know. "But no, I wasn't checking our navigation. I was enjoying the stars. It's hard to sleep with such beauty above me."

Her breath caught. "Liam was always the same way. He could hardly sleep on a clear night like this, especially at sea," she said before clamping her mouth shut. Captain O'Bannon shouldn't know such personal things about Liam.

"You must have been very close to him," Charles observed.

Fionola stayed silent, not trusting herself to answer.

"I assume you must have cared for him greatly to spend so long trying to track him down," he continued.

She should nod and bid him goodnight and head right back down to her pallet. Instead, she shifted to look at him, and in the process, her knee came into contact with his. Oh, that was a mistake. Even this innocent brush sent a white-hot bolt of lightning through her whole body.

Get up and leave the pretty Englishman alone, Fionola.

"Five years. I've been looking for him for five feckin' years. He was a close friend and a valued member of my crew."

Charles gave an incredulous chuckle. "A valued member of your crew?"

She knew exactly how ridiculous that sounded. No one chased after a member of their crew for five years, no matter how valued.

"Don't worry, Captain," he said with a sympathetic look. "I know Liam well. He's a good man with a generous heart, and I certainly wouldn't judge."

Oh no. He thinks... "We weren't—" she blurted, then stopped. He cocked his head and narrowed his eyes. "We grew up together. He was like a brother."

Still looking suspicious, he asked, "You grew up with the MacMurrough clan near Wexford?"

Yes.

"No, of course not. My father was a trader based in Wexford. Liam and I met in passing and became friends." This web of lies was getting more tangled by the second.

Fortunately, Charles accepted the explanation. Or at least decided to stop pressing for more. Another excellent opportunity to get up and walk away passed her by. Instead, she asked, "And you? In the belly of a ship, I know there are few human comforts. Any man would be forgiven for..." She trailed off, unable to continue such an embarrassing sentence.

Charles took a deep breath in and let it out before responding. "We were close friends. We gave each other comfort and kindness, but nothing more. I didn't share his feelings. He understood and didn't press."

She wasn't convinced. It wasn't something most men would readily admit, given the Church's views on such matters. The wrong person finding out could mean death, though such things were common enough on ships, nonetheless. She wasn't going to push him.

"Did he ever say anything about me?" *What a terrible way to change the subject, Fionola.*

He looked apologetic and said, "The only person he ever spoke of by name was Fionola. That doesn't mean he didn't think of you often. It's hard to talk about the people you love in a place like that."

So, he still thinks Liam was my lover. Fair is fair, I suppose.

"What did he say about Fionola?" she tried to ask casually, as if it was normal for a captain to ask about a lost valued crew member's sister.

"Do you know her?" His eyes were alight with interest.

Do I know her. Ha!

"A little. I knew her well when we were young, but I haven't seen her in many years."

He turned his gaze to the stars. "The woman he described sounded impossible—an expert sailor and swordswoman with a kind, fierce heart who spoke half a dozen languages and liked to go diving off cliffs. I've never met a man that could claim all those things, let alone a woman. He liked to tell me stories of their adventures at sea in their father's ships, traveling the known world. I secretly hoped someday I'd get to meet her. Truth be told, I'm a little bit in love with her, just from his description."

Fionola burst out laughing because truly, how else could she respond? She had to remind herself to keep her voice low. Usually, her façade felt natural and seamless, but with this Englishman, all her poise seemed to crumble.

"You forgot to mention octopus hunting. Surely Liam talked about that." That was always the first thing Liam told people. *Meet my sister Fionola, the octopus hunter.*

Charles chuckled. "He did, but I didn't believe him. Don't tell me it's true."

"She is a bleedin' menace with a spear. I've seen her at it."

His eyes went wide. "Please tell me you know where to find Fionola. I need to meet this woman."

Her heart was going to beat out of her chest. Could he hear it? "When we rescue Liam, I promise I'll introduce you to her." And she would, if that day ever came. "I should leave you to your stargazing and head back to my cabin. Goodnight, Charles. I wish you sweet dreams of Fionola." *Because she will certainly be dreaming of you, damn it all.*

THE NEXT DAY, she avoided Charles. They continued heading south, still two days out from Honfleur. Nonetheless, she saw to it that Charles was well cared for. And she watched him, of course, though from a distance.

One minute, he was mending a fishing net. The next, he was using the net to catch fish for dinner, then patching clothing for other members of the crew, and sharpening knives and swords… It seemed to give him strength and purpose to be useful, and she appreciated that he felt the need to contribute. Soon, he too would be a valued crew member, despite his origins.

Meanwhile, she focused her energy on her plan for retrieving Liam from the *Gorgon*.

"We'll attempt a rescue by stealth in the port," she told Seamus. "We have slim chance of success, I know, but if it works, we don't need to risk open battle. If it fails, we can follow the *Gorgon* out to sea. How is our supply of lime?"

"We should restock in port," he answered. "We also need to repair several of our rope ladders. They were damaged when we engaged the *Midas*."

She nodded without really hearing. Her eyes were on Charles as he stood up to start pacing again.

"Good thinking, Captain," Seamus said, following her gaze.

"Hmm?" She dragged her eyes back to Seamus.

"I said good thinking. Charles can mend the rope ladders."

"Excellent," she said as if it had been her idea all along. "We'll need to think about arming him at some point."

Seamus furrowed his brow.

"Yes, I know he's English," she said. "But I think we can trust him. He loathes Black Stephen almost as much as I do. He says he's good with a bow. Perhaps we should test that. Do we have arrows to spare?"

Seamus nodded.

"Have him stand by the mast and shoot at a barrel in the stern. Hopefully he's decent and we can retrieve most of the arrows. We'll need to see how he does with a sword too, but let's wait a few days until he's stronger."

"Yes, Captain." Seamus turned to carry out her orders.

She hovered over navigation charts with Colm while the test took place, though she made sure she had an oblique view of the action. He shot the first arrow straight and true into the barrel thirty feet away. When he shot the second arrow, it hit a mere thumbnail away from the first. Seamus had him back up ten feet. Yet again, he hit right next to the original arrow. He was a good shot then. It wasn't a lie.

Seamus had him climb up onto the forecastle, sixty feet away from his target, which had been moved to the aftercastle. Everyone was watching now. They had to clear the deck to make sure no one got shot. She gave up on pretending to peruse the charts and looked on as Charles hit his target and then hit it again, and then once more. He got some clapping and congratulations from the crew. He was impressive, but the true test would be whether he could hit an object in motion. Seamus, thinking along similar lines, grabbed three empty clay pots from a crate, put them in a sack, and climbed the rigging to the crow's nest with them.

From his perch, Seamus tossed the first pot in a wide arc off to starboard. Charles drew the bowstring back, aimed, and the tiny pot broke into shards and fell into the sea. There was loud applause from the crew this time. Her heart began to beat faster, and she held her breath as he drew again. She couldn't stop herself from noticing the way his arms looked in his rolled-up sleeves. Thank heavens her face was veiled or her feelings about this man would be obvious to all.

Seamus hurled the second pot with all his might, sending it out across the ocean much faster than the first. Yet again, Charles released, aiming at where he estimated the pot would be. There was a crack, and once again shards fell into the waves. She took a deep breath and let it out slowly trying to calm her excitement and stirring heat.

For the final pot, Seamus waited for a gust of wind then tossed it up high, forcing Charles to look almost directly into the glare of the sun. They could all see the pot curving in the wind. Once again, she held her breath, her heart beating loudly in her ears as she watched, fists clenched by her sides. Draw, release, crack. It was done.

He was magnificent, and she wanted to eat him up with a spoon.

Saint Brigid, please help me in my time of need!

Uncle Colm cleared his throat. "Our newcomer is an impressive shot. We could use him in the crow's nest next time we engage."

"Hmm?" she said, unable to tear her gaze away from Charles.

"The crow's nest, Captain. We should put him there for our next engagement."

"Of course," she answered, dragging her eyes back to the charts, resolved once again to ignore Charles completely.

"Captain," Colm said in a low murmur. "You seem quite taken with our talented new friend. Be careful in front of the crew, or you might give yourself away."

A sharp spike of anger and alarm tore through her. "You will never speak of this again, Colm," she said with quiet intensity, pinning him with a glare. "Do you understand?"

Colm looked abashed. She loved her uncle. It pained her to reprimand him, but he'd gone too far.

"I understand, Captain," he said quietly, with his eyes down.

"I've looked at enough charts for now. I'm going below. Tell Seamus to knock on my cabin door if he needs me."

CHAPTER SIX

"MERCHANT VESSEL OFF starboard," hollered the young man standing in the crow's nest, keeping watch. His name was David, Charles had learned yesterday. The boy didn't know how old he was, but his voice still broke into a higher register on occasion. He told Charles the captain found him starving in the streets of Calais and took him in. The more Charles learned about the captain, the more he respected the man, even if he was a pirate.

At the news of the ship, the deck began to buzz with activity. "What's happening?" Charles asked Thomas, who was in the midst of teaching him the hand signals they used to communicate during attacks.

Thomas smiled. "I do believe we're about to capture a nice fat prize."

"But we already passed three merchant ships this morning. Why this one?"

"Ah, but none of those were flying Black Stephen's flag," Thomas answered, his smile growing.

But they would certainly have been nice fat prizes. Why would they only go after Black Stephen's ships?

"The captain doesn't hold with theft, you see," Thomas continued as if Charles had asked his question aloud.

Charles guffawed.

"No, really! He'd never rob an honest merchant. But Black Stephen's men build fortunes on the backs of the Irish, stealing men's lives and livelihoods to fill their pockets with gold. I'd wager we'll find a shipment slaves in the belly of that ship."

"I'd wager the same. How that man gets away with flouting the law of England, I do not know."

"England may have outlawed slavery, but Ireland didn't. Black Stephen skirts the law and trades in slaves with the Irish and the Vikings. The captain has no compunction about robbing slavers and giving any riches we find back to the men whose lives they stole."

Charles stared, incredulous. "And here I thought we were pirates."

Thomas bobbed his head side to side. "It's all a matter of perspective. Certainly, the rest of the world sees us as such. Myself, I prefer to think of us as liberators."

"Liberators?"

"I can see you're skeptical," Thomas said with a little laugh. "I was a priest before joining the *Draconis*, you know. Well, technically I still am, as I don't think anyone has ever bothered to have me formally defrocked. I joined the crew when my friend Ronan was captured and pressed into service aboard one of Black Stephen's ships. I had to go after him."

Thomas cast a longing look at Ronan, who was coiling rope beside the aftercastle, and then he reddened and looked down at the deck. "Luckily, I knew Captain O'Bannon. We grew up together near Wexford. I turned to him for help, and he agreed. We found Ronan quickly. If only we had been so lucky finding Liam."

"We'll find him," Charles said, as much to convince himself as Thomas. "We have to find him."

"We will," Thomas's agreed and then sighed. "Black Stephen is committing a terrible sin enslaving people this way," he said, crossing himself. "Everyone is made in God's image. Everyone is born free with an immortal soul, and when we pass from this world, we all face God's judgment, stripped of wealth and position, our hearts laid bare. Some say that bad fortune is God's punishment here on earth for the sinful, that those who are pressed into service deserve their fate. But I cannot believe that God in Heaven, who sent his only Son to die for our sins, the same God that told us to 'love thy neighbor as thyself' would ever see this as a fit punishment for a man's sins. I know many would see my views as heretical, including many in the Church, but I would remind them of Paul's words to the Corinthians: 'If I have faith that can move mountains, but have not love, I am nothing.'"

Once again, Thomas's gaze strayed to Ronan.

Charles shook his head and smiled. "Are you telling me you became a pirate for love?"

Thomas laughed. "I suppose you could say that," he said rising to his feet. "You'd best get your bow and arrows and climb up to that crow's nest. There's work to do."

Charles moved quickly, climbing up the rigging as soon as David was down, still pondering his conversation with Thomas. Was it possible he'd fallen in with a ship of nice pirates? Could such a thing even exist? Then he remembered Captain Edward's screams as Captain O'Bannon extracted information from him. Maybe "nice" was the wrong word. Principled, perhaps? He had to admit, it made him feel just a little bit better as he prepared to engage in his first act of piracy. His loathing of Black Stephen knew no bounds.

Charles knew his job and was determined to carry it out to the best of his ability. An archer was much more important for a day attack than at night. There were limits to what he could do in the dark without risking the crew's safety, but in the light of day, he could see the enemy clearly, just as they could see him. He'd need to look sharp to remove any unexpected threats to the *Draconis*'s boarding party.

It was quieter up in his perch. The captain's voice barked orders from the forecastle, but the wind muffled the sound. He had his earplugs at the ready in case he needed them during battle, though he hoped he wouldn't.

The distance between the *Draconis* and its prey was closing rapidly, and the buzz of activity on the deck below died down as everyone took their positions and prepared for the fight. The boarding party stood on the forecastle, the captain first among them. The forecastle and aftercastle were each defended by an archer and two swordsmen. Additional crew members stood at the ready with small clay jars of lime and with grappling hooks. Everyone on deck was masked or veiled to keep the lime off their faces. Fortunately, he had little to worry about, being so high above the fray.

The deck of the other ship was coming into focus. It was slightly longer than the *Draconis*, but it sat much lower in the water. It sported two triangular sails instead of one square one, and the crew complement appeared to be minimal. They were scrambling and pointing at the *Draconis*. Moments later, four men armed with swords and shields came up on deck and stationed themselves along the port side that faced the *Draconis*. Several more descended below to the protection of their cabins. The rest of the crew appeared to be running pell-mell to pull weapons from a chest in the stern—no bows or crossbows, he noted.

Charles only counted ten men on deck. There were likely slaves chained below, but they would be no help in this battle. *No help at all*, he thought with a grim smile. With the advantage of height and the fact that the enemy had no archers, this looked to be an easy win for the *Draconis*.

They were almost in range, and the captain looked up at him, signaling to take out the armed men. Charles signaled his acknowledgment and nocked his first arrow.

Just a little bit closer…closer…There!

He let his first shot fly, and the man closest to the bow crumpled with a bolt in his leg.

Pulling another from his quiver, he drew and released. The man standing next to the first staggered back, as it protruded from his shoulder.

The crew of the other ship ran for cover, leaving only the two remaining armed men guarding the side. They raised their shields high to defend against Charles's arrows.

Seeing that his shot was blocked, he signaled to the archers in the forecastle and aftercastle. They stepped forward and took aim at the unguarded sides of the two men. One arrow missed its target by a hair. The other glanced off the edge of the man's shield as he realized the new direction of danger just in time.

The captain signaled the archers to hold as the other ship drew close enough to begin bombing it with lime. Its deck exploded in a cloud of powder as the *Draconis*'s crew lobbed pot after pot onto it. The flummoxed crew began cursing and shouting as the stinging dust got into their eyes, noses, and mouths.

Charles's stomach clenched and his heart raced at the noise, and he quickly stuffed his beeswax in his ears to block it out. He couldn't afford an episode now.

The captain and boarding party swung their grappling hooks, and soon they were scampering across the ropes to the other ship. The captain took the lead, neatly dispatching the closest of the remaining armed men with his sword as soon as he climbed on deck. As the rest of the crew joined him, Charles briefly lost track of what was happening below. There was too much dust and chaos. He continued to watch, though, trying to discern friend from foe in case he needed to take out any unexpected attackers.

As the dust settled, he saw that the captain and boarding party had subdued the remaining crew. Charles counted two dead and four wounded amongst the enemy. The rest of the crew submitted to being tied up and secured to the main mast. Thinking the action was complete, Charles lowered his weapon and relaxed his stance.

Just then, he saw movement. Someone was sneaking out from behind a barrel, knife raised high, aiming straight for the captain's back. Charles raised his bow once more, and the arrow flew true. The attacker collapsed mere feet behind the captain, an arrow in his neck. The captain started, and turned to see the felled enemy at his feet. Looking up at Charles, he touched his forehead in a gesture of thanks.

Charles saluted in return, almost giddy with pride. "Saved the captain's life on my first attack," he sang to himself, indulging in a little childish gloating while no one could hear. If he wasn't in a crow's nest, he might even have done a little dance. Or maybe not. It wasn't the sort of thing a grown man should be seen doing. But it felt so unbelievably wonderful to be useful again, to have purpose, to use his skills, and have them acknowledged.

Looking back down at the other ship where two bodies lay still, his thoughts sobered. Three members of the boarding party headed down the hatch to deal with any crew members that might be hiding and to liberate any slaves or prisoners that might be aboard. He could hardly breathe while they were out of sight.

Long minutes went by, and Charles watched the hatch, keeping an arrow at the ready in case something went awry. At last, the captain led a ragtag group of fourteen haunted, filthy men onto the deck where they milled around aimlessly in the sunlight, each struggling to come to terms with their new reality, he knew.

Soon after, Seamus led two richly dressed men up through the hatch with Ronan following, knives in both hands glinting in the sun. These men were tied up as well. The fighting was done, and the *Draconis* won handily.

The captain and boarding crew made their way back to the *Draconis*, and a prize crew of five replaced them as bundles of food and clothing were passed to the other ship on ropes.

As Charles climbed back down to the deck, the crew of the *Draconis* retrieved the last of the grappling hooks, and the two ships parted ways.

The captain walked straight up to him, piercing him with those fierce, enigmatic eyes. "Thank you, Englishman. You proved your worth today. I am in your debt."

The captain turned and strode up to the parapet of the forecastle, followed closely by Seamus.

"Friends, brothers," he roared, and every head on deck turned towards him. Charles edged closer, anxious to hear what the captain had to say. "It's time to celebrate! Bring out the ale. Bring out your pipes, lutes, and drums because ye, my friends, are the finest bleedin' crew on the Irish Sea," he yelled over deafening hoots and hollers.

"Today we took the *Rosemary* away from that gobshite Black Stephen." The cheering grew thunderous as the crew stomped their feet and beat on barrels. "Their captain took one look at us and went running to his cabin where he cowered until Seamus and Ronan pried him out. We took the day without a single casualty on our side." Seamus smirked and whispered something in the captain's ear. The captain held up his hand. "Wait, wait... Seamus tells me there was an injury. Apparently, Ronan got a splinter in his hand breaking down the captain's door."

As the crew roared with laughter, Ronan faked a melodramatic faint into Thomas's waiting arms.

"If you ever leave the *Draconis*, you could always join a mummer's troupe, you dope," the captain said, clapping his hands. He held up his hand and waited until the laughter died down to continue.

"Ye, my friends, are the best and bravest crew a captain could ever ask for, and I am honored to fight by your side. Today, thanks to your efforts, we freed fourteen men. Fourteen feckin' men! Tonight, they will breathe free, cleanse the stench from their bodies, drink ale, and fill their bellies with good food. Ye remember what it was like—that first night of freedom. Many of ye wore shackles yourselves not too long ago." Quiet murmurs and prayers followed the captain's words, and Charles realized for the first time just how many of his crewmates must have been enslaved on ships liberated by the captain from Black Stephen's clutches.

"And I have to tell ye, my friends," the captain continued after a long pause. "We plucked a plump and juicy prize today. Ye all just got a little richer. There was the usual ale and wool, but there were also dyes—woad blue, kermes red, and Tyrian purple. Not to mention high-quality blocks of *alym roche* fixative. Even after the freed men's portions, today's takings will give you each enough to live on for a year."

Ale was flowing freely by this point, and the men clapped each other on the back in celebration. Charles realized with a start that this meant he had money again. If he wanted to go home to Winchelsea, he would have the means to do so as soon as he got his portion, though whether his father would receive him was an open question. What story had Black Stephen told his family about his disappearance? Would they know he had a price on his head? If so, going home could cost him his life. All the same, it felt good to know home was within reach for the first time in years, even if he didn't dare venture there.

"But I know none of ye do this for the money," the captain said, waving a magnanimous hand.

"I do it for the money," chimed in a short, thick man with a very crooked nose.

"Well, all right then, none of ye do this for the money except Malcolm."

"I'm an honest crook, Captain." Malcolm swept into a ridiculous bow.

"So you are," the captain answered. "At least most of the time," he said with a wink. "But enough speechifying for one night, eh? Hand me a tankard, Seamus." Taking it in hand, he lifted it high. "To the *Draconis*! May we maraud these waters until we've taken every last ship from that poxy bastard, Black Stephen. *DRACONIS!*"

Every member of the crew roared an answering "*DRACONIS!*" with tankards raised high.

As if on cue, three of the men struck up a tune, one on lute, another on pipes, and the third on a drum. Several of the surrounding men recognized the tune and started singing the filthiest sea shanty Charles had ever heard. The captain made his way down from the forecastle and caroused with the crew.

Charles settled down with a tankard of ale, leaned against a barrel, and watched the fun. He hardly knew what to do with himself. When was the last time he'd felt festive? He couldn't even remember. And he'd certainly never been at a party like this. Barons' heirs generally weren't allowed anywhere near this kind of fun. The most he could hope for at home was a racy troubadour lyric to make the silly, boring ladies blush.

Charles smiled and shook his head as he saw Thomas and Ronan sneaking down the hatch hand in hand for some private time below decks. Clearly those two had found their bliss in life at sea. Would he ever be so lucky?

As usual when he started feeling maudlin, he found himself thinking of Fionola. Where was she now, and what was she doing? Was she looking up at the same moon, her heart full of longing, just as his was?

While he was woolgathering, the captain took a seat beside him. Charles jumped as the captain snatched his tankard.

"Daydreaming about Fionola?" the captain asked, taking a deep swig.

"Actually, yes."

The captain choked on his ale. "Lucky guess," he said, gasping, then took another swig to wash down the first. "Dare I ask…?"

Charles chuckled and shook his head. "Nothing untoward, I assure you. At least not right now," he said, giving the captain a confiding smile. "If you asked me what I *dream* about Fionola…" He could feel his face reddening, and he looked at the deck. Even to the captain, he didn't dare confess the loving detail with which he had dreamed every curve of her body, touching her, tasting her, making tender love to her. "But just now, I was only wondering where she is and whether she might be looking at the same moon."

He and the captain stared at the moon together in drunken silence for a long moment. "Foolish, I know," he said at last. The captain leaned against him and handed his tankard back.

"Not foolish," the captain said, staring at nothing in particular off stern. "Thank you for saving my life today. I am in your debt," he said, continuing to stare off to stern.

"Think nothing of it, Captain." Charles took a deep swig of ale, trying to ignore the complicated storm of feelings brewing within him. It had been so long since he'd been able to do anything at all except hard labor, and today, he saved his captain's life. "Introduce me to Fionola someday, and we're even," he said, taking another swig.

The captain was silent, staring off in a revery of his own.

"Thomas told me today why we only go after Black Stephen's ships," Charles said to break the silence. "Shocked the hell out of me. And here I thought we were just plain pirates, out for booty."

The captain turned his drunken stare and looked him in the eye. He didn't say a word, just looked.

Charles cleared his throat. "I liked your speech tonight. I'm proud to be a part of your crew. I never thought I'd see the day when pirates had the moral high ground, but…"

The captain turned his gaze back to stern. "I should go…do…something," he said and shoved himself to standing. He staggered off to Seamus.

What an unusual man.

The crew certainly loved the captain and with good reason, but his behavior toward Charles was such an odd mix of warmth and distance. Hopefully with time, Charles could win the captain's trust. In the meantime, he would thank the Lord for his good fortune landing on the *Draconis*. At that moment, he couldn't think of anywhere else he'd rather be.

CHAPTER SEVEN

FIONOLA PACED THE deck like a caged animal, ready to pounce. A week and a half had passed since she had learned Liam's whereabouts, and they were approaching Honfleur. Did she dare hope that she would see her brother at last? They were so close.

But it wasn't the first time she'd been close. Every time before, she had failed. This time had to be different. And they had to be cautious too. Black Stephen was well aware of the threat posed by the *Draconis*, and he'd offered the princely sum of one hundred gold pieces for Captain O'Bannon, dead or alive. Fortunately, he had no idea Captain O'Bannon was Fionola MacMurrough, or the price would be double. But Honfleur was a large port with multiple wharfs. As long as they didn't tie up in the same one as the *Gorgon*, the other ship would never even notice they were there.

For days, she'd been snapping at everyone, demanding they go over the plans again and again, finding fault with every little thing the crew did. Even Uncle Colm was steering clear of her. There was nothing more to do until they arrived, and she knew it.

What she needed was a distraction, any distraction.

Well, maybe not any, she thought as her eye strayed yet again to Charles.

She cursed under her breath, watching him and Ronan fight

with wooden swords on deck below. A churning heat settled between her legs as she watched, and she squeezed her knees together, wishing it away.

This was ridiculous. How could she possibly indulge such feelings at a time like this? Or at any time? Everything depended on her maintaining her disguise as a man. Not to mention her deathbed promise to her mother. And, for God's sake, he was an Englishman!

And she was Captain O'Bannon, protected by her fighting skill, a false beard, and rumors of a deformed face. Some thought she had a hair lip. Others thought it was a terrible injury. She let them speculate. The more rumors the better—anything to deflect attention from the truth.

But Charles had had to come along and ruin everything.

She grabbed a dagger from her sleeve and jabbed it into the parapet of the forecastle, then noticed what she was doing and sheathed it. But she couldn't look away from the sword fight below.

Ronan was good with a sword by all accounts, and Charles had trounced him three times in a row. Charles's reactions were a bit sluggish from disuse, but his form was impeccable. It was clear he'd noticed the way Ronan's left thumb twitched every time he started to lunge. It allowed him to use Ronan's momentum against him and set him off balance time and again.

Charles had his own tells, though. They were subtle, but she could see the way his right shoulder tensed as he prepared to block. He took a deep breath each time he went on the attack. There was the slightest hint of a smile each time he saw an opening in Ronan's defense. He was looking a little too pleased with himself for his performance against Ronan. Did she dare give in to temptation and teach him a lesson?

No sooner had the thought crossed her mind than she found herself storming down the steep stairs to the deck.

Moments later, Ronan and Charles paused as she approached and they backed away, giving her a wide berth.

Wise of them, given her mood.

"Captain," Ronan said with a respectful bow of his head, panting from his exertions.

"Captain," Charles said with a polite nod. "If we're in the way, just let us know and we'll clear off."

She clenched the pommel of her sword with a death grip. "Actually, I was thinking I might test your skills myself."

Charles's eyes strayed to her hand, gripping the sword.

Ronan hurriedly handed over his wooden sword to stop her from drawing steel against Charles's wooden blade. "My sword is yours, Captain."

She released her pommel and took the wooden sword without a glance at Ronan and positioned herself in front of Charles, staring him down. Yes, this was just what she needed—a little combat to chase away her restlessness.

He raised his sword. She did not.

His look of confusion made her smile widen beneath her scarf. "Well?" She beckoned with her empty hand.

The rest of the crew gathered to watch, forming a circle around them.

Charles wore a bemused expression but shrugged and then lunged.

Yes, come at me, Charles.

She pivoted backward at the last moment, and his momentum carried him right past her and straight into the onlookers in front of him.

Catching himself, he turned to face her, sword at the ready. He looked at her, his expression a mix of incredulity and respect.

"You can do better than that," she said, standing still. "I haven't even raised my sword yet."

He tilted his head to the side and narrowed his eyes. Once again, he lunged toward her, and this time, she grabbed the wrist of his sword arm and twisted, while she pivoted to pull him off balance. He landed on the deck, and she stood holding both wooden swords. It wasn't fair and she knew it, but if she fought fair, she'd be dead.

Charles pushed himself up from the deck and stared at her with a furrowed brow. "Captain, I don't understand. I thought we were sword fighting."

She shrugged. "I thought so too, but so far you haven't managed to engage."

The crew laughed. They'd seen this little performance enough times that they knew what to expect.

She tossed back his sword and opened her arms in invitation, her sword dangling casually from her right hand.

He stood holding his sword by his side and took a step toward her without raising it, and then another step. What was he up to? He was in easy striking distance now. Surely, he hadn't given up already.

Lightening quick, his sword swung in an arc toward her neck. It was too late to dodge, so she blocked. His face was inches from hers, his lips so close. Too close. Thank God her mouth was covered so she couldn't do anything foolish.

She twisted her grip and disarmed him once again.

"*Tsk tsk*," she said handing him back his practice sword. "You must be very rusty."

"Does he do this to everyone?" Charles asked Ronan who was shaking with laughter next to Thomas.

Ronan guffawed at that. "Does he do this to everyone?" he repeated, bending over, and slapping his knee, unable to catch his breath.

"You're not giving up, are you?" she taunted. Charles's irritation was getting the better of him. She could see it in his face.

He took a deep breath. "Of course not, Captain."

For a long moment, he stood still and watched her. And God help her, she watched him right back, in all of his long, muscular glory, his lovely eyes boring into her. She bit her tongue, needing some sharp sensation to pull her back from the warm revery that was overtaking her.

Saint Brigid, save me.

She blinked, and a moment later, she was on her back on the deck with no idea how she got there, and Charles had his wooden blade at her throat. Her crew gasped and *oo*-ed and *ah*-ed around her.

What did…? How did…?

For a moment, she marveled at what he'd just done. She had to respect his skill taking advantage of her moment of distraction like that. But then she remembered her peril.

I can't let this happen in front of my crew. They can't see me falter, or everything falls apart.

Grabbing the flat of his blade, she yanked him off balance, as she used his momentary distraction as he stumbled to jump back up and lift her own sword. This time, she attacked.

Her sword flew as she forced him to retreat, his proper, perfect form leaving him vulnerable to her tricks. He was too predictable. He fought like a nobleman at a tourney, following the rules as if it was a game. She wanted to ruffle him, make him lose control and answer her with the same fury and passion that consumed her.

Rational thought abandoned her, and she fought with muscle memory and instinct alone. She was the better swordsman. She knew it before she'd challenged him. But for some reason she found herself prolonging the fight, passing up obvious opportunities to take him down. Some madness made her want the dance to continue, his full attention on her, each thrust bringing him perilously close, each parry a tease that drew her on.

"You're toying with me, Captain. Why don't you end it?" he asked, breathing heavily, and bathed in sweat as he tried to keep pace with her onslaught.

Christ's teeth. Why didn't she?

"I'm teaching you a lesson." If only she knew what the lesson was.

She pressed him back and back and back. The crew moved around them as they traveled across the deck.

The mast was three feet behind him. Two feet.

It was time to end it. Past time.

One foot.

His back collided with the mast. She knocked his sword from his hand, holding her own to his neck. With her other hand, she grabbed a fistful of his tunic and pulled him so close his hot breath warmed her cheek.

"You fight too bleedin' clean," she said in a rasping voice, his heart beating beneath her hand. "There are no rules out here, Englishman. There is only your body and your sword. Use them well."

She released him and pushed him away as if he burned her. And perhaps he did. She had hoped the fight would quell the fire inside her, but it had only fanned the flames. Throwing down her sword, she made her way swiftly to the hatch, ignoring the backslaps and congratulations of her crew.

Solitude. That's what she needed. A moment to hide herself away and be free of everyone's expectations, away from the ever-present temptation of this man.

She stormed into her cabin and locked the door behind her, tearing off her scarf and beard.

Exercise. That will help me. Maybe if I exhaust myself this ache will go away.

She tore off her cotte and shirt and dropped to the floor, wearing just her breeches and the cloth that bound her breasts. In the heat and dim light of her room, she toiled away until her muscles screamed. Then she started all over again.

When she'd worked herself until her limbs trembled with exhaustion, she wiped away her sweat with a cloth and dressed again. The ache of wanting was only slightly diminished by her exertions, damn it all.

She knelt down beside her pallet and prayed to every saint she could name for deliverance from temptation. Still the heat and restlessness would not abate. No wonder her mother made such a fuss about virtue. The temptation to throw it to the wind was far greater than she'd ever dreamed.

What was she going to do? What could she do? It was impossible to indulge these feelings, and yet they seemed to take over, driving everything else away, at the most inconvenient moments.

She needed advice, or at the very least a chance to unburden herself. There was only one option, really.

⫸⫷

"THOMAS, I NEED your help," she said, pulling her old friend away from scrubbing the deck.

Thomas stood and gave her an all-too-understanding look.

"I need to go to confession," she murmured so that only he could hear.

Nodding, he led the way down to the hold, and they sat side by side on wooden crates.

"Forgive me, Father, for I have sinned," she said to the wooden deck beneath her feet. "It has been two weeks since my last confession."

Thomas sat in silence and waited.

Suddenly, her tongue was thick in her mouth, and words wouldn't come. She wasn't afraid. That would be absurd. How could mere words scare her? She was Captain O'Bannon, scourge of the Irish Sea and the English Channel. And this was Thomas, her best friend, who she'd always told everything, even before he became a priest.

She took a deep breath and let it out.

"I'm having feelings about a man," she began and then stopped.

When she didn't say anything more, Thomas prompted, "A man?"

"Charles." There. She said it out loud. "I'm having sinful, indecent thoughts about him. I've been trying to ignore them, hoping they would go away, but they keep getting stronger. I must put a stop to it. I can't afford to have these feelings."

Dear Lord in heaven, make these feelings go away before I do some-

thing I regret.

Thomas said nothing.

"I want to kiss him, touch him, feel his arms around me, even though I know it's impossible and wrong." Saying it out loud drained some of the aching desperation she felt. Thank God for Thomas.

"Why?" Thomas asked after a long silence.

"Why what?"

"Why is it impossible and wrong?"

She took a deep breath. "Because I am the captain of this ship and I live as a man. Everything falls apart if I indulge these feelings. And even if I lived as a woman, there's the promise I made to my mother to defend my virtue at all costs. Not to mention the fact that he's English. As for why it's wrong, you're the priest. Shouldn't you be telling me?"

Thomas laughed. "The Scripture says, 'First cast out the beam out of thine own eye; and then shalt thou see clearly to cast out the mote out of thy brother's eye.' Far be it from me to condemn you for your thoughts when my own sins of the flesh are so egregious. At least you have a path to virtue. There's nothing wrong with touching, kissing, or embracing if you marry."

"If I *marry*?"

Had Thomas lost his mind?

Tilting his head to the side, Thomas asked, "Yes, marriage. You've heard of it?"

Ever since her near-miss with Black Stephen, the very idea sent chills down her spine. Even Seamus's harmless proposals put her stomach in a twist. Not that she planned to stay alone forever. But it was impossible to contemplate in her current circumstances.

"Christ, man! Are you suggesting I marry Charles?"

The expected shiver of horror didn't come. Instead, warmth suffused her as she imagined standing beside him on the steps of a church, gazing into his eyes and making the ancient vows.

"I'm saying marriage is the only way to indulge these feelings without sin," Thomas said, interrupting her reverie. "Me, I'll always be a sinner and a sodomite."

"I thought this was my confession, not yours," she said, giving him a friendly nudge with her elbow.

He smiled and shook his head. "My apologies, Captain. Please continue."

"I already told you the juicy part. The rest is just the usual. I killed some men in battle. I stole a ship full of goods from that bastard, Black Stephen. Etcetera." She drifted into silence, feeling like she should say more but not sure how.

"Well, what are you going to do about it, Fionola?"

It was so odd to hear her name aloud. She wished there was a way to simply be who she was instead of pretending to be a woman or pretending to be a man. Neither felt right. She wanted to be the captain *and* Fionola. Was that so wrong? She wanted to live the life she'd chosen and have room for love. The life she'd crafted so carefully suddenly weighed her down like an anchor.

And then there was this idea of marriage. She'd always assumed she'd marry someday, but her current life made it unthinkable. And she'd never met a man who tempted her to consider it. But could she give herself to the right man in holy matrimony—one who accepted her as she was and didn't try to tie her down? Possibly. With the right man under the right circumstances. If only the right circumstances weren't impossible. It was absurd to even think about, but she couldn't let it go.

"I don't know." She shook her head and ran her hands over her face. "No matter what I choose, I feel like I'm living a lie. And he's a bleedin' Englishman. Just because my family owes fealty to King Henry doesn't mean I want to marry one. Not that any of it matters because I can hardly do anything about it while I'm Captain O'Bannon."

He took her hand in his and squeezed. "As your friend and not your priest, I can tell you that we don't get to choose who we love, not that I'm suggesting this is love. At least not yet. But even when our love will turn our whole lives upside down, we can't deny the truth in our hearts. I remember the day I finally admitted to myself that I was in love with Ronan. It felt like the end of everything. And it was. It cost me my vocation, my family, my friends—except you, of course. It nearly cost me my life. But here on the *Draconis*, I've built a life that feels honest, a life where I have love *and* purpose. I pray that you can find the same." He squeezed her hand again.

Thomas understood better than anyone. He always had. She wasn't too convinced he still had sway with the Father, the Son, and the Holy Spirit, but he was the only priest she ever took comfort in confessing to.

"Aren't you going to tell me to say some Hail Marys?" She turned to look at him, giving him a wry smile.

"Fine, Fionola. If you insist. How many do you think you should do?"

She pursed her lips and tilted her head to the side. "Twenty?"

He laughed at her. "Twenty it is. The Lord has freed you from your sins. Go in peace."

"Thanks be to God," she said with a sarcastic sigh.

She stood up, and so did he.

"And thank you, Thomas," she said earnestly, pulling him into a hug, "for being a good friend."

It wasn't an easy conversation, but unburdening herself gave her some relief. Whether she was O'Bannon or Fionola, she still had to save Liam and destroy Black Stephen. By the time she found her brother and ended Black Stephen's reign of terror, she could only pray that she would know the truth of her own heart.

CHAPTER EIGHT

HONFLEUR AT LAST. Fionola was ready. This time, she would not fail.

The assault on the senses was immediate as they docked and paid the harbor master the required fees, taxes, and bribes to prevent any trouble in port. At the mouth of the Seine, it was one of the busiest ports on the northern coast of France.

No sooner had they tied up the *Draconis* than a bevy of hawkers closed in, competing in volume in the hopes of drawing the attention of the crew. Some tried to entice them to inns, taverns, and brothels, ready to drag them bodily if they made the mistake of getting within arm's reach. Others offered all manner of street food from fresh fruit and vegetables to flaky honey pastries and ripe, stinky cheeses. Still others sold fake amulets and relics, promising the purchaser miraculous healing, endless good fortune, protection from enemies—all for a modest price. All of this, and they hadn't even left the docks yet.

She took a deep breath and steeled herself to plunge into the chaos. Leaving Seamus to oversee the sale of the goods in the hold and the reprovisioning of the ship, she took Charles and Ronan and headed south through narrow streets lined with stone warehouses and taverns, dodging horse droppings and drainage channels carrying raw sewage to the sea.

Soon they arrived at the city's main thoroughfare, and

weaved their way through carriages, riders, oxen-pulled wagons, donkey carts, and pedestrians. They passed the Custom House and continued on until she saw the Church of Saint Catherine.

"We turn here," she yelled over the din, grabbing Charles and Ronan by the wrists and dragging them left onto a long, porticoed market street. The stink of the docks receded, replaced by earthier smells of horses and pack animals. At last, she saw Alexandre's shop, and she sighed with relief as they stepped inside. A sense of peace and order settled over her as the noises of the street became muffled.

"Captain O'Bannon, welcome. Welcome! May God's blessings rain down upon you and your crew. May I offer you wine to refresh yourselves?" Alexandre greeted them in French.

He was a cadaverous old man with a thin strip of hair combed over his nearly bald pate. He beckoned them into the cool shadows of his shop, away from the bustle of the open stall in front. The walls were piled high with fabrics of every description. Snapping his fingers, two boys came running. The first followed the old man's gesture and went to tend the stall out front. The other went to get wine for the guests.

"Alexandre, God's blessings be upon you and your shop," she answered in French. "I would like to introduce you to two of my crew members—Ronan and Charles."

Alexandre's gaze turned sharp, but he answered mildly, "I'm honored. Honored! Please sit and be at ease." He gestured toward rickety wooden chairs along the wall.

She knew Ronan didn't understand a word, though Charles smiled and nodded as if he understood perfectly. So he spoke French. Interesting. It was further evidence that he was keeping secrets about his past. After all, French was the language of the Norman aristocracy. Perhaps there was something to Captain Edward's story about Charles claiming to be the son of a baron.

They all nodded politely at Alexandre's gesture, and all four of them sat down. "Have the winds been friendly in your travels, Captain?"

Fionola knew from experience that Alexandre would be magically deaf to any mention of business until the boy returned with their wine. She chafed at the slow pace. Every minute she spent here was another minute of captivity for her brother, but it would do no good to try to move things along. "Yes, the winds have been friendly and the weather fair. I could ask for nothing more. And what of you? Have you been healthy and prosperous since I last saw you?"

"Oh yes. Oh yes," he answered with an ingratiating smile. "I am healthy and prosperous. Thank you for asking." He settled into silence and openly studied Ronan and Charles. It was obvious to her that he suspected they were up to something, and he wasn't wrong. But he was discreet as long as she paid him generously, and she planned to make today's business quite lucrative for him.

Ronan shifted and opened his mouth to speak, but she shook her head and he obeyed. He and Charles kept silent and looked into the middle distance, ignoring Alexandre's bold perusal.

After several long, awkward minutes, the boy returned with a wine skin and four pewter goblets. He poured the garnet-colored liquid carefully for each of them and handed over each cup with a little bow. Fionola took a sip of the bright and fruity vintage and motioned at Charles and Ronan to do the same.

Alexandre inhaled deeply and savored it as he drank, smiling at her in a way that made the hairs on the back of her neck stand on end. "Now," he said at last, "what brings you to my shop today?"

"I bring new merchandise from the west that may be of interest to you—wool, linen, silk, dyes, and *alym roche* fixative. My ship is docked in the harbor, and my man Seamus, whom you know, is under orders to give your buyer first pick and to negotiate a very fair price. I can't afford to be so generous with all of my business dealings, but you are such a longstanding friend and business partner..."

Alexandre took another sip and licked his lips. "A fair price?"

"Practically a gift." Most of the bounty from the *Rosemary* went back to Gan Ainm, the island off the coast of Wexford they called home, but the goods she brought on board should have been sufficient to tempt him. He'd always been a reliable customer for her stolen goods.

"Ah, but you are too generous, far too generous, my friend. Of course, I cannot accept such a gift until I know what it is that I might do to show my gratitude. Is there not some small favor with which I might be of assistance?"

Wary as always, old man. Let the bargaining begin.

"Oh no. I could never accept anything in return. I do this only to show my gratitude for our partnership." She sipped her wine and looked Alexandre in the eye. "Though perhaps, if it wouldn't be too much trouble, you might be of service to a passenger of ours, a wealthy merchant from London. I'm afraid his trunk was ruined when he forgot to blow out a candle in his cabin. It caught fire. Such an unfortunate accident. It's a blessing we were able to put out the fire before it damaged the ship."

Alexandre watched her with an impassive face. "A blessing indeed. Such a blessing. Praise be to God Almighty." He took another sip and waited for her to continue.

"Our passenger needs new clothes befitting his station. By any chance, might you have anything that would fit a man of approximately this size?" she asked, gesturing at Charles. "I brought my man along to save our merchant friend the trouble. He has much more important business matters to attend to. I wouldn't want you to go to any trouble either. I only hoped you might have something lying around that we might purchase. For a fair price."

Tilting his head and looking at the ceiling, he asked, "He's from London, you say? Such peculiar fashions they wear in that part of the world, quite peculiar. But perhaps I might have something that would suit his taste. I assume he also lost shoes and accessories in the fire?"

Fionola smiled. "How did you guess? So unfortunate." She

took another sip. Almost nothing was left in the cup, but she couldn't let him see she'd finished until their business was concluded. "And there was one other small favor he asked of me. He seeks to visit a merchant of his acquaintance on a ship called the *Gorgon* that is docked here. Do you know of anyone that might be able to make an introduction to its captain?"

Alexandre nodded slowly. "So far, what you ask is a mere trifle. Is there anything else I can assist your passenger with?"

"No, thank you, Alexandre. If you could do these things, I would be deeply grateful. I must ask that you remain discreet about our arrangement. Our passenger values his privacy and is quite embarrassed about all of this."

"Of course, Captain," he said, draining his cup.

She nodded and drained hers as well.

Alexandre whistled, and one of the boys came to collect their cups. At a signal from her, Ronan also handed over a heavy purse to the boy. Alexandre never touched money himself. He merely glanced at the purse and nodded in approval. Then he murmured instructions in the boy's ear about sending the buyer to the *Draconis*. The deal was done.

With a few deft motions, Alexandre took Charles's measurements and disappeared into a storage room. He returned several minutes later with a fine linen shirt, deep blue woolen hose, and a matching deep blue cotte with pleated arms and gold embroidery at the collar and hem.

"Try on the cotte," he said, pressing it into Charles's hands. Charles clearly understood without the need for Fionola to translate. He did speak French then. Interesting.

The fit was a little bit tighter than ideal but adequate for their needs. She tried not to stare at the way his muscles rippled beneath it.

"That will do nicely," she said. "Our passenger will be most grateful."

Charles took it off again, and Alexandre wrapped it up in a bundle with the rest of the clothes, a pair of pointy leather shoes, a leather belt with a silver clasp, and a floppy blue velvet hat.

"My man will be ready to take your passenger to the *Gorgon*'s captain in two hours. He will meet you beside the Custom House, and he will be wearing a red scarf around his neck."

"Thank you. May God watch over you and grant you health and prosperity until we next meet," she said with a little bow.

"And you as well. And you as well," he said, returning to his customary place in the stall in front.

As Fionola launched herself back into the chaos of Honfleur along with Charles and Ronan, some sixth sense told her that things were going too smoothly. Something was sure to go awry. She looked back at her companions. They seemed more than capable of carrying out their assignment, risky as it was. It was no good looking for trouble before it arrived. All she could do was trust her crew and pray her instincts were wrong.

CHAPTER NINE

CHARLES LOOKED DOWN at his finery and tried not to panic. It had been years since he last donned such clothes. Could he truly play the role the captain expected him to? He knew he was the only one aboard who could pull it off, with his aristocratic English accent, but putting on the clothes of a noble only reminded him of how far he'd fallen. He was a mere echo of the Charles de Vere who'd left Winchelsea two years ago.

"Stop preening like a peacock, you tool, and get up on deck. The captain wants to see you," Ronan said, eying him with amusement. "Or should I say, 'The captain requests the pleasure of your company, my lord?'"

Ronan wore the plain linen cotte and hose of a manservant, shedding his usual seaman's garments. This might have been the first time Charles had seen the man wear shoes. Ronan swept into a mocking bow.

Charles gave a strained laugh. How had he ever accepted the deference of others as his due? To be called "my lord" now, even in jest, only deepened his discomfort with donning the trappings of his former life. He was a changed man and could never go back to what he'd been for so many reasons.

And yet here he was. A peacock indeed.

Taking a deep breath, he tamped down his discomfort and headed off to see the captain, followed by "his man" Ronan.

The captain narrowed his eyes as they approached, examining their appearance, then walked around behind them before circling back in front again. At last, he nodded.

"I suppose your disguises will do. Let's go over the plan one more time. Charles, tell me your story."

"I am Lord Brendan de Lucy of Romney." Charles had chosen the name of his cousin, to whom he bore a striking resemblance. He needed a credible story in case he was recognized. After all, this was far from his first visit to Honfleur, though he wasn't as well known here as at Calais.

"I'm looking for investments on behalf of my father and am interested in financing the *Gorgon's* next journey along the coast of England," he continued, thinking back on all the times he'd engaged in such dealings on behalf of his own father.

The captain nodded. "Mind how you speak. You have the most polished manner of any of us, but that doesn't mean they won't suspect you if you slip up."

Charles looked the captain in the eye. "Have no fear. I know how to speak and behave. I could convince them I was a baron if I had to."

The captain's intense gaze sent cold sweat trickling down his back. Had Charles said too much, struck too close to the truth? What did the captain suspect about him? Resisting the urge to look away, Charles breathed out slowly to calm the pounding of his heart.

At last, the captain turned his attention on Ronan.

"And you," the captain said, stepping close to Ronan. "Try not to act like the pompous ass you are."

"Yes, Captain," Ronan answered, smirking.

"Remember you're supposed to be a servant. Show some deference and humility for once. And don't you dare mock Lord de Lucy here for his finery. A manservant doesn't mock."

Stifling laughter, Ronan bowed to Charles. "I would never mock your lordship."

The captain's eyes flashed dangerously. "I mean it, Ronan. If you can't do this, I'll send Thomas."

That sobered Ronan up. Clearing his throat, he said, "I will do as you ask, Captain. No mocking. I shall be the humblest manservant you've ever seen."

"You'd better be." The captain exhaled slowly. "And what are you going to do once you're on board the *Gorgon* and Charles is distracting Captain Gregory?"

"Look around. Joke with the crew. See if I can figure out how many men they will have on board guarding the ship at nightfall."

The captain nodded. "Most of the men should be on shore, so it should be a skeleton crew. Charles, make sure Liam is truly there, and get to know the layout of the ship. Don't speak to Liam or indicate you know him in any way. Carry all the concealed weapons you can, and I want you both to get out of there at the first sign of trouble. Understand?"

"Yes, Captain," they said in unison.

"Captain," Ronan said, leaning forward, "I still don't understand why you aren't going yourself. I know how much you want to see Liam."

The captain took a deep breath. "Too many people in this city know me and know the *Draconis* is my ship. No one would believe I am either a noble or a servant. The ruse wouldn't work. Believe me when I say I will be the first off the ship tonight when we attempt our rescue. Until then, Liam's fate rests in your hands."

Ronan nodded. "We'll find him for you, Captain."

"Good. Now go. God willing, you'll be back in a few hours, and we can plan our rescue properly."

As Charles stepped onto the docks with Ronan close behind, it was as if he'd stepped back in time. Everything depended on him becoming the nobleman he once was, and he deliberately attempted to banish all vestiges of the last two years from his mind. He strode with purpose through the winding streets, ignoring the nods and bows of passersby, until he found the small square with the fountain with three fishes spouting water where they were to meet their contact.

No sooner did they approach the fountain than a rough-looking young man with missing front teeth and a nose that had been broken several times approached them.

"My lord, I work for a man named Alexandre and have been sent to see you safely to the ship you seek."

The man's loose garments failed to entirely hide the multitude of weapons he carried. Fortunately, Charles and Ronan were also well-armed. If this man attempted anything, he would soon learn his mistake.

"Come. I will take you to the *Gorgon*, Lord..."

"Lord Brendan de Lucy of Romney," Charles said, hoping no one heard the false note in his commanding tone.

"Lord de Lucy, if you would follow me," said the youth, gesturing with his hand.

They wound their way along narrow, cobblestone streets, past shops, and tidy stone homes, which steadily grew rougher as they approached the docks of the Bassin de l'Est.

The salty air grew thick with the smell of fish as they made their way past dockworkers carrying barrels, crates, and sacks between ships and warehouses that lined the docks.

The *Gorgon* was docked at the far end of a jetty, sitting high in the water, suggesting its goods had just been unloaded. It was an enormous cog vessel, half again the size of the *Draconis*. Its two sails were furled, and a gangway reached from the deck to the jetty.

Charles shivered despite the heat as he saw Black Stephen's flag flying on the mast. He could do this, he reminded himself. There was no reason for anyone on the *Gorgon* to recognize him aside from Liam, and Liam would not give him away. They would not lock him up and strip him of all humanity. He was armed, free, and dressed as a noble. They would not touch him.

Clenching his fist, he tamped down his turbulent emotions. This was not the time to give in to his weakness. Liam was depending on him.

Ronan reached out and touched his shoulder as their guide came to a halt. "My lord," he said quietly, "I am certain our business today will be successful."

Taking a deep breath, Charles unclenched his fist and nodded.

"My lord, this is the *Gorgon*. I will leave you here and await your return over by that warehouse there," their guide said, pointing. "If you require my services, call out for Michel and I will come."

Charles nodded, and Michel disappeared.

Forcing one foot in front of another, he climbed the gangplank. He would not fall into Black Stephen's clutches again, not now or ever.

"Good sir," Charles called out to a rotund sailor, leaning against the rail, whittling something with a knife.

The man looked up. "What do you want?" the man snarled.

"My name is Lord Brendan de Lucy, and I wish to speak to your captain about a business matter. I promise to make it worth his time."

With a sneer, the man hitched his head to the side, inviting them onto the deck, then he turned and disappeared down the hatch without a word.

Liam was down there, unless something had happened to him. Somehow, Charles had to get a tour of this ship so that he could lay eyes on his friend at last, even though his heart warned him to get off the vessel as quickly as possible.

There were only four men on deck. Presumably the rest had disembarked and were enjoying the entertainments of the town. There might be more below, but Charles hoped it was a skeleton crew, the minimum needed to guard the ship.

Several minutes passed, and the men on deck ignored them as they waited. Then a man climbed up through the hatch who looked terrifyingly like Captain Edward, his tormentor. Bile rose in Charles's throat, but he marched forward with a smile.

"Captain, thank you for taking the time to speak with me," Charles said with a condescending nod of his head. After all, a noble shouldn't bow to a mere captain. "I am Lord Brendan de Lucy of Romney. It's a pleasure to make your acquaintance." Nothing could be further from the truth, but Charles owed it to his friend and the whole crew of the *Draconis* to play this to the hilt.

"Captain Gregory at your service, my lord." The man bowed obsequiously, eying Charles with undisguised greed. "My man here says you wished to speak with me about a business matter?"

Good. Charles's disguise was holding up, at least so far.

"Indeed, Captain. My father sent me here to look for investment opportunities, and I've heard good things about your ship. I was wondering if you might give me a tour. I may be interested in financing your next voyage if I like what I see."

"Of course, my lord," the captain said with a rapacious grin, rubbing his hands together. "It would be my pleasure." He gestured toward the hatch.

"Sebastian, wait for me here," Charles said to Ronan, following the captain. Cold sweat streamed down Charles's back as he descended the ladder, but he focused on his breath and managed to keep his head. He only needed to play this role for a few more minutes if everything went smoothly.

The captain lit a candle and showed him the front hold, which was empty at the moment. Charles couldn't have cared less, desperate as he was to escape, but he made a show of inspecting every corner.

"Our lower hold is through here," the captain said, gesturing toward another hatch, which was near crew quarters.

"Lord Charles," a familiar voice that was not Liam's called out as he approached the hatch.

Charles froze.

"Shut it, you," Captain Gregory snarled.

"It's me, Arthur," the voice called out again, making Charles's insides turn to liquid. "You have to get me out of here!"

Squinting in the candlelight, Charles caught sight of a barred space that must have been the hold where they kept slaves. At least eight emaciated men were crowded together inside with more in the dim murk behind them. The captain's candle lit their faces as he looked between Charles and the prisoners.

There was Arthur, plain as day, with Liam beside him, tugging on his arm. Arthur had been part of Charles's crew when he first sailed for Ireland. The man was loyal to a fault but never did know when to keep his mouth shut.

"Here. What's this?" demanded Captain Gregory. "Why does this scum think your name is Lord Charles?"

"Because he's Lord Charles de Vere of Winchelsea," Arthur said, as Charles did his best not to wince. "You've come to rescue me, haven't you? You've got ransom money to pay?"

Charles's heart broke into a thousand pieces as he said, "You must be mistaken. My name is Lord Brendan de Lucy."

Captain Gregory's eyes narrowed. "Charles de Vere, eh? I've heard about that dirty traitor. Betrayed Lord Stephen, he did. And the crown too, from what I hear. Seen him myself once or twice on my cousin's ship. Come to think of it, you look a lot like him." The captain's hand went to his sword. "If you're Lord Charles de Vere, Lord Stephen would pay me handsomely for your return. He's here in Honfleur, you know. His messenger said he'd stop by my ship this afternoon. He could be here any moment."

Black Stephen was here? A cold bolt of terror turned Charles's blood to ice. The churning in his stomach and the pace of his heart told him an attack was coming on. Not now. If he lost control, all hope would be lost.

Breathing deeply, he felt for the knives up his sleeves and started backing toward the ladder up to the deck. "You are mistaken, Captain. I'm a distant relation of Lord Charles. Perhaps there is a family resemblance. My man can vouch for me. Let me call him." He reached the foot of the ladder and yelled, "Sebastian."

Ronan came running and slid down the sides of the ladder, landing with a thud. "What is it, my lord?"

Ronan stood in front of Charles, facing the captain, hand

sneaking into his waistband to grasp a hidden knife. And Charles blessed his lucky stars that he didn't have to face this alone.

"The captain here thinks I'm someone I'm not," Charles said slowly, attempting to keep his voice calm and even, "someone named Charles. Can you please assure him I am Lord Brendan de Lucy?"

For a moment no one moved. Charles prayed as hard as he ever had that this wouldn't come to blows. They were outnumbered, and even armed as they were, their chances of escaping a fight on board this ship were slim.

Then Ronan burst out in loud, boisterous laughter. "I swear to you, Captain, that this is Lord Stephen de Lucy. I've known him since he was a lad. But don't you have some distant relation named Charles, my lord? Dim fellow. Ugly too. It's a shame about the family resemblance. No offense, my lord."

The captain furrowed his brow and looked back and forth between the two of them, but he didn't draw his sword.

Charles forced a guffaw. "Quite right, Sebastian. I wonder what ever happened to him. I certainly hope he isn't the traitor the good captain is speaking of. Though if he is, I'm sure he blundered into it. He never was the sharpest blade in the armory."

"But Lord Charles," Arthur implored, rattling the bars, "you have to save us."

That was exactly what Charles intended to do if only he and Ronan could get out of this alive. Liam pulled Arthur back with as much force as he could and whispered something in his ear. Not once did he make eye contact with Charles, thank heavens. All would be lost if Liam confirmed Arthur's story.

"My lord," said Ronan, "I don't think your father would want to invest in this ship after all. Too many vermin aboard." He glanced at the men in the hold. "Perhaps we should be going."

"Yes, perhaps we should," Charles said with his most pompous, baronial smile. "Good day to you, Captain. Thank you for your time."

Charles climbed the ladder first with Ronan following. The captain was close behind.

They traversed the deck as quickly as they could without arousing suspicion. When they reached the gangplank, the captain yelled, "Stop."

They ignored him and walked briskly to the dock and nearly walked into a figure from Charles's worst nightmares, Lord Stephen de Burgh, his black silk cotte trimmed with black velvet sweeping around him as he reached out and grabbed Charles's arm in an iron grip.

"Watch where you're going, you stupid oaf," said Black Stephen, digging his nails painfully into Charles's arm.

Charles unwillingly turned his gaze to the face of his enemy as he tried to pry his arm away, taking in the heavy brow, the cruel blue eyes, the aquiline nose, and the jutting chin. Black Stephen's eyes narrowed as they took in Charles. The man's vicious grip tightened as he growled, "You."

With superhuman strength, Charles yanked his arm free, ignoring the tearing of fabric and clawing of skin as Black Stephen tried to hang on.

Hardly aware of what was around him, Charles took off at a run. Blood pounded in his ears and his vision blurred. The fit had him in its thrall, and his body was no longer his own. All he knew was that his feet kept pounding away beneath him as he fled blindly from the source of all his fears.

"Stop them," Black Stephen roared behind him, and Charles ran even faster, barely aware of the two men who joined him in his flight. Were they enemies or friends? It didn't matter. Charles had to get away at all costs.

A hand reached out and grabbed him, yanking him into a dark alley, and a hand covered his mouth, muffling his scream.

"It's me, Ronan," a familiar voice murmured in his ear. "We have to hide."

A corner of Charles's mind tried to obey, but his body struggled to break free. He was a caged animal, unable to control his reaction to being trapped. He sank his teeth into the flesh of the hand over his mouth.

Ronan grunted but held him all the tighter, wrapping an arm around his waist and pulling him against his chest. "Shh," Ronan whispered. "It's going to be all right. You're safe with me." Ronan's low, soothing voice was completely at odds with his iron grip.

The soothing words trickled into Charles's awareness, and he managed to stop flailing. Who knew Ronan had a softer side?

"It's all right. I'm here. Just breathe." Ronan's arms held Charles tightly as he gulped for air. His heartbeat began to slow as Ronan kept up a steady stream of murmured assurances. At long last, Ronan's grip relaxed.

Charles took a deep breath and let it out. "Where are we?" he whispered.

"Hidden for now," said a low voice he didn't recognize. He turned to see their guide, Michel, crouched behind Ronan. "But they're still looking. We need to get you out of here and back to your ship. Lord Stephen's nephew is baron here. You need to leave Honfleur as soon as possible or the entire town will be out looking for you."

Charles's heart sank. They'd failed. There was no chance of rescuing Liam, or Arthur, now. Shaking his head and running his hands through his hair, he turned to Ronan.

"I'm sorry I bit you. Did I break the skin?" A bite could lead to infection, and infections could kill. If he broke the skin, they needed to get Ronan to a healer to leech out the bad blood before foul humors set in.

"Fortunately, no. I have rough sailor's hands. You didn't make a dent."

Thank God.

"What now?" Charles asked.

"We find a place to hide until dusk," said Michel.

"We can't lead them back to the *Draconis*," Ronan added. No, they could not, or the whole ship would be in danger.

"Any sign of our pursuers?" Charles peeked out from behind the barrels, and Ronan did the same.

"Over there! I see them," came a shout in the distance.

"We have to move now," said Ronan, pulling them further into the shadows.

"Follow me, gentlemen," said Michel.

And so they did.

CHAPTER TEN

FIONOLA PACED THE deck, staring in the direction Charles and Ronan went, and flipping her dagger over and over in her hand. Where were they now? Had they seen Liam yet? When would this interminable day be over so that she could stop waiting around and go rescue her brother?

She stepped to the rail and stabbed her dagger into it.

Seamus came up and stood next to her. "Can I interest you in a meal and a drink, Captain? There's an excellent tavern nearby. You look like you need distraction."

Yes, she did. The wait was killing her. Liam was here in the same city, within walking distance even. In mere hours, she might see him at long last, feel like a whole person again. He had always been her other half, and she felt his absence like a phantom limb. She was counting every minute until Charles and Ronan returned, unable to settle down or think of anything else.

"Aye. I could use a drink." Only one. She couldn't afford to be addled, but she was no use to anyone wound up tight as the string of a lute either. A beverage to take the edge off would help relieve the pressure that made it impossible to focus.

They took a private table in the courtyard beside the tavern. Afternoon light filtered down through the leaves of an apple tree that grew in one corner of the courtyard, surrounded by fronds of lavender sage, spikey rosemary, and low mounds of thyme. A server came by with bread and camembert. Seamus ordered a carafe of wine and bowls of salted lamb stew.

Under any other circumstances, she would have found the surroundings soothing and enjoyable, but today, she had to make a conscious effort not to grind her teeth. Mercifully, the wine arrived quickly.

"You carry too heavy a burden, Captain," Seamus observed, pouring her a brimming cup. "I could help lighten the load."

Not this again.

"You do more than enough, Seamus."

He shook his head and sighed. "Drink. You need it."

So she did. With the day's heat and her empty stomach, the wine went straight to her head. Tendrils of sickly sweet oblivion tugged at her frantic mind. It was so tempting to give in, but she needed to keep her wits about her. Anything could happen on this reconnaissance visit, and she couldn't afford to let the drink dull her senses. The stew arrived, and she started scooping it into her mouth with hunks of bread. She hardly tasted it as she ate, though the food did much to settle her churning stomach.

As they settled back with their wine, grazing on the remaining bits of bread and cheese, Seamus's gaze took on an unwelcome intensity. "You know I would do anything at all for you, Captain. Ask me to traverse the nine circles of hell, and I'll do it. I…" He paused. "I won't touch on past conversations. You've made yourself clear."

Yes, she had. Abundantly clear. And yet here he was, once again looking dangerously close to making another unwanted proposal of marriage.

"I could be a partner to you. You don't have to be alone. I could give you comfort, support. You know I love you—" he cleared his throat—"like a brother," he said, looking around to make sure no one overheard.

"I know." She sighed and took a drink. "You are my partner, and you do comfort and support me. It's not about you, Seamus. My life makes it impossible to consider…a closer partnership."

He looked down and took a deep drink. "Perhaps when you have rescued your brother…" he said, trailing off.

She didn't need to reply. One glance at her face, and he scooted his chair back.

He was silent for a long moment and then looked up at her with a smile.

"Captain, did you hear the one about King Louis?"

She chuckled and shrugged, relieved that he was finally dropping the subject.

"He was touring the provinces and saw a man who looked like him. 'Did your mother ever work at the royal palace?' he asked the man, who replied, 'No, but my father did.'"

She laughed, even though she had heard it before.

They spent another hour joking and drinking before they headed back to the *Draconis*, and Fionola started to feel more at ease. The minute she was back on the ship, though, her anxiety returned full force.

"Any news?" she asked Thomas who was staring at the docks with an intensity to match her own.

"Nothing yet. It's early still." His fingers worked methodically over his rosary as he kept his gaze locked on the docks.

She pulled over two crates and motioned for Thomas to sit. "Then we wait."

They sat together in companionable silence and watched the world go by.

⤷⟫⟩⟨⟪⟵

AN HOUR PASSED, and then another, and another. The sun was getting low in the sky.

"I'm worried," Thomas said, breaking the silence of their vigil.

"I am too. Something has gone wrong."

Dear Lord, please let them come back safely. Saint Brigid, please intercede for my crew and my brother.

"Should we investigate?" Thomas's voice sounded light and friendly, but his forehead remained wrinkled with worry.

"Not yet." She hated that they had to wait, but they always knew this was a possibility. They'd sent Charles and Ronan to avoid anyone making a connection to the *Draconis*. "If they aren't back yet, it's because someone is following them, and they are trying to protect us."

"There are other reasons they might not be back." Thomas looked like he was about to squeeze his rosary into dust.

"I know you're worried, but it does no good to speculate. We wait."

The sun continued to sink in the sky, and Seamus brought them dinner—fish and grilled vegetables on baguettes purchased from the baker down the street. Neither of them was able to stomach much as they continued their watch. After an hour, Seamus took what remained of their food to beggars on the dock.

Various crew members that had been out and about in the city returned one by one, but still there was no sign of Charles and Ronan.

Near midnight, two furtive shadows approached the *Draconis* and then climbed aboard. Thomas uttered an audible sigh of relief as Ronan's head popped up over the railing. As he climbed onto deck, Charles appeared behind him.

"We need to leave. Black Stephen is here, and he saw Charles," Ronan said. "He's sent half the town after us. I think we lost them, but I can't be entirely sure."

"But Liam—" she began.

"He's on board the *Gorgon* and safe," Charles said. "But Ronan is right. We can't attempt a rescue here. If Black Stephen finds out Captain O'Bannon is here, all will be lost. We should leave now. We can catch them as soon as they leave port."

It killed her to know Liam was so close and still have to wait to rescue him, but Charles and Ronan were right. They needed this to succeed, and their best chance was at sea.

"Seamus," she yelled, and he came running. "Check whether

we have everyone. If anyone is still on shore, try to track them down as quickly as possible. We need to leave." Turning to Charles and Ronan, she asked, "Are you injured?"

They both shook their heads. *Thank God!*

"Malcolm," she called out, seeing him heading toward the hatch. "Get these two some food, water, and wine." Malcolm looked like a cranky child that didn't want to do his chores, but he obeyed. "Now," she said turning back to Ronan and Charles, "tell me what happened."

Charles nodded. "Liam is alive and doing as well as can be expected. I think it did him good to see us."

Thank God he started there.

"We had some bad luck but also some good. Our guide did his job admirably, and thank God, or we would be Black Stephen's captives right now." He shivered despite the warmth of the night, and she touched his shoulder to comfort him. She shivered too as she touched him, though for entirely different reasons. Poor Charles. He'd suffered so much. That bastard, Black Stephen, would pay for all he had done.

"Everything went as planned until we visited the hold," Charles said. "We saw Liam, and I could tell he immediately recognized us, but he kept quiet. But there was another captive who knew me. He was a former member of my crew, and I didn't know he was on the *Gorgon*. He called out my name, and the captain of the *Gorgon* realized he remembered my face. Fortunately, Ronan bought us enough time that we were able to get off the *Gorgon*."

"Thank God," chimed in Ronan.

"Then we ran into Black Stephen on the dock. We barely escaped, and he sent men after us. Apparently, he's related to the baron of Honfleur, and soon half the city was on the lookout for us. We led them on a merry chase with Michel's help until we finally lost them in the east of the city up by the Bassin de l'Est. We laid low there for several hours to make sure we lost them all before we dared return."

Fionola took a deep breath and let it out. "Thank Christ are both safe and unharmed. We'll have to take the *Gorgon* at sea. I pray Liam stays safe for another few days until we can reach him. Seamus," she called, seeing him coming up from the hatch. "Are all accounted for?"

"Yes, Captain," he said, casting a glance of obvious relief at Ronan and Charles.

"Then we leave now."

"As you wish, Captain."

And so, in the dead of night, they left the harbor and headed out to sea, sailing back and forth across the potential routes of departure for the *Gorgon* at a reasonable distance where their activity was unlikely to be remarked. As she headed back to her cabin to rest for the night, the tension within her finally unclenched. But she didn't have Liam yet. She'd come so close and just missed him. Why the relief? Then she remembered the tingling feeling she had as she touched Charles's shoulder. *Oh no.* No good could come of this. No good at all.

CHAPTER ELEVEN

THREE DAYS AFTER they left Honfleur, the silhouette of the *Gorgon* loomed beside the *Draconis*, black against a starry midnight sky. Charles's heart pounded as his friends hurled the first pots of lime onto the *Gorgon*'s deck, grateful for the wax plugs in his ears. Fortunately, his job up in the crow's nest didn't require listening, just a careful, watchful eye.

Was Black Stephen on that ship? Charles hoped so. It would be lucky beyond belief if they were able to rescue Liam and take their revenge on that evil bastard in the same night. But he couldn't get his hopes up. Black Stephen might well have stayed in Honfleur.

It was a clear night with a quarter moon, and visibility was good, at least until clouds of lime obscured his view of the *Gorgon*'s deck. Even then, he could have picked off several of their crew as they writhed, but the captain's orders were to take as many as possible alive. There had been too many near misses over the years. It was possible, though highly unlikely, that Liam was no longer on board, and she didn't want any potential source of information killed.

From a height, he watched as the *Draconis* crew's grappling hooks found purchase on the *Gorgon*, and shadowed shapes began crawling across the water. He watched the silhouette of the captain as he directed his men with hand signals and then set off across one of the rope ladders himself. Then from the corner of his eye, he saw a subtle movement in the crow's nest of the neighboring ship and heard a muffled cry from below on the ropes. Too late, he realized what it meant. They had an archer too.

With a muffled cry, the captain fell from the ropes into the sea, hitting his head on the side of the *Gorgon*. "No," he said in a hoarse whisper as he knocked his arrow and let it fly at the figure in the crow's nest across the water. He watched the silhouette of the other archer collapse and then scrambled along the crossbeam as fast as he could manage and dove.

The icy water was a sharp shock as he plunged beneath the surface. The pressure of the water squeezed the air out of his lungs. He swam up to the surface quickly, taking deep gulping breaths. The captain was starting to sink.

Diving for him in the dark, Charles wound an arm around the captain's chest and pulled him to a rope ladder someone had thrown down from the *Draconis*. The captain was limp in his embrace, and two arrows pierced his left shoulder. To get up the ladder, he was going to have to carry him.

Taking care to avoid the arrow shafts, he hefted the surprisingly light form of the captain over his shoulder and climbed as quickly as he could manage. Colm appeared at the rail and helped him maneuver the captain's limp form down to the deck. As Charles climbed over the rail, shouts grew nearer. The chaos on the *Gorgon* was spilling over onto the *Draconis*. Something had gone terribly wrong. His friends were putting up a furious fight, and he wanted to join them. But Colm put a hand on his arm, shaking his head. "Take the captain to his cabin and keep him there as long as you can, at least until you've tended to his wounds. We can't lose her."

Charles noticed the odd use of "her" but dismissed it. Colm was distressed, and there was nothing unusual about a slip of the tongue under such circumstances.

"I seem to recall the captain saying he'd kill me if I went in his cabin," Charles answered, scooping the captain up from the deck. Clearly, they couldn't stay put.

Colm smiled at him, a look of daring in his eye. "Are you afraid? The captain is unconscious and badly wounded from the looks of it. Do you think she's in any state to fight back?"

Charles narrowed his eyes, weighing his options, noting once again the curious use of "she."

A sword fight was drawing too near, and Colm brandished his own sword to fend them off. "Go now. I'll cover you," Colm yelled to Charles over the racket.

With Colm's help, Charles made it to the hatch, and from there, he headed straight to the captain's cabin in the stern. It was the safest place to go. Colm wasn't wrong. There, he'd be able to bolt the door and buy some time to try to revive the captain. Below decks, the only noise was the thunder of feet as the battle raged overhead.

He laid the captain down gently on his pallet and lit an oil lamp before bolting the door behind them. In the soft lantern light, he got his first good look at the captain. His curly, red hair was slicked back and soaking into the pallet. He must have lost his helm in the sea. An arrow had pierced the flesh of his left upper arm and come out the other side, and another was lodged in his chest near his left shoulder. Neither wound looked fatal, but the captain's breathing seemed labored.

Charles knelt down and tugged away the sodden cloth that covered the lower half of his face and rolled him on his side, checking his breathing. To his immense relief, the captain's breathing was shallow but steady. Charles bent down to take a closer look and noticed the captain's beard was askew.

A false beard?

He'd heard the rumors amongst the crew about why the captain kept his face covered, but he was not expecting a false beard of all things. He unfastened the beard from where it was looped around the captain's ears and gasped. The face beneath was unmistakably feminine. And beautiful. And...familiar.

He stared long and hard, unable to make sense of what he saw before him. The captain was a woman, and not just any woman, but an extraordinarily beautiful one. How had she managed to keep her secret all this time? Surely someone would have noticed.

And yet he hadn't suspected a thing.

He supposed he'd seen what he expected. No one would have guessed a woman would choose to live like this. And yet here she was. And her face was so familiar. He couldn't quite place her until…

"The captain is Liam's sister," he murmured, as the pieces came together in his mind.

It was Liam's face but softer, smoother, with full and perfect feminine lips and a more delicate chin. It was a proud face, just like her brother's. They had the same cheek bones and impossibly long lashes. He'd imagined her so many times during his imprisonment, dreaming of a woman he would never meet. But here she was in the flesh. "Fionola," he whispered.

Fionola, the sailor in men's clothes, the sword fighter.

Fionola, who spoke half a dozen languages.

Fionola, the woman he'd fallen for before he ever met her.

"Jesus, Mary, and Joseph," he whispered.

At the sight of her loveliness, fierce determination filled him. Having found her, he could not lose her. Not ever.

But there was no time for sentiment. She was wounded and needed his care. Taking a knife from his belt, he cut through the fabric of her cotte and shirt so that he could pull it away from her wounds. She had an unusually muscular physique for a woman, though he supposed he shouldn't be surprised. Her arms were thinner than most men's but still strong and sculpted. He never realized before how attractive a well-muscled arm could be on a woman.

As he continued cutting, he was startled to find more fabric beneath the shirt—bindings, he realized, to hide her breasts. The arrow in her chest pierced these as well, so he had to cut them away. He tried to leave her as much modesty as he could manage, but admittedly it wasn't a lot. Her lovely breasts tantalized him beneath the torn wet fabric that remained, and his body started to respond to the sight of a woman after so long without.

Damn it, not now.

He was here to save her, not make love to her for God's sake.

Focusing on the wounds helped. They were a problem to be solved, an urgent matter to occupy his mind.

The arrow in her arm was the easier of the two. It was a simple flesh wound. He needed to remove the arrowhead, pull out the shaft, then clean and bandage the wound. Simple. Looking around, he found a pitcher of water and a basin. He could use the torn fabric of her bindings as bandages. He dripped water on the arrow where the shaft met the head until the glue loosened, and the head fell off in his hand. Setting it aside, he put a hand on her arm around the wound and wrapped her other around the shaft. This was going to hurt, and there was no way around it. He could only hope she remained unconscious. Best to get it over with.

Holding her arm still, he pulled, drawing it out as quickly as he could manage without doing further damage. She hissed in pain but didn't move until it was fully withdrawn.

No sooner had he set aside the bloody shaft than he felt a blade at his throat. He turned slowly and carefully to look at Fionola. Her eyes were wide open and full of rage. She held the blade with her good hand. Where she'd pulled it from, he couldn't guess.

"What are you doing, Fionola?" he asked as calmly as he could manage, realizing a moment too late it was a mistake to call her by her name.

"You have no bleedin' right to be in here or take off my clothes or call me by that name," she said, her voice strained with pain but filled with fury. "I told you it was death to enter the captain's cabin. And now you've not only come in here, but you've stripped me half-naked." Her voice was higher than usual, all pretense of being Captain O'Bannon discarded. He tried not to notice how radiant she was in her fury.

God grant me the strength to resist this gorgeous and deadly woman.

Charles closed his eyes and exhaled. "I accept the consequences for my actions, whatever you decide they should be, Captain, but I beg you not to kill me until I've gotten that second arrow out and bandaged you." The blade remained at his throat, and his patience and control began to wear thin. For heaven's sake, she was only hurting herself by preventing him from continuing.

"And since it appears you've already decided to kill me," he said, his frustration with her delays building, "I have to say you have a curious notion of virtue, if being the lone woman on a ship full of pirates isn't a problem but allowing a man to save your life is." The blade pressed harder. She was really going to do it. The captain was going to kill him for rescuing her.

"Don't mock me, you gobshite," she said, in a voice trembling with outrage. "You have no feckin' right to do what you did. I should kill you." The knife scraped higher on his neck, as if she was giving him a shave, but the fatal stroke didn't come.

"Captain, your arm is bleeding where I removed the arrow, and I need to bandage it. And, in case you've forgotten, you have another arrow sticking out of your chest. Your crew needs you." Would the reality outside their door help her see reason? "Not to mention Liam. He will never forgive me if we rescue him, and he arrives on board only to discover I've allowed his sister to bleed to death."

"What happened?" Her eyes widened, and the pressure of the blade eased slightly.

"The attack on the *Gorgon* went poorly. God only knows what's happening on deck right now. I'm sorry, but we didn't succeed in rescuing Liam. And the ship has sustained damage."

Letting out a string of Gaelic curses, she very nearly slit his throat with her involuntary reaction.

"Will you please lower your knife so that I can bandage you and stop wasting time?" He looked her in the eye, trying to match the fire in her gaze with steel in his own, but instead he melted in her flames.

Dear God, I want to kiss you.

"I will on one condition," she said.

"Yes?"

Kill me, whip me, send me off with the crew of the Gorgon, *take my remaining toenails. I don't really care as long as you don't make me stand here any longer watching you bleed.*

"You have to marry me."

He stared at her in stunned silence, certain he'd misheard. If he wasn't already kneeling, he would have stumbled to the floor. He was still reeling from discovering she was a woman, but this…

"You've seen what you should not, what no other man has ever seen. I have killed for less. I swore an oath no man would touch me but my husband. Make it right and marry me, and I'll let you live." Looking into her eyes, he read anger, but something else as well. Could it be interest?

"But you know my mind isn't right," he objected. She couldn't be thinking straight. Perhaps it was the blood loss.

"I don't care." A moment of softness flitted across her face before she resumed her stony stare.

"I should tell you my father is Martin de Vere, Baron of Winchelsea," he blurted. "I'm his only son and his heir." He couldn't marry her without her knowing the truth of who he was.

"Are you refusing me because you think I'm not some bleedin' high-born lady? I'll have you know I'm the granddaughter of King Dermott MacMurrough of Leinster, and I'm every bit as good as you." The knife scraped against his neck again.

"No, Captain, but you should know the *Wind Song* was my ship before Black Stephen took it and turned it into the *Midas*. Lord Chester and I overheard him plotting against Lord Pembroke. He plans to betray his liege lord and make himself high king of Ireland. He even suggested he might take on King Henry if he succeeded. Lord Chester snuck away, but I foolishly tried to raise the alarm. He told his men *I* was the traitor. They captured me and tied me up. I thought he would kill me, but he decided against a quick death. He preferred to watch me waste away, enslaved, and humiliated. He never thought I would survive as long as I have. No doubt he's regretting leaving me alive especially now that I've escaped. So I must warn you. Having me on board heightens your danger."

He waited for the blade to slide across his neck, dispatching him once and for all. After all, he was a liability to everyone on this ship. Black Stephen would have no mercy if he were found here.

"Why are you telling me this now?" she asked in a harsh whisper.

"I know your secret. It only seemed fair to share mine."

The blade remained still as silence stretched between them.

"You did an honorable thing by telling me," she said at long last, her green eyes—such a lovely, enigmatic green—softening.

Hope swelled in his heart at her words.

"You don't care that Black Stephen is chasing me?"

"I'm his runaway bride. Who am I to judge?" Her mouth curled into a half smile.

Charles's eyes widened. She'd nearly married that black-guard?

"Your honesty shows you are an honorable man," she said, relenting somewhat with the blade. "You are loyal to King Henry?"

"I am. Not that anyone will believe me after whatever tales Black Stephen is telling about me."

To his surprise, she nodded. "Good. A man should keep his oaths. My family has sworn fealty to King Henry, and I will not betray that oath. I've no wish to make an enemy of the English crown. I can only hope the king someday recognizes Black Stephen for the treacherous feckin' snake he is and cuts off his head."

So she was loyal to the king. That was unexpected after all that had transpired, but he was glad of it.

"Now it's time to prove your worth again. Do you accept my conditions?" She narrowed her eyes at him and waited expectantly.

"But why marriage, Captain? If it's simply to keep your secret, I'll swear any oath you want." Her green eyes flashed fury. For a moment, he thought he was done for, but the knife didn't move.

"I swore an oath to my dying mother that no man would touch me except my husband. You took my clothes off when I was unconscious, and now I'm lying here half naked in front of you. The only honorable solution is for you to become my husband. Otherwise, I must kill you." She stared him down. "Well? Any more excuses?"

"None. If this is what you want, I am yours." He held his breath as she lowered the knife and sheathed it in her belt, letting out a sigh of relief when it was done.

CHAPTER TWELVE

THE DECISION WAS made. Fionola had fulfilled her promise to her mother. She would marry, God help her. But how was this going to work? Her quest still depended on her maintaining her disguise.

A burst of pain from her wounds made her close her eyes and hiss through her teeth. There were more immediate problems to worry about than her impending marriage.

"I have a pot of honey over there for wounds," Fionola said, pointing to a latched cabinet near her feet.

Charles retrieved it and dabbed it carefully on the entry and exit wounds on her arm. The viscous liquid soothed the angry throbbing of her injury.

As he turned his attention to the remaining arrow, she put her hand on his. "What kind of arrow was it?"

How bad was this going to be?

"Bodkin," he said, holding up the flat, diamond-shaped arrowhead from the first wound.

"Thank Christ they didn't choose barbed," she said, closing her eyes tight shut for a moment. "Have you done this before?" She looked at him, hoping he had some battlefield experience. But then he was a baron's son. It was unlikely he would have been tasked with dressing wounds.

"No," he admitted. "I know what to do in theory, but I've

never had to do it myself." As she suspected. She appreciated that he was forthright about it. "I know we have to use a thin blade to widen the hole, and I'll need to slide a finger along the shaft and hold the arrowhead in place as we draw the arrow out. Otherwise, it would stay lodged in the wound and cause infection."

She nodded, bracing herself for the pain to come. "Use this," she said, handing him the small blade she'd used to threaten him. "It's the thinnest I have."

He took it and rinsed it in water, then stood hovering over the wound, unmoving. "I don't want to hurt you."

Foolish man. He wouldn't hesitate with any other member of the crew. It was only because she was a woman.

"Give me my belt so I can bite the leather while you work."

He immediately obeyed.

"I'm ready. Do it. Do it now," she said, using the full command of her captain's voice. When he hesitated, she grumbled, "Do I have to put the beard back on?"

"Of course not, Captain," he whispered, looking abashed.

She bit her belt as he eased the blade into the wound beside the arrow shaft, hardly breathing, letting out a low *"mmph"* as the blade reached the depth of the arrowhead when the pain became too much. Fortunately, the arrow didn't reach the shoulder blade, and he wouldn't need to pry the head out of bone. As he drew the knife back out again, new blood soaked into the shredded remains of her clothes. If he didn't hurry, she was going to pass out from blood loss. He needed to finish this as quickly as possible.

"Now slide your finger in and take it out," she said through gritted teeth.

He nodded, clenching his jaw. "Here I go."

It was worse than she imagined. She couldn't help making a low noise from her throat as his finger penetrated the wound. But fortunately, he ignored her and carried on. This was an intimacy she prayed they would never share again.

After what felt like an eternity, the arrowhead moved. She held her breath so as not to scream as he drew it out at long last.

"It's done," he said, dropping the arrow on the floor, and she opened her eyes and took a deep breath, setting aside her belt. The throbbing lessened now that the arrowhead was gone.

"Now stitch me up. There's needle and thread over there," she said, pointing.

Charles winced each time he pierced her skin, though she remained still and silent. She clenched her jaw and hardly breathed. Fortunately, he had a steady hand, and it was over quickly.

Once again, he dabbed a generous dribble of honey over the wound and bound it securely with cloth. For the first time since she fell into the sea, she could breathe easily again.

"Good," she said. "I have to get up on deck." She tried to sit up, but pain exploded through her torso. She fell back down with a hiss.

"Take a moment, Captain. You've been badly hurt, and you're not ready to rise yet," he said in a soothing voice.

"Like hell I'm not." Yet again, she tried, and failed to rise, grunting. She had to get to her crew and see what had happened. This was no time for her to be incapacitated. But her body would not allow her to move. Not yet.

Charles went to the basin to rinse off his bloody hands and returned with a damp cloth he used to clean her. Her eyes followed his every movement. His wet shirt was plastered to his chest and nearly transparent, and she couldn't take her eyes off him. The contours of his chest were a marvelous distraction from the pain. She had a sudden temptation to trace each curve with her tongue.

Her lips parted slightly, and she licked them at the thought. Charles put down the cloth and knelt by her side, taking her right hand. She curled her fingers around his and caressed his palm. Touching him sent delicious tendrils of warmth all through her. She wanted to touch him more. No wonder her mother was so insistent on extracting a promise from her. She'd never so much as kissed a man before, but somehow her body knew what it wanted. The temptation to touch and taste every inch of him grew almost unbearable.

"Brave, fierce Fionola, will you do me the honor of becoming my wife?"

She smiled. "I thought you already agreed."

"I did, but you didn't," he said, smiling like a smug aristocrat then bringing her hand to his lips.

Pleasure washed through her like a lapping wave. Charles pressed his lips to each of her calloused fingers then brushed them against the inside of her wrist. The wave grew in strength.

She let out a tiny, breathless sigh, the most feminine noise she had ever made. It almost made her want to laugh, but the hunger in his gaze sent a torrential flood of longing through her. She craved more, so much more.

Cupping his cheek, she guided him closer and closer. If he was going to be her husband, then she deserved a proper kiss. What would it be like to taste his lips against her own?

She wanted this. She wanted him. His lips touched hers.

Oh, sweet Jesus.

He tasted like the sun breaking over the horizon at dawn, a piquant promise of warmth and fresh beginnings and delights as yet unknown. He savored her lips slowly, drawing out this first taste. She responded tentatively, holding back the crashing tumult of need that pounded through her veins.

"Mm...yes," she murmured as he kissed along her jaw and buried his face in her neck, drowning in sensation and loving every moment.

"Yes, you'll marry me, or yes, more of this?" he whispered in her ear before tracing its shape with his tongue and sucking on the lobe. She ran her fingers through the lengthening stubble on his head, and she pulled him back toward her lips. Mother never mentioned it would feel like this.

"Both," she said as she drew him in, and her tongue darted out to lick his upper lip, unable to resist a taste. His reaction was immediate. As his lips consumed her, she kissed him back with all the force and fury coursing through her veins. His tongue tasted hers, and hers twined with his. She let herself be carried away in the current as everything gave way to the swelling, spiraling passion between them.

She was kissing Charles. Could this possibly be real? Surely this was another fevered dream, and she would wake up to the reality that she was Captain O'Bannon, alone and aloof, any moment now. But never had her dreams been so real. She could see him, taste him, touch him. She could feel his warmth, hear his murmurs of pleasure as they feasted on each other. She nipped and licked with abandon, not caring what he thought of her. His response became wilder by the moment.

She wanted his body against hers, every inch of him pressed against her, especially against the churning heat between her legs. But today, she would have to content herself with this kiss.

There was a battle raging up on deck, and even if there weren't, she was wounded. And he wasn't her husband yet. This could only go so far. Everything would have to wait until they were safe, healthy, and married.

Slowly, he pulled away. "Captain?" he asked, panting.

"Hmm?" She was drunk on the taste of him and wasn't ready to stop, but he backed away.

"Do you think you can stand yet? You should put on dry clothes and go check on your crew, and I should join the fight if it's still going on."

The fight. The *Draconis*. Liam. *Feck*.

This was no time to lose her mind over a man. Captain O'Bannon was needed on deck. The thought doused her passion like the icy water of the North Atlantic.

She jolted upright and then winced in pain. Taking a deep breath, she steeled herself and stood up, trying to hold the shreds that covered her chest with her good hand. "Turn around," she ordered, losing the battle to maintain decency and walk at the same time.

Fortunately, he followed his captain's orders, and she had a moment's relief from his burning gaze.

Turning to her sea chest, she opened it with her good arm and pulled out a clean shirt, cotte, and hose. The ones she was wearing were in shreds and soaked through with blood and seawater. She wriggled out of the hose, both fearing and hoping that Charles was breaking his promise and watching. Getting out of her cotte and shirt was harder, but the garments were so shredded that she managed to shrug out of them after another minute of effort.

Getting into her clean clothes was another matter entirely. She stepped into her hose easily enough and pulled them up with her good arm, but when it came time to tie the drawstring, she was flummoxed. It took two hands to tie, and her left hand refused to move.

After several minutes of escalating oaths and struggle, she rasped, "Saint Sebastian's bloody nipples. I need your help."

She peeked over her shoulder, and he remained turned away. "Am I allowed to turn around without being threatened at knifepoint?"

"Yes," she snapped.

His feet padded against the wooden floorboards as he turned and approached her naked back. She kept her gaze resolutely forward. "How can I help?" he asked in a husky voice.

"My left arm is useless right now. I can't do anything with it except wiggle my fingers. I can't even tie my breeches." *Damn it all.*

"And you want my help to tie them?" He came up right behind her, close enough that she could feel his heat but not quite touching.

"Yes," she admitted through gritted teeth. A war raged within her. Her traitorous body wanted nothing more than the touch of his hands and lips, but her duty demanded she keep her head.

His hands grazed down from her waist to her hips, then moved slowly to the front, caressing the bare skin of her taut abdomen as he went. She thought she might burn to a crisp at his touch. Her cabin was an inferno, and she wanted to burn.

When he leaned into her and kissed her shoulder, she didn't object. As he tied the string slowly, she melted into him, surrendering to his embrace. His fingers trailed along her soft skin as he pulled his hands away, leaving her panting.

"What next, Captain?" he murmured in her ear, voice dripping with seduction.

"My shirt," she said in an embarrassingly breathy voice. "I don't think I can bind my breasts right now. I'll just have to hope no one notices."

"May I come around to the front, Captain?" he asked, all humility and concern.

She was silent for a long moment as he nuzzled her neck, and she lost the ability to form words. Her mother would be appalled, but what else was she to do? "Yes," she managed at last.

Keeping his eyes down, he walked around in front and picked up the shirt. Then his gaze trailed slowly upward. Goosebumps prickled on her skin despite the warm night. Her pink nipples hardened at his gaze as if he had caressed them. When he reached her face, she leaned toward him for a kiss, unable to stop herself. But he denied her, tapping a warning finger against her chest that he traced downward between her breasts and on down until it reached the band of her breeches. Her mouth dropped open, and she panted with need. But he smiled and shook his head.

"Your shirt, Captain," he said, gently feeding her limp left arm through a sleeve and holding the other sleeve ready for her right. Careful to avoid any pressure on her wounds, he pulled the loose neck of the shirt over her head, letting his fingers linger against her skin as he let it slip down to cover her hungry flesh. *Such a pity.*

"And my cotte," she said quietly, even though everything in her wanted to abandon duty and strip off the clothing she had just donned.

He picked up the thick, sleeveless tunic and gently fed her left arm through, just as he had with the shirt, and then helped her pull it over her head. This time, he let his fingers trail down her front, and her breath caught as he brushed her nipples before letting the hem of the cotte fall to her knees.

"Anything else, Captain?" he asked, averting his gaze to his feet as if he hadn't torn down every last defense with the gentle touch of his fingers.

She grabbed the front of his cotte and pulled him into a furious kiss. How dare he do this to her! She was aching with want, and her passions only seemed to grow as he gave in to her tender assault. There was something she needed, something he wasn't giving her. She couldn't name it, but her hunger for it was almost unbearable. Unable to take another moment of this sweet torture, she pushed him back. "I have to put on my beard, scarf and hood, and we have to go," she said.

"Yes, Captain." He stepped back while she finished the final touches of her disguise.

"Help me strap on my belt and sword," Fionola ordered gruffly, struggling to become the captain once more. "And stop looking at me like that or someone will notice."

"I will keep my eyes down, Captain." He had better because otherwise it would be plain for all to see.

With her belt fastened and sword swinging from her hip, she turned without meeting his eyes. "Let's go."

CHAPTER THIRTEEN

S HE WAS GOING to marry Charles. *Saint Agatha's bloody breasts.*
What was she thinking? He disobeyed orders and uncovered her secret. Anyone else, she would have killed. But not him. This attraction she felt outweighed her common sense. It wasn't enough to have mercy and let him live, sworn to secrecy. No, she had to obey her mother's dying words and demand marriage, as if such a thing was possible in her current life. How would it even work? How could Captain O'Bannon marry a man?

One problem at a time.

Fionola straightened her spine, bracing herself to face her crew. She was dressed like the captain again, beard and all, but never had she felt less confident in her disguise. Surely, they would see the heat and desire that seemed to radiate from her center. Her body was a bonfire. Charles walked several steps behind her, and even without touching him, sparks crackled between them.

She was weakened too. Her injuries throbbed and ached, an active reminder of her useless left arm. At least it wasn't her sword arm. She could still defend herself in need. But could she still command the crew's respect?

The noises from the deck had died down, no longer the thundering thuds of battle. She prayed that meant they had subdued the members of the *Gorgon*'s crew that had come aboard and not that she had lost her ship. Her crew's fighting skills were undeniable, and she trusted Seamus's leadership in her absence.

She clenched her fist, thinking of Liam still imprisoned by those bastards. Next time they caught the *Gorgon*, they would be fully prepared. They would not fail. This time, it seemed they would be lucky to escape with their lives and their ship intact.

Cautiously opening the hatch, she peered out to assess before climbing out. She saw her crew, bedraggled and downcast, but free and in control. The weapons chests and food and water barrels stored on deck were all gone, and a section of the deck was charred where someone had attempted to set fire to it. They would have to find a safe port quickly to restock and make repairs, or they would soon find themselves in dire straits. Her breath caught as she saw five still figures laid side by side next to the forecastle. She climbed out onto the deck, moving swiftly, needing to know who they'd lost.

The crew's eyes rested on her as she looked at the faces of the dead. Three were unfamiliar and presumably members of the *Gorgon*'s crew. Two were not. They were both recent rescues from a ship they'd captured two months ago—Fergus and Malcolm. Fergus was from Cork originally, she remembered—a young sailor whose ship was captured and appropriated by Black Stephen two years ago. Malcolm was a horse thief from Inverness—reformed—he swore, but she was glad nonetheless that he couldn't ply his trade at sea.

Her heart ached at the loss. This was dangerous work, and they all knew the risks, but her crew were like family, even the recent ones. She added their names to her mental list of crew members she had lost as captain. These two brought the total up to twelve. She said a silent prayer and blinked back the tears that she could never permit herself to shed.

Colm came toward her, eyes full of concern. "Captain, you're safe! I was so worried. I told them you were injured. How is your shoulder?"

She cleared her throat and said in her best captain's voice,

"It's seen better days, but I'm hard to kill." A couple of listless crew members managed to muster a grim chuckle. "Where's Seamus? I don't see him."

"Over there," Colm answered gesturing toward the aftercastle. "He's alive, but I'm afraid he's in rough shape."

No. Not Seamus.

She ran, ignoring the pain it caused as the motion jolted her shoulder. Thomas was hovering over him, securing a bandage around his midsection. Seamus's eyes were open, but his breathing was labored, and he barely seemed aware of his surroundings.

She knelt beside him. "Seamus?" she called quietly, putting a gentle hand on his shoulder.

Seamus blinked and managed a slight smile. "Captain, I feared the worst when I saw you go down. I don't know how I could have gone on if I'd lost you. But you and me," he said in a breathy, strained voice, "we're hard to kill." He took several labored breaths and turned his gaze to Thomas. "And you thought a little scratch like this would bring me down. Tell him, Captain. Tell him we're tough as nails." He raised a hand and clapped it onto her left shoulder.

Pain exploded through her, and her vision went white. She focused on breathing in and out, clenching her teeth together to avoid crying out. His hand dropped away immediately, and her vision cleared. Poor Seamus looked horrified.

"I'm so sorry, Captain," he whispered. "I didn't realize. What did those gobshites do to you?"

"Shot an arrow through my arm and another into my shoulder. Knocked me off the ropes into the water. Charles rescued me," she murmured, keeping her voice low.

"Captain, I—" He stopped and closed his eyes, apparently changing his mind about what he was about to say. Instead, he asked, "Does that mean Charles knows?" She shot him a warning look, then carefully nodded.

Seamus glanced over at Charles who was helping to clear

broken detritus from the deck. "You might consider him to stand in for me at least until I'm back up on my feet. He's proved his loyalty and skill as a fighter, and he knows his way around a ship. He was a little twitchy at first, but the men like him. And I get the sense he's no stranger to command."

No, the baron's son was not a stranger to command. She closed her eyes. It would mean working with him in close proximity, a dangerous prospect. On the other hand, she was going to need help in the weeks ahead; *months*, if she were being honest with herself. Wounds like hers didn't heal quickly. He'd already been in her quarters and seen…a lot, and she'd have to bring him back for every bandage change, every time she changed her shirt.

It might be best if Charles was first mate to give cover for his being granted entry where everyone else was denied. Not to mention that soon they would be married. How they were going to keep that secret, she had no idea, but that was a problem for another time.

She reached a decision and nodded her head. "Colm, go get Charles and bring him to the aftercastle." Colm immediately turned to obey. "Seamus, I need to know. Did we find out where the *Gorgon* is headed next?"

The answer was written in Seamus eyes. "I'm sorry, Captain."

She let out a string of invective that made Seamus wince. They'd missed Liam again, and God only knew they were going to catch wind of the *Gorgon*'s whereabouts again. She was going to have to wait for news, and she hated waiting.

Taking a deep breath, she said, "I need to address the crew. Is there anything I should know about what happened before I do?"

Seamus groaned. "It was bad. They expected us. Our little visit in port tipped them off. Fortunately, we were able to retreat and cut ourselves loose from them before too many could climb over to our side. You should know we lost David in addition to Fergus and Malcolm. An arrow got him in the back, and he fell overboard around the same time as you. We couldn't save him."

David. Sweet little David. He'd been with the crew for a year now. He couldn't have been more than fifteen. She found him starving on the streets of Calais. He was an orphan, and they took him in. This was only the second time she'd allowed him to join when they took a ship. Her chin sank to her chest. She wasn't supposed to have favorites, but this hurt worse than the rest combined.

Thirteen deaths since she started sailing as O'Bannon. It was too many.

With a deep sigh, she rose to her feet and straightened her back in spite of the pain radiating from her wound as well as her heart. She was the captain. This was no time for personal grief. She would save that for the privacy of her cabin. Right now, she had to console and reassure the crew.

Fionola climbed the ladder to the aftercastle, her left arm dangling at her side. Charles was there waiting, staring down at the deck.

"Captain," he said in a carefully neutral tone. "Colm said you wanted to see me."

Looking out at the boundless night sky over his shoulder, she ignored her intense desire to bury herself in his arms. "Seamus was badly injured in the fight. You're going to be my first mate while he recovers."

"I'm honored you'd consider me, Captain, but don't you have others who have served you longer who would be better suited to the role?" She felt, rather than saw, his eyes on her.

"You're questioning my orders?" she said quietly to his shoulder.

His gaze returned to the deck. "No, Captain."

"Good."

She turned and walked to the crenellated parapet of the aftercastle, facing the bow. Motioning with her good hand, she brought Charles to her side. It felt strange to be so very aware of someone even when she wasn't looking.

She forced her attention back to the crew before her.

"Friends. Brothers," she boomed in a voice that carried all the way to the forecastle. She watched as every eye turned toward her. "Today we fought the *Gorgon* and lived to tell the tale," she thundered.

"Hear, hear," several of them shouted.

Win or lose, they always craved the same thing, a tale of bravery and sacrifice, of bravado and heroism in which they, the special few, triumphed in spirit if not in fact, while the glorious dead went on to a better life hereafter. It bound them together and filled them with determination to fight another day. It also bound them to her and her mission. Without the myth she wove, it would all fall apart. And so, she set aside her pain, exhaustion, and became Captain O'Bannon, pouring all she had into giving them the story they needed.

"The enemy knew we were coming. The odds were against us." She paused and smiled. "But then, they usually are." A few bleak guffaws echoed from the deck.

"Still, we did not hide. We did not shy away," she continued. "We looked our enemies in the eye and challenged them on the deck of their own ship. We fought Black Stephen's slaver bastards like the very devil." There was a roar from her audience, and she knew she had them.

"Some of us were injured." She looked down at Seamus. "Some of us did not come back," she said, gazing down at the still bodies, crumbling inside as she tried to project solemn determination. Her crew murmured their prayers for the dead as she watched. She said a silent prayer to St. Brigid to intercede.

"Malcolm. Fergus. David."

Not David. Please, not David.

She squeezed her right hand into a fist to fight the turmoil threatening to overtake her. Charles noticed and knew. She was sure of it.

"They were our brothers and they died fighting for the freedom of their fellow man. Heaven will give them a hero's welcome. And we will remember their names for the rest of our lives. We will tell our children and our children's children of their deeds this day." The crew was shouting their agreement and passing around ale to drink to their fallen brothers.

"No one is as brave as the crew of the *Draconis*. No one is as fierce, and no cause so just as ours. This summer alone, we've taken six ships and forty-two slaves from Black Stephen." The yelling of the crew reached a fevered pitch. She was almost done. Almost.

"We will continue the fight, Brothers. We did not win the day, but we lived to fight again. Stand tall. Stand strong. Stand together, and remember this day," she roared, and the crew yelped and stamped and beat their fists. They hugged and drank, and a few even had tears in their eyes.

When the din began to die down, she announced, "Tonight..." She waited several moments for their attention to return to her. "Tonight, we must see to the enemy dead, secure our prisoners, and care for our wounded. We are setting course for Gan Ainm so that we can recover and regroup. Charles will be my first mate until Seamus is ready to pick up the mantle again."

Some eyebrows rose at that news, but no one dared say a word about her orders.

"He will direct you in what must be done," she continued. "Tomorrow, we will mourn our brothers and say our goodbyes. But tonight," she said, looking into the individual faces of her men in the moonlight, "once the work is done, you must rest so that you can greet the glorious dawn as warriors once again."

She unsheathed her sword and brandished it over her head. Taking a deep breath, she yelled, "*Draconis!*"

The crew repeated her cry in a rousing roar.

"*Draconis*," she called out again, feeding off the energy of the crew's deafening response.

"*Draconis*," she shouted one last time, shaking her sword for Malcolm and Fergus, but most of all for David.

She hardly heard the din of the crew's final response as she sagged against the parapet, the last of her energy spent. Charles caught her, wrapping an arm around her waist to support her. That would not do. She could not be weak in front of the crew. Not now. Steadying herself, she stood straight and gave him a warning look. He withdrew his arm but stayed close.

"Good speech, Captain," he said in a low voice just for her.

"I'm going to my cabin," she responded quietly. "Take care of the work that needs doing tonight, and then knock on my door and wake me to give me your report."

"Captain, I—"

"You have your orders."

Holding herself together with the last of her strength, she made her way down the ladder to the deck then slipped through the hatch before any of her crew could waylay her. Moments later, she was in her cabin, door locked, and she collapsed on her blood-soaked pallet fully clothed.

CHAPTER FOURTEEN

I T FELT LIKE no time at all had passed when she heard two quiet knocks on her door. When she tried to sit up, she forgot her injury and made the mistake of putting weight on her left arm. The pain that had faded into the background when she was still came roaring back to life, and she couldn't stifle a low groan.

"Are you all right, Captain?" Charles's muffled voice came through the door.

Pushing herself up with her right arm, she felt around for her flint and lit a candle, memory and awareness returning. Pain shot threw her arm as she struck the flint to light the candle. Why was he disturbing her sleep?

Oh yes. She'd ordered him to report to her cabin when he finished his work for the night.

Forcing herself to her feet, she shuffled over to the door with her candle and unlatched it, reflexively checking that her beard was in place before opening it.

"Your report?" she asked in a gruff voice, blinking the sleep out of her eyes. But then she made the mistake of looking at him, and it took a supreme effort of will to resist the urge to throw herself into his arms. It was embarrassing, really. She thought she was long past any such feminine weakness. She reached reflexively for her sword to center herself but realized it was resting on the other side of the cabin.

"We've changed course and set sail for the island. I under-stand it's near Wexford?" His voice was quiet and neutral, as he stared at the candle, avoiding her gaze.

"Yes," she confirmed. Exhaustion, grief, pain, and desire all seemed to be struggling for the upper hand within her. She lacked the energy to fight any of them.

"Thomas prayed over the dead from the *Gorgon*, and we let the sea take them. The men are taking turns standing vigil over the bodies of Fergus and Malcolm. We cleared the lower hold in the bow and moved the grain sacks to crew quarters to form beds for the wounded, and we moved our prisoners to the hold. They've been fed and watered and had their injuries tended to." She wanted him to look at her, touch her, give her comfort and relief from the roiling feelings she couldn't deny, but he kept his distance, impassive and detached, a man doing his job. She had to admire him for this, just one more thing to add to the growing list of things she appreciated about Charles.

"How is Seamus?" She said a silent prayer to St. Brigid for his recovery, a spike of guilt and anxiety stabbing through her exhaustion.

"Sleeping. Ronan says if he survives the next two days with-out infection, he stands a good chance of recovery." He left the other possible outcome unspoken, but she knew what he didn't say, nonetheless.

"Thank you for your report. You should get some rest." She turned to close the door. It was all too much, and she stumbled, with hardly had the strength to keep herself upright. But she clutched the door and stayed on her feet.

"Wait," he said catching the door before it closed and looking her in the eye at last. "May I check your bandages? I would be remiss in my duties if I allowed the captain to bleed to death in his sleep."

Yes.

She knew she should refuse. If she let him in, she had no hope of resisting temptation, but she couldn't muster more than a moment of hesitation, glancing around the corridor to make sure no one was watching.

He came in, and she latched the door behind him. They were alone, and the echoes of their earlier encounter reverberated around them, filling the silence.

He took the candle from her hand and used it to light the oil lantern.

"You'll check the bandages, and that's all," she said, knowing she didn't mean it.

"Yes, Captain." His voice made something within her squeeze and clench.

"You promise?" Her promise to her mother hung by a thread. Was it breaking her oath to give in at least a little bit to the temptation of her betrothed? After all, he would become her husband in the very near future.

"Yes." He stepped behind her and untied the scarf covering her face then pulled off the false beard, hanging them on a hook by the door. "Fionola." He said her name like a prayer. "May I take off your cotte?" he whispered in her ear, his lips brushing against it.

At her nod, he put his hands on her hips and began gathering up the fabric. She leaned back into his warm embrace, helpless to resist. Once he had the hem in hand, he ran his hands up her sides, caressing as he went. His lips whispered against her neck, and she let out a shuddering sigh. She was lost.

As he eased the garment over her head and slid it down her throbbing left arm, tears gathered at his tender touch, and she blinked them back furiously. No one had ever treated her with such care since her mother died. And as captain, she had to carry the collective weight of her crew, even when her own strength was gone.

"Shh, Fionola," he murmured. "You are strong for the crew, but you don't have to be strong for me. What happens behind these doors is between us. You don't have to be the captain right now. Let go." He wrapped his arms around her from behind and kissed her hair, and she sank against him.

This is weakness you can't afford, she chastised herself. But she couldn't bring herself to leave his arms. Charles didn't say a word or move a muscle, just holding her in his warm embrace.

"I need to lie down," she said at last, giving in to bone-deep weariness.

"Wait," he said, leaving her to stand on her own for a moment, and the sudden absence of his warmth made her shiver. She watched as he went over to her pallet and flipped it, hiding the enormous blood stain from view. "There. You can sit, but I need to check your bandages before you lie down."

Seating herself, she once again surrendered herself to his gentle, caressing hands. He knelt before her, and ran his hands up her thighs, spreading her legs, and positioning himself between them. His fingers lifted the light fabric of her shirt, brushing the bare skin of her torso as they went.

He pulled the shirt over her head and then ever so gently down her left arm, and she was bare to him from the waist up, her nipples mere inches from his mouth. Even though this was no more than he'd seen before, she felt so much more exposed, and the longing for more contact became almost unbearable.

Turning his head, he blew a soft breeze over her left nipple, watching it pucker in need before hovering his lips over it, as if he was going to take it in his mouth. The heat of his breath whispered against her skin. So close... so close...

He turned away and lifted his hands to examine her bandages.

Blood hadn't soaked through either bandage, and he left them as they were. He probed around the wound with his finger, checking for fever or tenderness that might indicate infection.

"Good news," he said, reaching up to caress her cheek, tilting his beautiful face up toward hers. "You might just survive the night. I'm done checking your bandages, Captain. Shall I leave now?"

He waited, a supplicant before her. His left hand rested high on her thigh, his thumb making slow circles agonizingly close to the center of all her hunger.

"Please stay," she moaned before even realizing she'd made a decision.

"Shh," he whispered, brushing his lips across her nipple with a feather light touch. She trembled in response as tingles and heat engulfed her. "We wouldn't want anyone to hear."

And with that, he sucked her nipple into his mouth, teasing and tormenting it with his tongue, grazing it with his teeth, and robbing her of all conscious thought. The world contracted until nothing was left but the sensation of his mouth against her skin. Suddenly she understood why virtue might be hard to maintain. Her mother had always talked about the sinful lusts of men and the dangers they posed. She'd never imagined she herself might want this, that a man's kisses and caresses could make her body hunger like this. She'd never wanted anything in her life with the ferocity that she wanted him—his mouth and hands against her skin, his body pressed against her molten center.

His hand left her thigh and traced up to her other breast, brushing, circling, caressing, and the impossible sensation doubled. But she missed his seductive touch on her thigh. The intensity of the pleasure had increased, but she felt further from the unknown fruition she sought.

She wrapped her legs around his waist, pulling him against her, desperate for something she could not name. Without knowing why, she moved her hips against him, and he moaned softly at the motion.

Pulling his mouth away from its work, he nuzzled between her breasts, his breathing rough and ragged. "Fionola, would you permit me to compromise your virtue just a little bit more? I swear I won't take your maidenhead until we're wed, but you need more than this to find any relief tonight."

"What would you do?" she asked, knowing she would let him do almost anything but unwilling to fully relinquish control. If they didn't consummate, was she still keeping her oath?

I'm sorry, Mama!

"I would take these off," he said, dipping a finger beneath the waist of her breeches and giving a gentle pull, sending a thrill to her extremities. "And I would touch you here," he said, reaching a hand between her legs to cup her where she felt the most heat and need. She breathed in sharply, making a startled noise in the back of her throat. Involuntarily, she pressed into his hand, moving against him. Yes, this was what she needed. This was where her hunger pooled. If he would only keep touching her there…

The last of her self-control snapped.

"Yes," she whispered. "Do it."

He stood and pulled her to her feet, his fingers making quick work of the tie at her waist, and he pushed the fabric to the floor, caressing as he went. She was completely bare. Her wild curls had completely escaped the leather thong that tied them back, and they cascaded over her shoulders tickling her flesh, Stepping back, he looked her up and down with his eyes heavy with desire, his mouth slightly open and the bulge beneath his clothes very apparent. "Oh, Fionola," he sighed, shaking his head as if in worshipful awe.

Suddenly, she was very aware of the fact that he was still fully clothed while she was fully exposed. That had to change immediately. "Now you take off your clothes," she ordered with a rough voice. He pulled his head back in surprise. "I want to see you too."

Without taking his eyes off her, he tugged off his tunic and shirt, discarding them on the floor. Oh, yes, there was that sculpted torso she saw in the distance that first day. "Mmm," she purred in appreciation. He hesitated when he reached for the tie to his breeches.

"Shy?" she asked with a little smile. "It's not like I haven't seen you before."

"You haven't seen me like this. Have you seen an aroused man before?"

He was trying to preserve her innocence. How sweet!

"I live on a bleedin' ship with twenty or more men at any given time and no privacy. Do you have any idea how many times I've walked in on Thomas and Ronan fecking in the hold? No one besides you has ever seen or touched me. I have guarded my virtue with vigilance. But I'm no stranger to how men touch themselves and each other."

His jaw dropped, and she could practically see all the uncomfortable thoughts racing through his head. "But you're right," she said to snap him out of it. "I haven't seen you like this." He swallowed. "Yet," she added staring at him every bit as boldly as he stared at her. "Those. Off. Now," she commanded in her captain's voice, staring at his breeches.

As he untied his drawstrings and pushed them down, she stood and circled him slowly, taking time to appreciate his magnificent shape. His powerful back was crisscrossed with scars from whipping, as she knew it would be. Many of her men bore such scars, though he had more than most. She paused in her circuit to trace the puckered skin with her fingers. He had endured more than any man should, but he was a survivor. She respected that.

"I know you're touching me, but I can barely feel it," he said in a rough voice. "I can hardly feel anything on my back. Too many scars."

She trailed her hand down to the delicious curve of his bottom. She'd wanted to touch it ever since she first saw him naked. The sensation of him beneath her hand made warmth pool in that secret place where he'd touched her. "Do you feel it when I touch you here?"

"Yes," he whispered, standing still, and surrendering to her caress.

Unable to resist, she licked his powerful shoulder and grazed it with her teeth. He made a low rumbling noise in response, but he didn't move, letting her explore his body at her own pace. Stepping around to the front, she trailed her fingers over his hip, kissing and tasting his powerful chest. Feeling daring, she dragged her fingers along his shaft, which strained toward her. The sight of him triggered another explosion of heat at her core. He wanted her. Desperately.

"Do you feel it when I touch you here?" she asked, tilting her head, and looking up into his eyes as she ran her thumb over the soft, velvety head, smearing the bead of moisture that had formed there. *All mine*, she thought with greedy delight as he shuddered with pleasure.

"Fionola," he pleaded in a voice that shook with desperation.

She stepped away, leaving him panting, and lay down on the bed. "Touch me, and give me what I need," she ordered softly, spreading her legs in invitation. She wasn't sure what made her say that, but it felt absolutely right.

"Oh my God," he gasped, staring at her with an intensity that sent heat radiating out to her very fingertips.

Dropping to his knees, he reached for her, sliding a rough, calloused finger between her folds and sending lightning to her extremities. If she'd thought she was out of her mind with pleasure when he was suckling her breasts, the feeling now was multiplied tenfold. His tantalizing finger made soft circles around a throbbing nub of flesh that she'd never noticed before. When he brushed his finger directly over it, her back arched off the pallet, and she nearly fell off. A jolt of pain shot through her arm and shoulder at the sudden movement.

"Careful, Captain. Don't hurt yourself," he murmured, taking his finger away and gently helping her settle back into a comfortable position. "And don't forget to stay quiet. I know you don't want your secret to get out."

"Of course, I'll stay quiet," she whispered in annoyance.

He smiled at her. "We'll see."

Then his fingers began stroking her again, and he had to clap a hand over her mouth almost immediately to stifle a wail. Whatever his fingers were doing, it was too much. She couldn't keep still as he stroked and tapped and tickled her tender flesh. She had to get away. She had to get closer. She couldn't stand it and she needed more.

Oh God. Oh God.

Oh. She felt a finger enter her, new motion and pressure creating a deeper sensation while his thumb continued to stroke the throbbing nub that drove her wild.

She peered into his face. He looked almost as crazed as she felt. The sight of him sent her to even greater heights, and she had to clap her own hand over her mouth to stifle the sounds that came from her no matter how hard she tried to keep them back.

Another finger slid into her, and he covered her mouth with a furious kiss as her body shook and arched from the pallet. She closed her eyes and leapt off a cliff, her body floating through the air, suspended between earth and sea, falling, falling…

She gave a great sigh as her body was suffused with warm contentment, and her eyelids began to droop.

"Sleep, Fionola," he whispered, kissing her forehead, and that was the last thing she remembered.

CHAPTER FIFTEEN

SLEEP. HE NEEDED it so desperately, but lying in his hammock with eyelids heavy as lead, he still couldn't quite drift off. Too much had happened, and it all kept spinning through his mind. This morning, he'd thought the captain was a man, and Fionola was a distant dream. Marriage had been the furthest thing from his mind. Now Fionola was his captain and his betrothed, and she was without a doubt the most alluring and seductive woman he had ever met or even dreamed of.

"Touch me, and give me what I need," she'd said. Good God, he was getting hard again just thinking about it. She was a lioness, soft and languid and purring, but teeth and claws always at the ready. He never knew whether she was going to kiss him or cut his throat, and Christ, was it arousing.

And then there was the way she ordered him around. There were no shy, blushing requests, no coy prevarications. She knew what she wanted and demanded it in the bluntest possible terms. And every time she did, he felt it in his cock as surely as if she was stroking him. "Touch me, and give me what I need." *Fuck.*

He tried to imagine any of the fine ladies his parents had introduced him to saying such a thing. Even the friendly and knowing widows he'd bedded from time to time back home never would have dared say such a thing.

She'd never been with a man. He believed her about that. If

she had, she couldn't have been so surprised by her body's reaction to his touch. Also, he fully believed she was capable of dispatching anyone who learned her secret and tried to take liberties. He'd seen her kill and had felt her blade at his own throat. It was only by luck that she liked him enough to let him live. Liked him enough to marry him apparently. He couldn't help a smug smile at the thought.

What would it mean to be married to Fionola? When he'd imagined marriage back in Winchelsea, he'd assumed he'd be trapped in courtly boredom, tupping some prim, frilly damsel who wanted nothing but babies and fancy dresses from him. Noblewomen were so dull. Granted his sisters were noblewomen, and they were nothing like that. But they were special. He had yet to meet a noblewoman that could keep up with any of them. Fionola, though…. He liked the idea of introducing Fionola to them, especially to his oldest sister, Carenza. What would the strongest two women he knew think of each other?

Not that he could ever go back to Winchelsea. And even if he could, he couldn't imagine his family would be pleased by his marrying a pirate, no matter how brave and beautiful she was. Not that it mattered. After tonight, he was ruined for all other women. He'd been ruined for all other women before tonight, if he were honest with himself, because he'd been loving Fionola since Liam had first described her to him. Now he knew, no one else would do. He was hers, whatever she decided to do with him.

But then every man on this ship was also hers, he suspected. Even without the day's revelations and intimacies, that speech she gave would have worked its magic. Her entire crew was under her spell, ready to fight for her to their dying breath, even though not one of them knew how lovely she was beneath her clothes or the way she looked at the peak of ecstasy.

He wasn't just marrying a wife. He was marrying a leader of men, a captain with a crew whose loyalty was unwavering.

Did he mind?

No, he did not, he decided. As long as she allowed him to follow wherever she went, and let him share her bed at least occasionally, he would be quite content. Ecstatic really. After the last two years, it still felt miraculous to breath clean air and eat his fill. Never mind finding purpose serving a good and noble captain by day and making love to her by night.

But still, he had questions. Perhaps in the morning they could talk. For now, he would sleep. Or try to.

⫷⫸

STILL RUBBING HIS eyes, Charles reached the front of the breakfast line. "Aidan, can you give me two extra bowls? I—"

"*No one* gets extra bowls." Aidan shook his ladle, brandishing it like a bludgeon. "You think you're better than the rest of us?"

"No, I…It's for the captain and Seamus," he said, casting nervous glances at the other crew in line.

"Oh," Aidan said, his expression instantly solicitous. "Well, that's completely different. Why didn't you say so?" He pulled out a tray and placed three bowls of fish stew on it, putting hard biscuits beside each one. Two of the bowls received a precious sprig of parsley, plucked from the tiny herb garden he kept in a box on the aftercastle. He narrowed his eyes at the tray, then lifted a finger in the air. Turning his back to Charles, he rummaged around in the crates behind him and came back with two apples. Smiling at his work, he looked back up at Charles. "That one is yours," he said pointing at the unadorned bowl. "No thieving apples," he admonished for good measure.

Charles balanced the tray carefully as he went below decks. His first stop was to Seamus who had a tiny cabin next to the captain's.

Knocking quietly, Charles called, "Seamus, I have your breakfast."

"Come in. It's not locked," Seamus answered, his normally

gruff voice weaker than usual.

Squeezing in beside Seamus's pallet, Charles looked the man over in the lantern light. Seamus was sitting, clad in just his breeches with a cloth bandage wrapped around his waist. He had dark circles under his eyes, and his face was tense and drawn. Nonetheless, he attempted to greet Charles with good cheer.

"Parsley *and* an apple? Aidan must think I'm on death's door," he said with a strained smile. "Thank you for bringing it down."

Nodding toward the door, Seamus signaled for Charles to close it, a tricky maneuver in the tiny cabin with a still-full tray in hand.

"So now you know the captain's secret," Seamus said in a quiet voice. "Since you're still alive, I assume you've sworn to her to keep it?"

"Yes," Charles said cautiously, quite aware that Seamus would likely slit his throat if he knew the full truth about last night.

Seamus nodded. "Good. Break that promise, and I'll kill you. That is if the captain doesn't kill you first. Don't underestimate me just because my belly is stitched up like pillow."

There was nothing pillow-like about Seamus's belly, but Charles took his point. "Her secret is safe with me."

"The only people who know are you, me, Thomas, Ronan, and Colm. All except you and me are from Wexford and are part of her clan. I was her first mate for a year before she trusted me enough to let me know. And now you come along learning everything on a mere week's acquaintance." Seamus shook his head, running a hand over his face. "I think you're a good man. I recommended you as first mate until I recover. You do anything to hurt or betray her, though, and I'll gut you like a fish."

Charles swallowed. "I swear I will never intentionally hurt or betray her in word or deed."

Seamus gave him a long, hard look and nodded. "Go give her the stew before it gets cold."

Easing carefully out of the cabin, Charles took a deep breath before knocking on the captain's door. At some point, they were going to have to tell Seamus and the others. Would they let him live when the time came?

"Captain? It's Charles," he said, knocking twice. "I have your breakfast."

Moments later, the door opened, and the captain stood there, fully clothed. She backed away as he entered, keeping her distance.

"I figured out how to dress without you," she said once the door shut.

Putting down the tray on the small round table in the center of the room, he took a step toward her. She took a step back.

He stood still, momentarily confused by her retreat. It was almost as if she feared him, but that didn't make sense.

Remembering himself, he cleared his throat and smiled. "So I see. I'm pleased to hear it. I know you value your independence and privacy."

"Thank you for your assistance." She had trouble meeting his eye. "I wasn't myself yesterday," she said, staring avidly at the stew and gripping the back of the plain wooden chair beside the table. "I said and did things I now regret. Please accept my apologies."

His brow furrowed. "What do you mean?" His heart gave a warning lurch.

Please tell me you didn't change your mind, Captain.

"I would have thought in the light of day it would have been obvious. I can't... We can't..." She trailed off, squeezing her eyes shut and taking a deep breath.

No. Please. I can't lose you.

"Fionola, if I have caused you offense in any way—"

She held up her hand to stop him. "You saved my life and tended my wounds. Everything else that happened was only because I invited it, demanded it really. In the light of day, I realize what an enormous mistake I made. I beg you to under-stand and forgive my actions."

Her words pierced him like a sword. Had she offered him everything he desired only to take it away? No. The woman he loved wouldn't do that. She couldn't...

He took another step forward, and once again she stepped back. "I'm afraid I don't understand. Are you saying...are you saying you don't want to marry me?"

Everything in him tensed as he braced himself for her answer. She'd made him promise and gave her promise in return. Surely, she wouldn't break it. Twenty-four hours ago, matrimony was the furthest thing from his mind, but now, he couldn't imagine his future without it. Without her.

She stared down, still refusing to meet his eyes. "You must see how impossible it is. I can't marry you or anyone. It would jeopardize everything I've built here on the *Draconis*. I don't live as a woman, and I can't afford to start doing so. Setting aside the dangers from my crew finding out, there's also Black Stephen. He cannot find out I'm Fionola MacMurrough or even that Fionola is still alive. What would he do to Liam if he found me out?"

An understandable worry. He'd be lying if he pretended it didn't give him pause too. But the Fionola he loved was also Captain O'Bannon. He didn't want her to become someone else for his sake. He loved the impossible person she was with all her messy contradictions.

"We can keep it secret. I'm happy to stay on the *Draconis* as a part of your crew. You can be the captain to everyone else. Just let me be with Fionola when we're alone." Would that be enough? In a perfect world, he would have preferred for their marriage to be in the open, but he was willing to do whatever she needed him to do.

"What if I got with child? There's no way I could hide that."

He'd thought of that too. They could avoid children if necessary. A part of him would have liked them, but it was a small sacrifice to make for the chance to be with her. A tiny corner of his brain recalled his father's words about the future of Winchelsea, the succession, and his obligations, but he shoved the thought aside. He was a pirate now, not the heir to Winchelsea. His family didn't even know whether he was alive. They would have to find another way to secure the town's future.

He reached out and took her hand. She tried to pull it away, but he held tight. "There are ways we can be together that wouldn't result in children."

At last, she met his eyes. "I don't need a man in my life. I can't let myself need you."

Ah. Now we come to it. "Of course, you don't *need* me."

Her eyes widened.

"It was never a question of whether you needed me. You are the most capable, independent, and intimidating person I've ever met, man or woman. You don't need anyone. But Fionola…" He pulled her close enough to feel her heat, smell her salty, earthy musk, and he placed her uninjured hand over his heart. She inhaled sharply but kept her eyes on his. "Be honest with me. Do you want me?"

He needed to hear her say it. There was no mistaking the look in her eyes the previous night and her body's response, try as she might to deny it that morning. Her breathing grew ragged as he held her close. He could see the battle behind her eyes as she struggled to form a response.

"Yes," she whispered at last.

A wave of relief flowed through him. There was hope.

He leaned in, brushing his lips against her ear. "What do you want, Fionola? Say it."

She took a deep, shuddering breath. "I want you."

He stiffened at her words and fought to keep his breathing steady. "And how do you want me?"

"How?" Her voice was husky.

Good. Her resistance was melting. He began kissing his way down her neck.

"Do you want me as…a valued crew member?" Kiss. "A servant to change your bandages and bring you breakfast?" Kiss. "A lover to warm your bed and sate your desires until you tire of me?" Kiss. "A husband to have and hold until death do us part?" Kiss followed by a gentle nip. She arched against him. "I will be whatever you ask, but know this. My deepest desire is to spend the rest of my life with you, and I will never stop caring for you, no matter what you say today. What do you want, Fionola?"

He caressed her cheek and sank his hand into her curls, waiting for the answer, praying that he was right and that her feelings were as strong today as they had been the night before, despite her protestations to the contrary.

She let out a long, slow breath. "I want you as my husband, just as I did last night, but I have no idea how we'll make it work."

It was all the answer he needed. Lowering his mouth to hers, he kissed her furiously, taking vengeance for the heartbreak she almost forced on them both. There would never be anyone else for him. She was the woman of his dreams, his rescuer, captain, and lover, and he couldn't contemplate life without her. Why she wanted him, he couldn't guess. He could only be grateful that she did.

He backed into the chair by the table and lowered himself, pulling her into his lap astride him, his hands hungrily caressing every curve. She rocked against him, grinding against his tumescence, her breasts pressing against his chest. "I want you to touch me," she whispered, guiding one of his roving hands between her legs. "Touch me like you did last night."

He pushed up her cotte, then tugged on the strings of her hose until he could reach what he sought. Oh God, she was so slick with need. A tremor of white-hot desire shot through him. He desperately wanted to sink into her and feel her from within. There was nothing like it. As intoxicating as it was to watch her writhe against his hand, he craved more. But if this were all he could have, he would still count himself blessed.

She crushed her mouth into his, stifling the sounds she couldn't help making as he brought her to a swift and violent climax, her fingers digging painfully into his back, and her whole body bucking against him. Oh yes, she wanted him. *Thank Christ.*

As her shudders subsided, she collapsed against him, panting. He ignored his own painful arousal and held her close, burying his face in her hair. "Fionola," he said, breathing hard, "I've made no secret of my feelings for you. I confessed my love before I even knew who you were, and now that I know you, my love has only deepened. Last night, you offered me everything I wanted, everything I dreamed of for two long years, and then this morning, you threatened to take it all away. If you feel anything at all for me, please don't ever do that again."

She sighed against his chest and tightened her embrace. "I never intended to hurt you. You've saved my life twice in the last week and given me hope of finding my brother. Your loyalty to him means so much to me." She kissed his cheek. "From the day you arrived, you made me feel things. And last night... I never imagined such feelings." Brushing her lips against his, she touched her forehead to his. He couldn't stop himself from cradling her cheek. "I woke up this morning and remembered what I'd done— what we did together—the promises we made, the way we touched. It was clear to me that what I wanted could never be."

"Fionola—"

She silenced him with a long and tender kiss.

"But now... I still don't know how this can work, but you've made me realize that it would be harder to deny this than to live with the consequences. We'll marry when we get to Gan Ainm. I'll speak to Thomas."

Holding the woman he loved against him, knowing she would be his wife, he felt whole in a way he never had. Despite the challenges ahead, all he could manage to say was, "Thank you."

CHAPTER SIXTEEN

"I REQUIRE THE services of a priest," Fionola murmured to Thomas as he finished his breakfast on deck with Ronan. "Can we talk?"

Ronan gave her an inquiring look that she quelled with a sharp glance.

"Of course, Captain," Thomas said, handing Ronan his bowl and squeezing his hand.

This was insane. She couldn't become someone's wife. She had to find Liam. She had to captain the *Draconis*. Her mind kept searching for some way to reconcile what she wanted with the life she lived and the oath she'd sworn. The risks were enormous, but she meant what she'd said to Charles. They had to marry, and the sooner the better.

"What is it, Captain?" Thomas asked, as they settled into their usual makeshift seats in the hold. "Confession?"

She laughed. "I have a lot to confess, but no." She rested her forehead on her folded hands and tried to force herself to form the words.

A full minute passed, and she didn't manage to speak. Where should she begin?

"Well?" Thomas watched her with kindly concern.

He was such a good friend. Why was this so hard?

"It's about a wedding I need you to perform when we get to

Gan Ainm." It was a start. Not exactly a full revelation, but an improvement on the awkward silence.

Thomas raised an eyebrow. "Of course, but...whose wedding? I didn't know anyone on board was recently engaged."

Out with it, Fionola. He's your oldest friend.

She took a deep breath and let it out. "Mine."

"Don't tell me you've had a change of heart about Seamus." He clutched her arm.

She laughed. "No, not Seamus."

"Then...well...I...you can't mean Charles."

"Yes, I am marrying Charles." There. She'd said it. The wheels were in motion. There was no taking it back.

Thomas's jaw dropped. And then he closed it. And then it dropped again. Finally, he seemed to regain control of his mouth and said, "Fionola, I know I mentioned marriage as a theoretical option when we last spoke about him, but I never thought you would do something like this. You hardly know him."

"I agree, but circumstances require I take swift action."

His brow was so furrowed his eyebrows touched in the middle. "What do you mean? You didn't... He didn't..."

"No! Not that. My virtue is still intact." Blood rushed to her face. "Mostly," she mumbled, as his grip tightened on her arm. "Last night, when I woke up and found him tending to my wounds in my cabin, my clothes in tatters where he'd cut them away, I may have overreacted."

Now Thomas's eyebrows nearly reached his hairline. "Overreacted? What happened, Fionola?"

"I held a knife to his throat and ordered him to marry me or die for disobeying my orders and seeing what he shouldn't have."

There. That was all of it.

Wait no. Not quite all.

With her eyes closed, she added, "After he agreed to wed, we may have taken some unvirtuous pleasure in each other's company, though he stopped short of taking my maidenhead."

Now it was done.

Thomas stared for a long moment and then roared with laughter long and hard, tears gathering in the corners of his eyes. "Oh, Fionola! Only you," he gasped. It took him another minute to compose himself enough to speak. "So you're telling me, *you* have to marry *him* because you told him you'd kill him if *he* didn't agree to marry *you*. Have I got that right?"

She nodded, feeling very foolish.

"Well, I hardly know what to say," he said, shaking his head and chuckling. "I hope that you enjoyed your 'unvirtuous pleasure' with him after all that pining you were doing."

She bit her lip. "I had no idea I could feel like that." She momentarily hid her head in her hands, heat burning her cheeks, then looked back up at him cautiously.

"Very hard to stop once you start, isn't it?" he said with a wry smile. "Well, I knew you felt something for him. Does he have feelings for you?"

Oh yes, he does.

"Before he knew my secret, he confessed to me that he was in love with Fionola from Liam's description and stories. He said he dreamed of her on the *Midas*, praying someday he would meet her. You should have heard him the night after we took the *Rosemary*, wondering if Fionola was looking at the same moon. I was sitting right next to him drowning myself in wine to stop myself from kissing him."

She smiled and shook her head. "You can imagine his reaction when he saved me and stripped away my disguise. I may have threatened him into proposing, but the way he tells it, I granted his deepest wish."

Thomas's laughter subsided at last. "I'm glad to hear that, Captain. Plenty of marriages have been based on less. If you're determined to go through with this—"

"I am."

"—then I'd be honored to marry you." He pulled her into a fierce hug.

She hugged him back, burying her face in his shoulder. *Thank*

God for Thomas.

When he released her at long last, he said, "Are you going to tell the others?"

She knew what he meant. Should she? Ronan would laugh. Colm would tear up and ask to be the one to give her away. Seamus…might take a dagger to Charles.

"I'd like to, but I'm not sure how they'll take it."

Thomas gave her an all too understanding look. "You're worried about Seamus."

She nodded. "It's been over a year since his last proposal." *Not counting the one I prevented in Honfleur.* "But I still don't think he'll take it well. I'd like my groom to survive the wedding."

Even injured, Seamus was a dangerous man to anger.

"You should tell Ronan and Colm. Let me talk to Seamus. I'll make sure he understands violence is out of the question."

Yes, that would be best.

"Thank you."

"Are we done? I should get back on deck. The funeral will be at noon."

"Yes, we're done."

What else could I possibly say?

As they made their way back up to the deck, Charles glanced at her and Thomas, eyebrows raised. She nodded. He smiled, and she could swear all her clothes went up in flame.

Thomas noticed the direction of her gaze and turned to have a word with her betrothed. Good. She shouldn't be the only one having humiliating conversations this morning.

IT WAS NOON, and the entire crew stood at attention on deck. Thomas would lead the services, but the crew would look to her, nonetheless. Grief and resolve. That was what she needed to project as the crew said their goodbyes. The grief was easy enough because she felt it down to the soles of her feet. Malcolm,

Fergus, David. Those deaths would weigh heavily on her for the rest of her life.

She was a bit embarrassed, though, to have spent her morning laying the groundwork for her wedding instead of comforting the crew.

While Charles and Thomas had their little chat, she'd found Ronan and cornered him beneath the aftercastle. His reaction was more or less as she expected.

"Congratulations, Brother," he said, pulling her into a hug. "I look forward to seeing you in a wedding dress and laughing my ass off."

Ah, Ronan, my friend. You laugh your ass off at every opportunity. That's why I love you.

The conversation with Colm also went as predicted. He insisted her aunt would help her find a dress and cook a wedding feast for the tiny group that would attend the ceremony.

"Maeve would have my head if I denied her the opportunity," he said when she objected. "You know she thinks of you as the daughter we never had. And of course, you must let me give you away."

She smiled. Of course, he would make it a statement rather than asking.

Fionola's greatest regret, other than her failure to rescue her brother, was that her cousin Brendan had died before she was able to come to his rescue. Her grandfather had offered him as a hostage at the same time as Liam, and Colm and Maeve sold everything they had to try to ransom him. But when they caught up to the ship that took them, they'd learned Brendan had died of a fever weeks after he was taken, and Liam had been transferred. Thus began the mission that had lasted five years now and counting.

Yes, Colm would walk her down the aisle. There was no doubt.

Thomas stepped forward. The bodies of the deceased had been washed in precious fresh water from their barrels, and they were wrapped in rigging of the white silk that they took from the *Rosemary*. Since there was no body for David, Ronan had drawn him in charcoal upon the deck. The boy lay still, hands folded and a playful smile gracing his face within the rough outline of a charcoal coffin. As always, Ronan's work took her breath away. She blinked away tears that she could not afford.

Charles stepped up beside her, making no outward sign of greeting or recognition, but he allowed his knuckles to graze against hers, a touch no one would notice but a touch, nonetheless. She squeezed her eyes shut, cursing her weakness. No one could see her cry. Not ever.

Thomas offered Holy Communion to all who partook. Charles followed her closely as she took the bread and wine and prayed for the souls of her brothers in spirit. Malcolm, Fergus, David. Too many people she had failed. Starting with Ali.

The ceremony ended, and the bodies were committed to the sea. She watched as Malcolm and then Fergus sank below the waves. And then Ronan poured a bucket of water over the image of David and scrubbed a stiff bristled broom across it, smearing the charcoal. As the face became an unrecognizable blur, she reached her pinky to hook through Charles's. He had never left her side throughout the ceremony.

When the men began passing around wine skins, she let him go to propose a toast.

"To Malcolm," she began. "May he be surrounded by tempting horses and never tire of the chase." The crew drank.

"To Fergus, who was a righteous man and never sullied his body with this shit," she said, grinning at the ale. They all drank to that.

"To David..." Her voice failed her. The pressure and heat of tears built and built behind her eyes. Taking a deep breath and swallowing it down, she said, "To David who earned his place in heaven too soon. May his voice stop cracking and his beard grow thick. May he kiss a pretty wench and eat his fill at a heavenly banquet. He never had a chance to taste life's sweetest joys..."

Her gaze drifted to Charles, and she looked away swiftly. "But he deserved them all. To David."

She took a long, deep drink and then took the first opportunity when her men were distracted to flee below decks to compose herself. Charles started to follow, but she shook her head. She could tell he was tempted to follow anyway, but duty constrained him. She was still the captain, and he obeyed.

As she passed Seamus's door on her way to her cabin, the strangest sound emerged from it. Was Seamus weeping?

Cautiously, she knocked on his door.

"It's open," he said in a rough voice.

She squeezed herself into the tiny space.

"Captain."

"Seamus." He stared at her with a world of hurt in his eyes. "I came to check on you. How are you recovering?"

He turned his head away.

"Seamus?"

He closed his eyes. "You've known him two weeks."

She remained silent. There was nothing she could say.

"Two *weeks*. I've served you faithfully for two and a half *years*. I've proposed three times. Why him and not me?"

What could she say?

"I don't know. I never led you on, Seamus. I told you I didn't return your feelings."

"Two weeks."

There was no answer. She had no words.

As she turned to leave, he said, "I hope you're happy with him. I'll always hate him, but I won't try to stand in the way. If you don't mind, I'll skip the wedding."

She nodded and left, closing the door behind her.

In her cabin, she took off her scarf and beard and poured herself a drink of water. Sitting on her pallet, she closed her eyes and breathed deeply to calm the storm of conflicting emotions within her. She knew she should go back up to the crew. They needed her right now, and she had to be strong for them. But if she was a wreck, she was no good to anyone. In. Out. In. Out.

Her friendship with Seamus would never be the same. In. Out. Two weeks. In. Out. Malcolm. Fergus. David. In. Out. Charles. In. Out.

She let the feelings wash over her and waited for calm to return. Just as the storm began to die down, there was a knock at her door. Charles. It must be.

Opening the door, she saw her future husband waiting, his gaze focused on his feet. "Captain, Thomas asked me to find you. He wanted to know if you're ready to join the crew on deck. They need you."

He hazarded a brief glance at her face, and he seemed satisfied with what he saw there, nodding as he returned his gaze to his feet.

"Come in for a moment. I need to speak with you."

Keeping his gaze carefully averted, he complied. "What can I do for you, Captain?"

"I spoke to Thomas this morning. We'll marry when we get to Gan Ainm. Ronan, Colm, and Seamus know too." She paused. "I'd steer clear of Seamus. He didn't take it well."

"Oh?" He met her gaze at last.

"He's proposed to me several times. It wasn't easy news for him to hear."

Charles nodded slowly. "Thank you for telling me. I wouldn't have guessed. I have no desire to antagonize him."

The temptation to touch him became too much, and she reached out for his hand. He breathed in sharply. "I don't think you understand how hard it is not to kiss you senseless every time I'm near you," he whispered.

"Then do it."

A moment later, she was pressed against the bulkhead with Charles's mouth against her own, tongues entwined. The intensity of his onslaught made her moan into his kiss, as everything disappeared except the sensations of his body against hers. Dear Lord, she wanted to drown herself in him and never come up for air. She couldn't stop. She didn't want to stop. But she had to. Her crew needed her. She couldn't afford to lose herself like this.

With great difficulty, she pulled back. "We have to stop. I have to go."

"I know. You should go."

Neither of them moved.

"I'm going," she said. Still, she didn't move. She couldn't stop staring at his lips.

"Fionola?"

She grabbed the front of his tunic and pulled him into another kiss. How was he so delicious? Why did he make her feel this way? None of this made any sense, and she absolutely could not stop. He pressed his knee between her legs, and she grabbed his buttocks, pulling his hips against her own. The wanting only intensified as she gave in to her body's urges. His fingers were doing something heavenly to her left nipple through the rough fabric of her cotte and shirt while his leg rubbed against the molten center of her heat, further stoking the flames that consumed her.

There was a knock on the door, and they both froze.

"Captain? It's Ronan. Thomas asked for you."

"Tell him I'll be right there," she called as she straightened her clothes and grabbed her beard and scarf. In silence, he helped her put them on and tie them, then he kissed her hand and let her flee out the door.

When she arrived on deck, Thomas raised an eyebrow at her and shook his head. Damn it all, he knew exactly what they'd been doing and why she was blushing beneath her beard. Keeping Charles a secret from her crew was going to be impossible, and she had no choice.

CHAPTER SEVENTEEN

FOR THE SECOND time in a day, Charles stood in the captain's cabin with a painful arousal and no Fionola. When she'd fled this morning, his fingers were still covered in her creamy essence. The spicy scent of her was so tantalizing. Touching his tongue to it, he groaned in need. He could hardly wait to taste her at length, but that would have to wait until they were on Gan Ainm and had time and privacy. There was no way she'd manage to stay quiet enough here.

That thought did nothing to improve his current predicament. Here he was again, mere hours later, hard as a rock and alone once again. Was this what the future held? Would he be caught in an endless loop of desire and frustration with far less access to his wife than his body craved? He could not get enough of her. The slightest touch drove him to distraction, and for some reason, she seemed to feel the same. Dear God, the way she kissed him just now, as if he was a succulent fruit she couldn't resist… How was a man supposed to keep his sanity?

If he didn't want to give himself away in front of the crew, he was going to have to keep his distance from her today, not to mention the rest of the week.

They were still a good three days away from their destination.

With twenty men and no privacy.

And he could hardly look at or even think of her without a rush of lust.

Perhaps he should take up residence in the crow's nest.

When he returned to the deck, he was immediately aware of her presence on the forecastle, so he went in the opposite direction. Ronan was sitting in his usual spot sketching with a wineskin by his side. Charles went over.

"Mind if I join you?"

Ronan smirked and handed him the wineskin.

"I understand the captain told you?" Charles took a long, deep drink.

"He did indeed. You have my condolences. He's not going to make it easy."

Charles raised an eyebrow. "What do you mean?"

"The captain belongs to his ship and his crew. You'll always have to share him with the rest of us, and he is unlikely to give as much of himself as you crave. He'll intend to, but other things will always pull him away. If I'm not mistaken, you're already getting a taste of that." Amazing the man could read his mind. Was it that obvious? Or was it only obvious to those in the know? He hoped it was the latter.

Letting his breath out slowly, Charles answered, "I'd rather take what I can get than have nothing at all. The captain is a unique man, and he has my undying devotion, even if all I get from the bargain is the opportunity to watch him from afar."

Ronan took the wineskin back and drank deeply. "When I came down to get the captain, were you…um…having a chat with him? It didn't sound like you were watching from afar."

"Christ on the cross. You could hear us? I thought we were being quiet."

Charles grabbed the wineskin, and Ronan laughed and laughed.

"The captain's not my type, but I imagine he's quite the fiery conversationalist."

Dropping his head to his knees, Charles groaned. "Ronan, I

need your help. I have to keep my distance until we get to Gan Ainm. He and I can't keep having these little... 'talks'...or the wrong person is going to notice, and his secret will get out. But God help me, I don't have the willpower to stay away. Can you help distract me? Teach me to draw. Sword fight with me. Teach me every dirty sea shanty you know. Make me wash all your laundry. Anything to keep me out of the captain's cabin."

"Are you sure that's what the captain wants? Seemed like he rather enjoyed your...talk."

Charles took another deep drink. "We both want to make it to safety with no secrets accidentally coming to light. The less we talk, the better."

"All right, I'll help you," Ronan said, taking the wineskin again. "Though if you do decide to 'talk' with him, I recommend the front hold during breakfast. It's well away from sleeping quarters, and everyone is on deck for breakfast anyway. Just make sure you hang a scarf over the door so that no one disturbs you. You aren't the only ones seeking a bit of privacy from time to time."

THE JOURNEY TO Gan Ainm was flurry of furious, and pointless, activity. At Ronan's suggestion, Charles organized a swordsmanship competition, an archery competition, and a dirty shanty competition. He drilled the crew on battle tactics and tested them all individually on their hand signals, with Ronan's help, since he barely knew them himself. Ronan taught him to draw a passable seagull in charcoal, and they practiced sword fighting daily until they were both too tired to continue. On the second day, after a particularly grueling round of sword fighting, Ronan handed him a piece of whale bone and a knife and told him not to bother him again until he'd carved something.

Charles made a tiny skull like the one his grandfather had

worn and strung it on a string around his neck. "Death can come at any time, and life should not be wasted," his grandfather used to say. *No, life should not be wasted*, he thought, looking up at Fionola in the distant forecastle. No sooner did he look than she looked back. Their eyes locked. A few minutes later, they were in the hold together, scarf over the door, in a desperate embrace as they tried to sate each other before anyone discovered them. When they slunk guiltily and separately back up to the deck, he was relieved to see that no one was the wiser.

There was one more frenzied, furtive encounter before the end of their journey. On the day they were expecting to arrive at Gan Ainm, he brought her breakfast. After days of mostly successful avoidance, he let his guard down. With the journey's end so near, surely there was no danger in a friendly meal. Three minutes after he set down the tray, they were naked and entwined on the pallet, doing their best to maintain absolute silence.

When he reemerged on deck, Ronan looked at him and laughed, shaking his head. "Good talk with the captain?"

"What gave it away?"

"The bite mark on your shoulder. Keep the neck of your cotte laced up if you don't want the crew to notice."

An hour later, a cry went up that Gan Ainm was visible in the distance. Charles jogged to the railing to look. Squinting in the late morning sun, he was just able to see a dot on the horizon. Excitement filled him at the prospect of visiting a pirate's hideaway. He imagined a densely forested island with no visible structures and caves full of loot. He was ready to make love to Fionola in a secret cave on a pallet covered in covered in stolen silks beneath stalactites that cast strange shadows in the flickering candlelight. They would be surrounded by treasure chests overflowing with untold riches that they would guard with their lives against rival pirates.

As the details of Gan Ainm became clear, he was startled to see a small town with stone buildings and a proper port, not unlike Winchelsea. There was even a castle tower north of the town. This was nothing like the smuggler's dens he imagined as a child, playing on the tiny Dolphin Island in Rye Harbor.

"You look disappointed," Fionola said, stepping up beside him and making him jump. "Did you think we lived in caves?"

His face flushed.

"Oh, you did, didn't you," she said with a laugh, eyes wide. "Well, I'm sorry to say we're quite feckin' civilized. It's a proper town with a proper port just like you'd find anywhere in the Atlantic. Ronan jokes that I should declare myself the Countess of Gan Ainm and present myself at court in London, as if I could ever pass myself off as a noblewoman."

"But you *are* a noblewoman. Your grandfather was a king. And you do realize you're about to marry the son and heir apparent of a baron?"

She shook her head. "Don't remind me. I pray the day never comes when I'm forced to play baroness. Let me live my life as a captain. That's the only bleedin' title I need."

She stepped away to oversee docking. The *Draconis* lowered its sail and coasted into a berth in the harbor. A cold shiver went through him at the sight of the *Midas* docked nearby. He looked away quickly, but it was too late. His hand began to tremble in the onset of a spell.

Blood pounded through his head, and his heart raced as if he was in pitched battle. His breathing became fast and shallow as he sat down and then cowered by the railing, unable to hold back his reaction. Moments later, a friendly hand touched his shoulder. Ronan. As the spell passed, and he raised his head, his friend put an arm around his shoulder.

"You did well, Charles. I vomited when I arrived here and saw the ship where I was imprisoned in the harbor. Seamus was not pleased." Ronan jumped to his feet and offered a hand up. "Come. You'll be staying with Thomas and me until the captain makes you his blushing bride."

The docks were bustling with workers and traders loading

and unloading cargo. There was even a tiny custom house, which Ronan explained only charged fees to traders visiting the island. There were no customs or duties on the goods, but there was a high price for entry to help safeguard the black market that operated in plain sight.

"The Romans used this as an outpost," Ronan explained. "Then they abandoned it at some point. No one knows why. Fishermen from Wexford sometimes stopped here, but no one lived here. When the captain began rescuing the people from Black Stephen's clutches, he needed a safe place where they could live away from prying eyes. This seemed like the ideal solution."

The town had two streets. There was an inn and two taverns at the southern end of the docks. The street above was mostly residences. As they approached the island, Charles saw several farms—a wheat field, an orchard, a meadow where sheep and cows grazed. This tiny microcosm had everything it needed to be self-sufficient. Even women, he noted as they walked past street vendors and residences.

At Charles's curious glance, Ronan smiled. "How long do you think an island of men would last with no women? It's a good life here. Most of the women fled Black Stephen's pillaging. Others came at the invitation of the men who live here. Colm's wife, Maeve, has been here from the start, along with their daughters. You'll meet Deirdre and Molly soon enough. They live up at the castle with the captain."

Stopping at a charming, two-story stone house with a green door, green shutters, and a planter with fresh herbs out front, Ronan announced, "And allow me to welcome you to our home." He made an exaggerated bow.

Charles entered and looked around the clean, comfortable, and well-lit space. Paintings hung on the walls, mostly portraits, all clearly Ronan's work. The furniture was simple but well made. There were fresh rushes on the floor. The room smelled of freshly baked bread. Two fragrant loaves sat on the table in the middle of the room. "Thank you for your hospitality," he said, smiling at the homiest space he'd been in since his capture.

Once upon a time he would have disapproved of living so openly in sin, but his time as a prisoner changed everything. Wherever people found happiness, he could not begrudge them. And were their sins worse than anyone else's? He himself succumbed to lust out of wedlock just this morning. Was he not equally sinful in the eyes of the Lord?

At that moment, Thomas came through the door. "Charles! I'm so glad you'll be staying with us. I hope Ronan has been behaving himself as a host."

"He's been very gracious," Charles said with a laugh.

"Have you met Cian and Peter? Oh, and of course, Princess." Thomas whistled, and a sleek hound came running down the stairs, greeting Thomas with enthusiastic barks and licks. "This is Princess," Thomas said, giving her pets and a piece of cured meat from a cupboard. "Cian can't be far, since I see the fresh bread," he muttered. "Cian? Peter? Are you here? We have a guest," he called out.

A young man with loose brown curls and dimpled cheeks came bounding down the stairs and halted as soon as he saw Charles. "Well, hello, guest," he said, giving Charles a sultry look. "I'm Cian. It's truly a pleasure to make your acquaintance."

Charles smiled and nodded his head in greeting. While he didn't return the man's interest, he hoped they could be friends. There was a rascally gleam in Cian's eyes that made Charles immediately like him.

Ronan and Thomas exchanged a look.

"Don't get your hopes up, Cian. You're not his type," Ronan said in a dry tone.

"Really? Because he's definitely *my* type." He looked Charles up and down with undisguised interest.

Charles's cheeks heated and he turned his gaze to the floor for a moment before looking back up. His new friend was certainly bold.

"He's getting married the day after tomorrow," Thomas said,

looking up from scratching Princess between the ears. "To a woman," he added as if it needed explaining.

"Well, that's a pity. I'm a better cook than she is, I'll wager, and better at keeping house too."

Ha! Charles didn't doubt it. No one would have mistaken Fionola for the domestic sort.

"That's God's truth," Ronan muttered, holding back laughter.

"Lovely man, if you ever decide to broaden your horizons, I hope you'll remember me." Cian winked.

Flattering as the attention was, it was time to disabuse Cian of any hopes he might harbor.

"My name is Charles. It's a pleasure to meet you, Cian. I wish you luck finding a different lovely man that properly appreciates your skills and virtues."

Thomas gave him a worried look. "Cian is a bit…forward. If he's bothering you, just tell him, and he'll leave you alone."

Charles smiled. "No, I'm not bothered. My best friend is Liam, remember?" Oh, how Liam would laugh if he could see him at this moment! God's teeth, he missed his friend. "I just wouldn't want him to get his hopes up when my heart is given elsewhere." Ronan had to sit down; he was laughing so hard. "You're lucky to have found a place where you can live so openly."

"We can't. Not truly. We keep it quiet outside these walls. Even so, everyone knows. They just don't speak of it. Except for the other priest in his sermons," Thomas said with a sigh.

"We don't say the other priest's name," Cian whispered loudly.

"Most of the townsfolk ignore us and leave us alone." Thomas turned to Cian and gave him a pointed look. "Some of us are better at staying out of trouble than others."

Cian fluttered his eyelashes. "Can I help it if they love my buns?" Turning to Charles, he added, "I run a bakery. Everyone says my buns are irresistible."

"You're lucky Peter keeps an eye out for you," Ronan mumbled, "or you'd be in real trouble. The other priest is already out to get you."

"Don't worry. The other priest loves my buns just like everyone else. He's just jealous the others prefer my buns to his holy wafers. Which I also make by the way," he said as an aside to Charles. "Someday he'll come around and remember he's a man with appetites just like anyone else."

At that moment, a mountain of a man with arms thick as logs walked through the door. "Who are you," he demanded, stalking toward Charles who stumbled back in alarm.

Thomas stepped in between them. "This is Charles. He's staying with us as our guest for two nights. He's getting married the day after tomorrow."

Peter grumbled and stomped out of the room and up the stairs.

"Don't worry," Thomas said. "He's a bit standoffish. He'll stay out of your way."

"With Godric back in town, you probably won't even see him," Cian said with a smirk. "He's always grumpy when he needs a fuck."

"Shouldn't you be at the bakery making honey cakes or something?" Ronan said, taking Cian by the arm and propelling him toward the door.

Cian rolled his eyes but complied. "See you later Charles. Don't hesitate to stop by the bakery if you want to sample my buns. I promise they are delicious."

As soon as he was gone, Ronan grumbled to Thomas, "If he doesn't watch out, he's going to meet with an accident one of these days."

"He's his own man. We can't treat him like a child," Thomas replied. "But I'll talk to him. Again," he added, seeing the look on Ronan's face. "Let me show you to your room." He beckoned and led Charles to a bright room with a window looking out over a kitchen garden behind the house. The scent of fresh herbs wafted in through the window. "Our house is your house. Feel free to come and go as you please. You should go out and explore the town, perhaps see the tailor about some wedding clothes. I'll lend you some money, since you haven't received your portion from the *Rosemary* yet."

⟫⟫⟪⟪

WHEN CHARLES RETURNED that evening with a lighter purse and several bundles of purchases, it appeared no one was home. He set down his things in his room and then heard voices in the back garden.

"He's a nice enough man, but do you think he'll make the captain happy?" It was Ronan's voice.

"I hope so," said Thomas. "It won't be easy for them, but I've never seen the captain respond to anyone like this. I just hope it's enough to carry them through the difficulties to come."

"Well, we made a go of it despite the odds."

"Yes, we did."

Charles heard kissing and blushed, edging away from the window so as not to see or be seen.

"Let's go upstairs," Ronan murmured. "It's been a long month without a bed."

"Yes, it has."

Footsteps tapped up the wooden stairs. It wasn't a conventional household, but it was a happy one.

He made his way quietly back outside and had a leisurely drink at the tavern, chatting with friends from the *Draconis* to learn more about the town. Upon his return, his hosts had a simple and hearty dinner laid out—roast chicken, grilled carrots, mashed potatoes, fresh bread, and for dessert there were sweet buns, which were, in fact, sinfully delicious. Life in Gan Ainm was good, and he could hardly wait to make a home here.

CHAPTER EIGHTEEN

AS USUAL, MAEVE smelled of roses. Fionola breathed deeply as she surrendered to a long, soft hug from her aunt. "My sweet girl, I'm so happy for you. I can't wait to meet the man who captured your heart. I admit I had my doubts about whether this day would ever come."

"You'll like him, Auntie. He's a good man—kind, respectful, capable, strong…"

"Handsome?"

Fionola blushed. "Yes, he's handsome."

Maeve laughed. "Of course, he is. He'd have to be extraordinary in every way to turn your head. Though I must say I don't know how I feel about your marrying so quickly. I hardly have time to prepare." Maeve served up an overflowing bowl from cast iron pots and pans resting on the outer edges of the enormous hearth—her famous fish stew. "Eat. You're too skinny."

Nowhere on earth felt quite as homey as Maeve's kitchen. The rest of the island might call their home "the captain's castle," but the only part that Fionola felt was truly hers was her room. The castle's five residents agreed that all the rooms aside from the bedrooms belonged to Maeve, especially the kitchen with the low ceiling, enormous hearth, bread oven, and game birds and herbs hanging from the ceiling.

"It's going to be a very small wedding, just six guests in addition to Thomas, Charles, and me." She sat at the enormous trestle table Maeve used for food prep and dutifully dug in with a spoon. There was no chance Maeve would let her escape without making a decent dent.

"Does this mean you'll finally stop wearing that ridiculous beard and settle down?" Maeve avoided making eye contact.

"Auntie, we've talked about this." She should know better than to ask such questions, though the truth was Fionola herself hadn't fully thought through the ways in which her life was about to change. "I can't captain the *Draconis* as a woman. No one would follow me."

"But couldn't you hand it off? Maybe let Seamus take over as captain? You deserve to live your life." Maeve squeezed her uninjured shoulder.

"Not until we rescue Liam."

Maeve's hand dropped, and she went to putter with a kettle by the hearth. It was an old argument. Maeve wanted Liam home too, but she'd never been happy with Fionola's role in the search.

"Well, I hope you're at least going to dispense with the beard for your wedding," Maeve said into the fire.

"Of course, Auntie. And I was hoping you could help me with a dress."

The effect of her words was immediate. Maeve spun around and clapped her hands in joy, her eyes tearing up. "You'll be such a beautiful bride, my dear!" She ran to the door and called out, "Deirdre! I need you!"

Fionola heard running feet.

"Saint Brigid's eyelashes, Mum! You scared me half to death." Deirdre looked around the kitchen and squealed when she saw Fionola. "I've missed you so much," she said, carelessly flinging her arms around Fionola.

"Ow," Fionola yelped, flinching back.

Deirdre immediately dropped her hug. "What's wrong? Are you hurt again?"

"What is this?" Maeve came running over.

"It's nothing. Just a flesh wound."

"Let me see," Maeve demanded. Fionola tried to shrug away. "Now, young lady."

At a signal from Maeve, Deirdre ran to close the kitchen door. Reluctantly, Fionola pulled off her cotte and then her shirt, revealing the bandages around her shoulder and arm. Maeve's hand went to her mouth as she gasped.

"Your bandages need changing," Maeve said, unwrapping the linen Charles had wrapped so lovingly. "Who tended to your wounds while you were on the *Draconis*?"

"Charles. He rescued me."

Maeve pinned her with a look. "Now I understand the need for a hasty wedding."

"You're getting married?" Deirdre asked, gaping.

"Shh," Maeve said, gently pushing Deirdre away. "Go get clean linen, lavender oil, and honey. Oh, my sweet girl," she said turning back to Fionola, "what have they done to you this time?" She inspected the wounds, shaking her head and glancing up at Fionola every so often with a frown. "Are these arrow wounds?"

Fionola nodded. "We found Liam."

"No." Maeve froze in the midst of her flurry.

"He's on a slave ship called the *Gorgon*. We attacked off Honfleur, but it went poorly. They had an archer we didn't see in time."

"Do you know where they were going?"

"Sadly, no. I fell overboard, and Charles rescued me. He learned my secret when he removed the arrows. Charles used to sit next to Liam on the *Midas*, and he immediately knew who I was. I revived to hear him calling me by name. Given what he'd seen, I gave him a choice between marriage and death. He chose wisely."

Maeve hardly breathed through the whole recital. When it was over, she looked carefully at the wounds. "He did a good job tending to you. There's no sign of infection. Another few days, and we'll be able to take out the stitches." She pointed at the shoulder wound. As they waited for Deirdre to return, she said, "I thought this was a love match, but from what you said, he had no choice. Do you care for each other at all?"

"Yes, Auntie. We do. He's very happy about this. You'll see."

"And you? Are you happy?"

"I am," she said, avoiding Maeve's eyes. "But I'm also..." What was the right word for this churning feeling in her gut? "...concerned. I don't know how this will work. I want Charles to be my husband, but I can't stop being Captain O'Bannon. He says he doesn't mind, but I don't know how I'm going to manage to be his wife and the captain at the same time."

At that moment, Deirdre came running in with everything Maeve asked for. With pursed lips, Maeve went to work replacing her bandages with clean strips of cloth.

"I can't believe you're getting married. Tell me everything," Deirdre gushed, pulling up a stool directly in front of Fionola. "Also, you owe me a hair ribbon. Remember when we made that bet when we were eight about which of us would marry first? I won."

Fionola laughed. "How do you even remember that? I hardly remember anything from those days."

"Hand me that strip of cloth," Maeve ordered, and Deirdre immediately obeyed.

Deirdre turned her attention back to Fionola. "The boys always liked you better. I suppose I shouldn't be surprised you beat me to the altar."

"But the boys liked me as a boy."

Deirdre waved her hand dismissively. "They liked you better, full stop. So this man you're marrying, what's his name?"

Fionola cracked a grin. "Charles."

"Is he very handsome?" Deirdre's eager smile looked like it was going to split her face in half.

"Yes, he is."

"Do you love him very much?"

"I..." She searched the room, hoping for inspiration on how

to distract Deirdre from this line of questioning. She drew a blank. "I'm still figuring that out."

Putting her hands on her hips, Deirdre gave Fionola a withering look.

"I like him?" Fionola offered, uncertain.

Deirdre made a derisive noise. "Where's he staying? I might try to get a peek at him."

"He's staying with Thomas and Ronan, though I'm probably going to regret telling you. Or maybe he will," she grumbled. *Poor Charles. He won't know what hit him.*

"Excellent. I'll see you later!"

"Wait," yelled Maeve. "I need to find her a dress to get married in. Can you bring down your nicest dresses? I want to see if any of them fit her."

Deirdre huffed but headed upstairs to gather what she had.

Fionola was dubious. Deirdre was slightly taller but also skinnier. She wasn't sure she could stuff her arms into the skinny sleeves of Deirdre's dresses without splitting the seams. Frankly, the whole idea of wearing a dress gave her the shivers, but she wasn't going to get married in disguise. For her wedding, she would be Fionola, not O'Bannon. If she could stay stoic while Charles removed the arrowhead from her shoulder, surely, she could manage to wear a dress for a few hours without complaining.

Deirdre came back down with three dresses and lay them down on the kitchen table.

"I'm not sure I'll be able to fit in any of these. My arms are too big," Fionola said, perusing the pile of garments.

"Oh, I'm sure we'll find something. I don't think this one would suit you. It's the wrong color," she said, pointing to a yellow one that Fionola was certain must be her favorite. "Maybe this one?" she said, tugging on a red dress with bell sleeves. "You should be able to get your arms into it. The blue one is nice, but it has skinny arms. I'm not sure we could make it work."

Maeve and Deirdre made her strip and try on each of the

three. The yellow one fit the best, but they all agreed it was the wrong color for her skin. The red one was too tight and made Fionola feel indecent, even if the sleeves did fit. The blue one she couldn't even put on. Her biceps threatened to burst the shoulder holes.

"Molly is too short," Maeve said, rubbing her forehead. "None of her dresses would work. Maybe I have something that would suit." Fionola sat patiently on her stool and waited.

Maeve returned triumphant with a kermes red linen dress that was dreadfully wrinkled as if it had been stored in a trunk for too long. She also had a white linen shift, similarly wrinkled. "It was a gift. I've never worn it," she said, pulling it over Fionola's head, right over her shirt and breeches. "We'd need to take it in here and here, and I'd need to steam the wrinkles out, but this could work."

She pulled it back over Fionola's head and made her strip down and put on the shift. With a few pins, she marked the alterations and then pulled the dress on. Fionola felt like a walking pin cushion by the time Maeve finished. She had no idea what she looked like, but she figured Maeve was more trustworthy regarding this sort of thing than she herself was.

"Can I go yet? I want to see if I can catch a glimpse of Charles." Deirdre was drumming her fingers on her opposite arm and shifting from foot to foot, obviously dying to go spy on Fionola's mystery man.

Maeve threw her hands up. "Go! Leave me in peace. I have work to do." Deirdre practically flew out the door. "You too," she said to Fionola, easing the new garments over her head and injured shoulder. "But I'll expect you back for dinner."

THAT EVENING, FIONOLA returned from a long, solitary walk along the shore as the sun was setting. Colm, Maeve, and Deirdre were just sitting down to dinner. Where had Molly gotten off to? The castle was full of wonderful cooking smells, but dinner was simple pottage with bread and roasted chicken.

"What are you cooking, Auntie? It smells delicious," Fionola said as she took a seat.

"You'll find out tomorrow," Maeve answered with a mysterious smile.

At that moment, the door opened, and Molly walked in looking dazed, her light brown hair escaping her bun. "Fionola, it's so good to see you," she said, hugging Fionola's shoulders. Then she stood still, making no move to join them at the table.

"What happened to you?" Deirdre asked. "You look like someone hit you over the head with a cauldron."

Molly blinked several times and said in an unsteady voice, "Seamus just proposed."

Aunt Maeve dropped her spoon on the floor. "I need to get your father. Don't move." She ran out of the kitchen at surprising speed for a woman of her years.

"What happened?" Deirdre demanded.

"It was all very sudden and unexpected." She lapsed into silence and stared at her shoes, blushing.

Fionola hardly trusted herself to look up. She was pretty sure she knew why Seamus suddenly proposed marriage after years of being totally oblivious to Molly's interest.

"Well? Are you going to tell us more?" Deirdre asked, her voice getting higher by the moment.

Molly looked at Deirdre with huge eyes. "When he asked, I didn't want him to change his mind, so I said 'yes' without waiting for Da's blessing." She closed her eyes and clenched her fists. "How furious do you think Da will be?"

Fionola got up and folded Molly into a hug, squeezing tightly. "He'll be delighted, Molly. Just you wait. I'm very happy for you. You deserve every happiness. And I will personally murder Seamus if he ever makes you unhappy in any way." She released Molly and looked her up and down. "In fact, perhaps I ought to have a chat with him. Do you know where he might be?"

Wringing her skirts, Molly looked pleadingly at the others. "Actually, he's outside. Should I bring him in?"

"In a moment. I want to speak with him." Fionola strode out, leaving Molly with the others. She needed to have a few words with Seamus without his new bride-to-be.

Opening the door, she said, "Seamus," with a nod.

"Captain," he said, entering but not meeting her eyes.

In a heartbeat, she had him pinned against the door with a knife at his throat. "You hurt her, I kill you. Do you understand?"

"You think I don't know that, Captain?" he said, with no apology in his eyes.

Fionola looked him up and down. "I don't like the timing. Did you do this because you care for her or to get revenge at me?"

He met her gaze. "A little of both. I always liked Molly, but she pales in comparison to you. But after your news, I realized I was wasting my time. Molly cares for me, unlike you. And suddenly, that seems like the best reason in the world to choose a bride."

Shaking her head, Fionola scraped the blade against his neck. "She will never know she was your second choice. Do you understand?"

"Yes," he whispered, looking affronted. But she took that for a good sign.

She lowered her knife. "You're coming to the wedding tomorrow. You could have avoided it if you'd set your sights on anyone else, but you proposed to her. She's coming to the wedding, so you are too."

His jaw muscles bulged as he clenched his teeth.

"You made your choice, Seamus. Make her happy, or I will shove this in your kidney. Understood?" She brandished her knife.

He gave her a dirty look. She narrowed her eyes. He was a good man, and she couldn't entirely blame him. But really, did he have to propose to Molly the day before her wedding?

She brandished her blade again. "If you don't come to the wedding, Molly will wonder what's wrong. And if she suspects, it will break her heart. I like you, Seamus. I care about you. But if you break her heart, I swear I will send you to hell unshriven and let the devil roast you slowly over an eternal spit. Are we clear?"

He let out a long, slow breath and glowered at her. "Quite clear."

Fionola smiled. "Good. Go in there and make nice. And remember I will slit your belly, spill your guts, and strangle you with your own entrails if you give the slightest hint that you aren't desperately in love with her."

He gave her a bitter, brittle smile, and grasped his still-healing belly wound protectively.

"I'll be watching," she said, brandishing her blade one last time before sheathing it and putting on her own fake grin.

To her pleasant surprise, Seamus lived up to his promise. He was a devoted suitor to Molly, providing all the right assurances to Colm and Maeve before asking for their blessing. And then, after he received it, he declared his intention to attend Fionola's nuptials with Molly the next day.

"I wish you the same happiness I have found, Captain," he said.

She wasn't sure what to make of that and gave him a warning look. He responded with an innocent smile then kissed his bride-to-be on the cheek.

"I must go now," Seamus said, bowing his head to Colm and Maeve and squeezing Molly's hand. "I'll see you tomorrow at the wedding."

Fionola eyed him warily as he walked out the door. The next day would prove very interesting indeed.

THE CHURCH BELL rang for mid-afternoon prayers, and Fionola

stared at herself in Deirdre's mirror. Somehow, Maeve had transformed the red, wrinkled lump into something that both fit her and suited her, and Deirdre had transformed her wild curls into a seductive pile that made her look like a goddess.

The reflection in the small, polished silver mirror looked gorgeous. And utterly unfamiliar. There was no hint of Captain O'Bannon. She looked like a lady who would swoon if someone sneezed near her. "I can't do this," she gasped, tearing at the constricting lacing on the sides of her dress.

"Yes, you can," Deirdre assured her, taking her hand and pulling it away from the laces. "You look beyond divine. Charles will fall at your feet."

Fionola assessed the overall effect again, feeling particularly drafty in the nether regions. "I miss my breeches. I feel indecent like this."

Deirdre gave her a look.

Just then, Maeve came bustling in. "Everyone is here. It's time to go down. Oh, you look so lovely, my dear!"

Fionola blushed. "Thank you, Auntie."

"I have to go down and see to the guests."

All six of them. No, seven with Seamus. Such a fuss for so little!

"You just come downstairs when you're ready. We'll all be on the beach waiting," Maeve said and hurried out of the room.

Fionola looked at Deirdre. "I'll come down in a minute, but do you mind letting me have a moment alone?"

Deirdre shrugged. "Suit yourself. See you downstairs."

Alone in her room, she looked once again at the stranger in the mirror. They'd done a good job. She couldn't fault them. But did she really want to get married pretending to be someone she wasn't? How could she make herself look slightly less like a stranger?

She spotted her sword and belt, resting in the corner and smiled. Maeve would have some choice words, but no one would dare stop her. Grabbing the belt, she strapped it around her hips and slid her blade into the scabbard. Next, she grabbed the small knives she habitually wore up her sleeves. There. She felt slightly less naked and ridiculous.

Ready at last, she made her way down the stairs and out the door to the cove beside the castle. No one else ever came to this beach. Everyone considered it part of the castle grounds. There was no risk of being seen unexpectedly.

Colm was waiting for her. He raised an eyebrow at the sword but didn't say a word. Offering an elbow, he escorted her between the two benches with guests and placed her hand in Charles's.

How different this was from the wedding she'd fled five years ago! The man she'd been contracted to wed couldn't have been more different from Charles. Marriage to Black Stephen would have been hell on earth, and that was if she survived it without dying in childbirth or being dispatched for her inconveniently wayward nature. She knew without a doubt that Charles loved her for who she was, accepting her strange life as Captain O'Bannon and caring for her wellbeing with greater attention than she herself gave. Thank God she was marrying a good man.

Everyone stared at her, except Seamus who seemed deeply preoccupied with something just over the horizon. But the only person she noticed was Charles. He was wearing an outfit very much like the one he wore in Honfleur, except this time his hose and cotte were a deep plum, almost black, and it had silver embroidery in geometric shapes along the hem and cuffs. The sleeves of his fine linen shirt billowed in the breeze. She took it all in, but the thing that made her breath catch was the way he looked at her.

The heat and hunger that seemed to flare between them was stronger than ever, but there was something else as well, a worshipful tenderness, as if she was the most precious person below the firmament. She stared at him, captivated, unable to drag her gaze away until Thomas cleared his throat.

"Dearly beloved," Thomas began. "We are gathered here today to join this man and this captain in holy matrimony."

Fionola couldn't help an unladylike laugh at that. Charles grinned and squeezed her hand.

"Do you, Charles, take our captain to be your lawfully wedded wife?"

"I do," Charles said fervently.

"Do you, Fionola, also known as Captain O'Bannon, take this man to be your lawfully wedded husband?"

For a moment, she felt panic shiver through her, but she shoved it down. She wanted this. She'd demanded it. Whatever happened next, they would figure it out together.

"I do," she said in her most resonant captain's voice.

They spoke their vows and exchanged rings. Thomas pronounced them married. Fionola once again swallowed down a moment of panic that it was done, irrevocable. She barely heard Thomas announce they could kiss, but she certainly noticed the torrent of desire that flooded her as Charles pulled her into his arms and placed his lips on hers.

For a moment, she forgot anyone else was watching, and she kissed him with all the ferocious hunger she felt. His chest rumbled as he moaned quietly at her onslaught, tightening his own grip, and matching the fury of her embrace. If only she could tell everyone to go away now and leave them. All she wanted was to be alone with him so that they could give in to their spiraling passion.

Thomas cleared his throat and whispered for their ears only, "Seamus looks like he's about to murder someone. You might want to stop before he loses control."

Reluctantly, she pulled back, trembling slightly at the loss of contact. She stole a peek at Seamus who looked like he'd swallowed the entire contents of the weapons chest from the *Draconis*. Everyone else was looking away discreetly, ignoring their torrid display, except Deirdre, who was staring with avid attention. Fionola shook herself and stood tall, grabbing Charles's hand, and pulling him to her side.

In a loud, clear voice, she said, "I believe Maeve has cooked enough food to feed the entire town. Let's go feast!" Then she practically dragged Charles inside to the formal great hall. It was done. They were married, and tonight... Tonight would be a night to remember for the rest of her life.

CHAPTER NINETEEN

S CHARLES TURNED to walk with Fionola to the grand great
hall in the castle where they would have their wedding
feast, he could actually feel the blood draining from his face.

Seamus really is going to kill me.

But then he glanced at Fionola, whose hand descended to her
sword while she watched her former first mate with cold
appraisal, and corrected himself.

Fionola is going to kill Seamus.

"My injury pains me. I'm afraid I can't join for the feast,"
Seamus said, touching his bandaged belly gingerly. It happened to
bring his hand conveniently close to his sword.

Fionola glowered at him for a long moment, her hand resting
casually on her hilt, then said, "Thank you for coming. Go home
and rest like an aul wan if you must." She cracked a smile.

Seamus stared for a moment then chuckled. He and Fionola
grasped forearms and thumped each other on the back. "I'm not
the one wearing a dress, Captain."

She gave him a playful push, but they were both smiling.

Seamus turned to Charles, a warning glint in his eyes. "Take
good care of her, or you'll have me to answer to."

"As if I can't take care of myself," Fionola said, smacking his
arm.

Laughing, Seamus leaned in toward Charles. "She can. And

she's well-armed," he said, glancing at her sword. "Good luck surviving your wedding night."

Molly gave his arm a yank. "Come on, Seamus. Let's leave these newlyweds to their feasting. I'll walk you home."

She gave him a saucy look, and he grinned, pulling her away from the celebration and kissing her on the lips.

"Really," Maeve exclaimed. "They aren't even married yet," she said, shaking her head, but there was a smile on her face. "Inside, everyone. Inside. No need to give them an audience."

⟫⟩⟨⟪

THE FEAST WAS a delight. Charles had met the whole family that morning when he paid a visit, and he found breaking bread with them deeply moving. Maeve and Colm clearly loved Diedre, Molly, and Fionola deeply, and they'd welcomed him as a member of the family. He looked forward to getting to know Molly better at some point, but he suspected she wouldn't be around much in the near future.

Thomas and Ronan joked and laughed with Fionola and Colm, but they both seemed daunted by Maeve, who glared at them any time their table manners strayed from the height of decorum.

Ordinarily, Charles wouldn't want such a meal to end, but tonight he had other things on his mind. So did Fionola, who was squeezing his thigh beneath the table at that moment.

"Oh no, Maeve," he said, "I don't think I could possibly eat another helping of dessert. What about you?" he asked, turning to Fionola.

"Very full, Auntie," she told Maeve, patting her belly. "In fact, I'm feeling a bit tired. Perhaps we should retire?" she suggested, giving Charles a pointed look.

"Oh yes, of course. If you're tired, then certainly," he answered, grinning.

God yes. Finally!

Everyone at the table exchanged knowing looks. "Goodnight to the bride and groom," Colm said, raising a cup. "May they be joyful and fecund."

Fionola choked on her wine and needed a tall cup of water before she could stop coughing.

"To the bride and groom," said Ronan, raising his cup. "Be gentle with him, Captain. He's a delicate flower."

Charles's face heated, and he stared at the floor while Fionola bent over laughing.

"To the captain and first mate," said Thomas. "And to finding happiness in unexpected places."

"To my sweet girl and Charles," said Maeve. "Blessings on your marriage. May your love blossom forever."

"To my cousin," said Deirdre. "Thank you for the hair ribbon. I knew when we were eight that you'd beat me to the altar, though I confess I began to doubt myself when you started wearing that fake beard. But here we are. I'm glad to see you happy."

With that, they made their way up to Fionola's room and closed the door behind them.

The room was of modest size with stone walls and a wood floor covered in fresh rushes and herbs. A large, ornate canopy bed dominated the space, presumably booty from some ship's cargo. Otherwise, the room was quite plain and a little bit messy. Fionola didn't seem to be one for ornamentation or straightening up, not that it mattered. At least not on land.

He wrapped his arms around his bride and kissed her deeply. "*Mm.* The last week has been torture."

"For me too," she murmured into his chest, as he ran his hands down her back to her firm, shapely buttocks.

His arm knocked against her hilt. "Maybe we should take this off," he said with a smile, unbuckling her belt and leaning her sword and scabbard against the wall.

"I should put these away too," she said, removing a tiny knife from each sleeve.

"Were you wearing those the whole time?" he asked, in amused astonishment.

"Of course."

"Why?" He watched as she set the knives down on a small table.

"To kill you if you didn't follow through on your promises," she said with a smirk.

He laughed. "Did I give you reason to doubt me, Captain?" He came up behind her and began pulling pins out of her hair, releasing her glorious curls, and nuzzled her neck.

Her breath caught, and she leaned back into his embrace. "No. But I don't trust easily." She slowly swayed her hips back and forth, pressed against his growing arousal, and he swallowed hard.

"I've noticed. I'm grateful you've relinquished your blades for the evening." One of his hands settled on her hip while the other cupped one breast and teased a nipple through the fabric of her dress.

"Do you think I couldn't kill you with my bare hands?"

He gasped. By God, why did he find it so arousing when she reminded him exactly how dangerous she was? His cock was suddenly hard as a marble pillar. "To be honest, I never considered it," he said in a hoarse voice. "Perhaps I should have."

"Well, I promise not to kill you for performing the marital act." She turned around in his arms and kissed along his jaw.

"Did you just call it 'the marital act'?" he asked, unable to hide his amusement.

She narrowed her eyes. "Did I say something funny?"

"Yes, you did." He smiled broadly and pulled her close so that her whole body was pressed against his. *Mm.* She felt so good.

"What should I have said?" she asked, cocking her head. "That you can feck me?"

He breathed in sharply, pulling her hips closer still, trying to resist the urge to carry her over to the bed and sink into her right that moment.

No. This was her first time. He needed to go slowly.

"My dear wife," he said taking a deep breath and stepping back slightly, "what do you know about 'the marital act'?" He stroked her cheek and kissed her neck.

"Well," she began, "a man puts his cock in a woman's hole and fecks her until he spills his seed inside her, and if the woman is a virgin, she bleeds."

"Christ on the cross," Charles swore. "You really *did* learn everything you know from sailors, didn't you?" His fingers grasped the twin curves of her buttocks and squeezed.

"About fecking? Yes. Everyone else refused to explain it. I didn't believe what the sailors said at first, but then I saw one of them with a prostitute in an alley in Calais, and—"

He silenced her with a furious kiss, and she responded with equal fury. Her delicious lips and tongue were driving him to distraction. Unable to stop himself, he began backing her toward the bed. But when they reached it, he pulled back, panting. "I'm not going to fuck you tonight, Fionola."

"You're not?" She froze and stared at him.

"No, I'm not," he said, kissing her forehead and her cheek. "I'm going to make love to you."

She burst out laughing. "Charles, I'm not some delicate flower like the noblewomen you're used to. Make love..." She rolled her eyes. "That's like making a flower arrangement or making a honey cake. I don't want you to sing me feckin' love songs. I want your naked body pressing between my thighs."

"Oh fuck." At this rate he was going to come before he got his hose off.

She grabbed his shirt and turned him, then pushed him down on the bed. Careful not to put weight on her injured arm, she climbed on top of him, sitting astride him with her skirts hitched up.

Dear Lord, she had lovely legs. He so seldom got to see them, but here they were, peeking out from beneath all that fabric, somehow looking all the more naked because she was still clothed.

"Let me make you come, Fionola, and then I promise to make love to you until you start singing *me* love songs."

"Ha! That will never happen."

"I'm a patient man. But for now, I'll settle for you laying back and spreading your gorgeous legs."

She complied, giving him a wary look. "What are you going to do?"

"You'll find out in a moment. Yes, just like that." As he pushed up her skirts, he could smell the spicy tang of her arousal. He could hardly wait to taste her, lowering his head between her legs.

"You don't mean you're going to…"

"I most certainly am."

He licked, and she moaned. My God, she tasted sinful—sweet and salty with a touch of spice.

She jerked away from him, but he held on tight as his tongue continued to tickle and lap and drive against her relentlessly. She made a whimpering noise that spurred him on to even more vigorous torture. Writhing and gyrating, she let him drive her to the brink of insanity as he savored this secret part of her body that he'd been dying to taste.

Just as she was at the tipping point, he slowed, prolonging the sweet agony of the moment before—one slow lick and then another. At last, he had mercy on her and suckled her bud hard then grazed it lightly with his teeth. She succumbed to wave after wave of raw pleasure, and her reaction drove him to the brink. He needed to be inside her. He couldn't wait any longer or he was going to spend himself too soon.

As she lifted herself up and he reemerged from beneath her skirts, she was still catching her breath. "Charles, take your clothes off," she ordered in a husky voice.

Yes. "I'm yours to command, Captain," he said with a devilish smile. He stood and stripped off his clothes piece by piece, first peeling off the cotte, then shedding his shirt, and sliding out of his hose. She'd seen him before, so he had no fear of her reaction. Her eyes and smile grew wide as she saw his cock, twitching and straining for contact.

She reached out with her good arm and ran her hand down his naked chest, and he savored the feel of her touch. As her fingers trailed farther down, she traced them over his hot, hard arousal, and her smile widened. His breathing grew ragged at her caress. Her touch robbed him of all sense. There was nothing left but the firm grasp of her hand around his aching flesh. It was too much, especially in his current state of arousal.

"I want you naked. Now," he said, his voice rasping with desperate need. She gave him a sultry smile, seemingly amused by the challenge and hunger in his tone. "I want to see you as I enter you. I want to see all of you while I'm inside you."

He loosened the laces at her sides that held the bodice of her dress tight, and he pulled her to standing with her good arm. She was still dazed and languid from pleasure. With the same care as always, he helped her pull her right arm and head out of the garment and slide it down her injured left. He repeated the procedure with her shift, and at last they were bare. At last, he could feel the length of her against the length of him, and he wanted all of her.

He kissed her deeply, letting her taste herself on his lips, salty, carnal, and wicked. The way she kissed him back made every-thing within him scream for more. "Are you ready, Fionola?"

"Yes."

"Thank God."

He turned her around and seated himself on the bed, pulling her hips toward him until she was straddling him. His arousal rubbing against the sensitive places he'd just tantalized with his tongue, and she moved her hips, pressing against him, clearly needing more but not entirely sure how to go about it.

"Do it now. I'm ready," she ordered.

God, yes. Order me, Captain.

A shiver of anticipation ran through him as he moved her

into place.

"Yes, Captain," he said guiding her hips up and then positioning himself at her entrance with his hand, the tip just barely within her. "Take me in, Fionola. Slide down onto me at your own speed until I'm fully within you. You'll feel some pain because this is your first time, but I promise not to move until it passes."

And so, she slid down a little bit, stretching to accommodate him. He was desperate for more, but he knew he had to let her take her time, even if it killed him. She slid a little bit farther and paused. Charles's mouth hung open, and he breathed in quick, ragged pants. The effort to keep his word and hold absolutely still caused sweat to bead on his brow. She lowered herself even more, sliding down until she gave a startled gasp.

Gasping with the effort to keep his promise to hold still, he reached down and touched her to help ease her descent, and she clenched around him, making them both cry out.

So close. Oh, so close.

Rocking her hips from side to side, she slid down one last time with force, taking him all the way in. Another moan escaped him, and he bit his lip. *Oh, dear God!*

She gasped and froze, her eyes closed.

"How do you feel?" he asked, gasping for breath.

Instead of answering she took a deep breath, smiled, and began moving her hips. "Ready for you to make love to me until I sing."

And he had every intention of doing so if he could just manage to hold on and make this last. But oh, she made it so difficult. Being inside her was unlike anything he'd ever felt. It wasn't just the physical sensation that was different. In that moment, he felt a deep connection between them click into place like two magnets coming together. In his arms, she was softening, relenting, letting go. He was inside her and the captain was surrendering at last. They were one, and neither of them was alone.

Pressing up into her, he began to rock with her, guiding her and kissing her as she clung to him. She yielded control, letting him lead her in the rhythmic bliss that carried them both along. Whatever was happening between them was more than he'd ever experienced and something beyond words held them in thrall together.

Their movement sped up, and his yearning sharpened. He wanted this bliss to last, but his control hung by a thread. He needed friction, fruition. But that would mean the end of this, and so he held back, defying the torrent.

Then he looked into her eyes and stopped moving. "Fionola, am I hurting you?"

"What?"

"You're crying. Did I hurt you?" He thumbed away a tear.

"I'm not crying. I don't cry."

"My apologies. Of course not, Captain," he said gently, kissing her forehead. "But are you in pain?"

"No," she said, struggling to find words. "I...I feel too much. Don't stop. I need you."

He kissed her with all the raw desperation he felt, and she answered with equal intensity. Their bodies strained together, seeking a closer union. He turned them so that she was on her back. She squeezed around him as he thrust. Her body began to tremble, and he could feel something powerful building within her. Thank God. He didn't think he could last much longer. She writhed beneath him, and at last, the pulsation of her wave crashed within her, shattering her and leaving her dazed and boneless beneath him. At the very last moment, he pulled out, spending himself in the sheets.

When he was done, his chest heaved as he tried to catch his breath. He kissed her on top of her head and pulled her over to lie on top of him. She tucked her head beneath his chin, and he reveled in the delicious feeling of her body resting on his.

"I would sing, but I don't know any love songs. I had no idea it would feel like that," she murmured into his chest.

"I didn't either." He ran his hands gently down her back and squeezed her tight.

"But you've done this before." She propped her head up to look him in the eye.

He kissed her curls. "There is no one else like you on God's earth, and no one but you ever has, or ever will, make me feel so much."

Troubles aplenty awaited them outside these doors. Soon enough, they would have to return to reality and their search for Liam. But this moment was so perfect, he never wanted it to end. He held her close and breathed her in, knowing this momentary respite was temporary and determined to savor every last moment of it.

CHAPTER TWENTY

WHEN FIONOLA WOKE just before dawn to find someone in her bed, she panicked. A mere moment later, she had Charles pinned with her hands wrapped around his throat.

"Fionola?" he gasped.

She blinked, coming back to herself, and swiftly released him. This was not an auspicious start to their first day as a married couple.

"I'm sorry," she said as she sat back, still straddling his abdomen. She rubbed her injured shoulder gingerly. "I've never shared a bed before."

"Does it hurt?" he asked, nodding toward her shoulder.

She shrugged with her good shoulder. "It doesn't matter."

As she moved to climb off him, he grasped her thigh and pulled her back. "It matters to me," he said, gently caressing along her thighs and up her sides. His fingers traced the edge of the bandage over the swell of her breast.

Unable to resist his touch, she twisted to press her breast into his palm.

"Mm," he murmured, caressing and teasing. "How do you feel this morning? Are you sore from last night?"

She smiled. "Not sore. No." His arousal pressed against her bottom. Perhaps the morning didn't need to be a complete disaster. "I want more."

"Well, that's convenient because so do I." He grazed his fingers up her inner thighs and stopped teasingly close to where she wanted him. Did all men torture and tantalize their partners like this, or was it a specialty of Charles's? He wrapped his arms around her and turned them so that they were lying side by side, facing each other.

Dear Lord, look at that chest. At some point in the not-too-distant future, she was going to need to taste every delicious inch of him.

And then he touched her.

How did he manage to do this to her? She'd never been so helpless in her life as when she let him touch her. Everything else disappeared—all will, all awareness. Only pleasure remained, and she welcomed it even as it blew her apart in a thousand tingly pieces. She was terrifyingly vulnerable in this state. After a lifetime of defending herself against everyone that tried to encroach, she couldn't explain to herself why she let him in, let him incapacitate her like this. But dear God, it felt good.

"Come for me, Captain. Let me watch you come undone."

And she followed orders. Her. Captain O'Bannon.

As she caught her breath after a dizzying climax, Charles nudged her legs apart and eased into her. The sensation was so different, but no less intense. When he was merely touching or licking her, it was like touching lightning, every inch of her skin prickling with the intensity. When he was inside her, she felt like she must be glowing as everything within her became molten.

With Charles, she was swept away by the force and heat. Volatile. Radiant. Helpless in the face of something elemental. All she could do was surrender and let the sensations flow until she found the relief her body so desperately needed.

Once again, bursts of pleasure blinded her as they moved together. As the sensation began to dissipate, he pulled out just in time to spend himself on her belly.

"Does it bother you to do that?"

He slumped on the bed beside her, barely conscious. "Hmm?"

"Does it bother you not to leave your seed in me?"

He exhaled slowly. "It isn't easy. My body wants me to stay. But it doesn't bother me. I don't want to burden you with unwanted children."

"I might like children someday in the very distant future," she said, staring up at her canopy, surprised to hear herself speak her secret wish aloud. "Not before we find Liam, of course."

He propped himself up to face her. "Really? Because I would too, but only if you want them. Oh, let me clean you up." He stood up and went over to the pitcher and basin and poured some water on a cloth folded next to it. Returning, he carefully wiped up the pearly puddle he'd left on her.

"Yes, really," she said as he cleaned her up. "Maeve is right. I can't keep doing this forever. Once I have Liam back, I can hand things over to Seamus, and we can live as we please."

"But it would mean giving up being Captain O'Bannon," he said, setting aside the cloth. "I would never ask that of you. If you decide to remain the captain for the rest of our lives, I would still be content with our marriage."

She shook her head. "Thomas was right. I need to find a way to live as myself, and I am not Captain O'Bannon. Or rather I am not *only* Captain O'Bannon. I am also a woman named Fionola MacMurrough, and I have already spent too much of my life in disguise. I like being the captain, but I tire of the beard. I don't think I can give up the sea completely, but I can't give up being Fionola either."

He lay down beside her and kissed her sweetly. "Whether you are O'Bannon..." Kiss. "...or Fionola..." Kiss. "...or both..." Kiss. "I am yours." He kissed her deeply and thoroughly.

"Mm," she said as he released her. "We should head downstairs for breakfast. Maeve insists on punctuality. And she said she might take my stitches out today. I think the skin has healed enough, though I know it will take months for the wounds to fully heal."

AT BREAKFAST, MAEVE was all sweetness and care, giving them both extra helpings of everything, as if they weren't stuffed enough from what she'd already served.

"So what are you two lovebirds going to do today?"

Charles turned bright red and stared down into his plate. Fionola couldn't help but smile. She was thinking along similar lines. But perhaps they should get out of the castle a bit. There were other quiet places on Gan Ainm where they could do as they pleased undisturbed.

"I thought I would take Charles on a tour of the island. I don't think he's seen anything but the town."

"I haven't," he said, letting Maeve foist a third apple tart on him.

"Auntie, do you think we could pack a lunch?" She knew the answer before asking, of course. They would be lucky to get out the door with less than a wagon full of food. "A small lunch, something easy to carry," she added for good measure.

"Of course, my dear," said Maeve, already bustling to assemble a basket.

"I'd better go get my beard and scarf," she said and rose to leave.

"Wait," Maeve exclaimed, pausing in her work. "I need to look at your shoulder. Perhaps Charles can go get what you need."

Charles made a little bow to Maeve and went on his way.

Deirdre came running in, and Maeve pinned her with a glare. "You're late."

"Sorry, Mum," Deirdre said, her head down in contrition. "I'll help with the dishes to make up for it. Where is Da?"

Maeve huffed. "Come and gone. He's working on repairs to the *Draconis*, and there's still work to be done on the *Midas* to turn her into...I think they were going to call it the *Athena*?"

Fionola smiled. She insisted that the ships they stole be renamed for powerful women.

"Now that it's just us ladies, how do you feel this morning?" Maeve asked.

Ah, so that's why she sent Charles away.

"I feel good, though I confess was a bit startled to wake up with someone in my bed this morning."

"I'm surprised he's still alive," Deirdre mumbled under her breath.

"What was that?" Maeve asked, and Deirdre put on an innocent smile.

"Nothing at all, Mum."

Maeve fixed Deirdre with a long look but said nothing. Turning to Fionola, she said, "Take off your shirt, and let's take a look at those stitches."

Fionola obeyed, pulling off her cotte and shirt carefully. While her flesh might have healed on the surface, movement was still limited and painful.

Unwrapping the bandages, Maeve looked closely at the three scars—the large one on her shoulder and the two smaller ones on her arm. "I think we can take these all out. I'll go get my scissors." She bustled out, leaving Fionola alone with Deirdre.

"Quick, before she comes back, tell me everything," Deirdre whispered.

Fionola furrowed her brow. "What do you want to know?"

"Did it hurt?"

Fionola nodded. "But not much."

"Was it…pleasant?"

At that, Fionola blushed.

"I'll take that as a yes," Deirdre whispered, squeezing Fionola's arm. "Was it scary? I mean…I know you're not scared of anything, but was it…unnerving to let a man touch you like that and put his…his…" Deirdre made an obscene but accurate hand motion, "…inside you?"

"I—"

"Oh no, here comes Mum. Act natural."

Fionola had rarely been so relieved about an interruption. Maeve came in with tiny sewing scissors and tweezers and set to work on her shoulder. When she was halfway through, Charles returned with Fionola's beard and scarf and gave a start at seeing her half naked.

"Oh, I'm sorry. I'll just go somewhere else for a bit, shall I? Yes. Yes, I'll do that."

He disappeared, and all three of them burst into laughter.

"I don't think I've ever seen Charles so flustered," Fionola said.

"I don't know why," Deirdre said. "It's not as if he hasn't seen you."

Staring intently at the final stitches, Maeve said, "I suspect I'm the one that sent him running. It's one thing to see your wife half naked in the privacy of your bedroom and something else entirely to have her stern Auntie looking on while you do it."

Giggles overtook them once again.

"There. You're all done. You can get dressed and go find that husband of yours," Maeve said, standing back to check her handiwork. "And you," she said, turning to Deirdre, "dishes. Now please."

As FIONOLA ESCAPED the castle with Charles, she couldn't help wondering if she would come home to find Deirdre had eloped. With whom, she had no idea, but it wasn't going to be easy for Deirdre to be the only remaining focal point for all of Maeve's mothering. Fionola loved Maeve with all her heart, but it was all a bit much sometimes. She was glad she could go out to sea and escape for long stretches.

"Are we riding or walking?" Charles asked as they passed the small castle stable.

"Definitely walking," she said a little too vehemently.

He tilted his head to the side, and there was the tiniest hint of a sideways grin. "Do you have something against riding?"

She looked down at her boots. "Horses don't like me," she mumbled.

"What was that?" he asked, leaning in.

"I said, 'horses don't like me.'" She still couldn't meet his eyes, and she could feel her cheeks growing hot. It was embarrassing, really. They were a mode of transportation. That was all. Riding should have been like sailing, but instead, the beasts seemed to discover they had a mind of their own when she sat on them. The harder she tried to impose her will, the more willful they became in response. On the rare occasions when horses tolerated her on their backs, she'd come away with every muscle in her body aching from clinging to the beast for dear life for the duration of the ride. Why would anyone ride a horse when they had two perfectly good feet to walk on? Not that she would ever admit any of this out loud.

Charles couldn't contain his mirth. "I'm sorry," he said, laughing. "You're so good at everything. I never would have expected something so simple to confound you."

She looked at the sky in a silent prayer to Saint Brigid for something, anything to distract them from this conversation.

"What else are you secretly bad at?"

She let out a long, slow breath. "It's not secret. I just don't talk about it."

"Mmhmm." Still laughing, the cursed man.

"I'm also a terrible archer, terrible housekeeper, and a terrible cook. Are you happy?"

Reining in his laughter, he gave her a sweet smile and kissed her forehead. "Very happy, Captain."

A moment later, they arrived at the turn onto the road to the village. As they stepped out into the street, she and Charles slipped into their roles as captain and first mate again, waving to members of the crew as they passed, at least until they were out of sight of the last of the buildings. Then she shed her beard, tucking it into the bag with their lunch, and held his hand.

They spent the morning making a circuit of the island, passing a handful of farms, and walking through a forest of oak and pine. At last, they arrived at a high, grass-covered promontory that ended in a cliff overlooking the sea.

She stopped on a little plateau at the highest point. "Do you want to eat lunch before or after?" she asked as Charles put down the bag with the food.

"Before or after what?" From his grin, it was clear he had suspicions, and yes, that was part of the plan, but not the whole thing.

She said nothing and smiled in return.

After a long moment, he said, "Lunch after, I think."

Her smile widened. "Take off your clothes," she ordered, and she began stripping her own off. He looked around as if concerned someone might see them. "We're safe up here. No one ever comes here except me."

He started stripping down as fast as he could. When they were both naked, she gave him a long, tantalizing kiss and then broke away.

"Now follow me." She turned around and ran to the edge of the cliff and jumped off without looking back. She hugged the injured arm against her chest with her other arm to shield it as she hit the water. As she surfaced, she was relieved that she didn't seem to have done any damage.

She swam aside to give Charles room to make the jump.

"Are you mad?" he yelled from the top of the cliff. "You're still recovering from an injury."

"I'm fine," she yelled back. "Come and see for yourself."

He looked at the drop and then at her. "God's wounds, Captain. This is insane. Is there another way down?"

Laughing, she treaded water in the waves. "I've done this a hundred times. It's safe, I promise. If you're scared, try a running start."

He paced naked a few feet back from the edge of the cliff, running his hands through his hair.

"I bet your sisters would do it," she yelled. Even from this distance, she could sense his glare.

A moment later, he came plummeting down with a guttural yell. Someday, she had to meet these sisters of his. As he surfaced, she started swimming sideways toward the beach of the small cove beside the cliff. He swam after her, and his strokes were much stronger since he had two working arms. The distance was closing quickly, so she dove beneath the waves and swam over by a rock formation at the edge of the cove. Opening her eyes under water, and ignoring the stinging salt, she spotted a small octopus and caught it gently between her hands.

As she surfaced, Charles caught up and wrapped a strong arm around her from behind. His hand found her breast, and he nipped at her ear. "So I caught you," he murmured. "What's my reward?"

She laughed, held up the octopus, and draped it over his arm. It promptly wriggled back into the sea. "See? Not all animals hate me. Just horses."

He stared and laughed, and then laughed some more. "If ever I needed a sign from heaven that you are the woman for me…"

He trailed off, pulling her toward the shallows. As soon as he could put his feet down on the bottom, he turned her around, pulling her legs around his hips. His arousal pressed against her, hot and insistent even in the chilly water, and she melted against him, hungering for his touch, needing more.

Her lips found his, and they tasted and tugged and nipped at each other in a tender battle. This was no gentle love making. They had tipped over the edge to something far wilder and more carnal. His fingers dug into the cheeks of her bottom, and her own fingers raked his back. He carried her up to the beach and lowered himself to a flat sun-warmed rock. His finger reached between her legs to stroke, and she closed her eyes and wailed.

Moments later, she pulled his hand away and grabbed his cock. "I'm going to make you beg for mercy," she whispered in his ear, eliciting an animal moan from him as she placed him at her entrance and slid down, letting him fill her.

From that moment on, everything was instinct and sensation. She was vaguely aware of the furious motion of their bodies together as she rode him, but her attention was consumed by the sharpening hunger for a release that kept building and building. She needed all of him, and what she had didn't feel like nearly enough.

"Oh my God. Fionola. It's too much. I'm going to…. I have to…. Please, you have to let me go before it's too late."

But she was lost to everything except the waves of pleasure rocking her, one after another, as she reached fruition at last.

Something throbbed within her, the most delicious sensation she could imagine, as she came back to earth and looked down at her lover. Something hot and wet dripped along her inner thigh as the last tremor of their coupling rocked them both.

Charles's eyes were wide, and he was hardly breathing. "I'm so sorry."

Her brow furrowed. Why was he apologizing?

"I should have had more control. I should have pushed you away, but you were gripping me so tightly."

"What?" She was still dazed from their coupling and couldn't figure out what he was talking about.

"I left my seed inside you."

She looked down at the pearly liquid dripping along her inner thigh.

Oh no.

CHAPTER TWENTY-ONE

Three weeks later

"FIONOLA, WE CAN'T keep this a secret much longer. Maeve already figured it out, and now Colm and Deirdre know. We should at least speak with Thomas and Ronan. We need a plan."

Charles watched as Fionola drank a cup of water, plucked two mint leaves off a plant on the windowsill, and stuffed them in her mouth. She had just vomited in the chamber pot for the second time this morning. His guilt greeted him along with the morning sun, as it had every day since he lost control on the beach. He didn't mind becoming a father, but it was clear Fionola didn't want to be a mother, at least not yet. He'd never intended to burden her with this, especially when so much still hung in the balance regarding Liam.

Ever since their failed attack on the *Gorgon*, she'd been desperate for news of where it was headed next. Carrying a child hadn't dampened her determination to find her brother one bit. She questioned her crew endlessly about their efforts to track it down. At least, she did when she wasn't vomiting.

She sat down on the bed and put her head in her hands.

"Captain?"

She raised her head briefly to glare at him then closed her

eyes again and hung her head between her knees.

"Captain, you can't get on the *Draconis* tomorrow and set sail without a plan."

"Leave me alone," she said in a gruff voice.

"Don't you think someone is going to notice if the captain is suddenly seasick every morning? And what about when you start showing? I'm sorry this happened, but—"

A warning rumble came from her throat.

"—but you can't flee from it. Please let's tell our friends before they find out some other way."

He crouched down beside her and put a gentle hand on her back, not moving, just resting it there. She told him three days ago that when she was nauseous, friction from movement made her skin crawl. By afternoon, she was usually fine again, but morning sickness had incapacitated her for hours every morning for the last week.

"If you truly want to keep this secret, we have to go away somewhere."

"We have to keep looking for Liam," she said without lifting her head.

"Then we have to tell at least enough people to crew the *Draconis*. To do that, we need our friends, and we need a plan. Setting sail and attempting to keep this secret is not an option."

Taking a deep breath, she said, "All right. We tell Thomas and Ronan, and we come up with a plan. Go take care of it."

The captain was back, giving orders. It was a good sign. "Yes, Captain."

HALF AN HOUR later, Charles returned with Thomas, Ronan, and Colm to find Fionola sitting in the kitchen with Maeve and Deirdre, nibbling at a freshly baked ginger cake with an expression of disgust. Poor Fionola. Maeve's ginger cakes were delicious. Charles picked one up and started to eat.

"Captain, I have good news for you, but is everything all right?" Thomas asked, examining her face. "You don't look well."

Ronan looked her up and down and raised an eyebrow, amusement causing the corners of his mouth to turn up. "Congratulations, Captain. I've never met a man carrying a child before. My felicitations on your unique predicament."

Thomas's head jerked around, and he stared at Fionola at the word "child."

"How did you know?" Fionola asked, scowling at Ronan as she pushed the plate with the ginger cake away.

"I've never known you to have stomach troubles on land or sea, and you look like a man in shock, not a man recovering from a minor ailment. Mind if I finish that?" he asked pointing at her barely touched ginger cake. She pushed it over to him.

"When did you realize?" Thomas asked, taking a seat at last.

"A week ago. What is your good news?"

Thomas nodded. "We've gotten word of where the *Gorgon* is headed. It's currently at Brest. From there, it's headed to Calais, then on to Winchelsea."

The last word hit Charles like a thunderclap. He fumbled his ginger cake, and it dropped to the table. "Winchelsea?"

With an understanding look, Thomas nodded.

Oblivious, Maeve passed around a basket of warm rolls. "I think it's nothing short of madness for her to set sail in her condition."

"My dear," Colm interjected. "We can't wait nine months to go after Liam. We might not ever find the *Gorgon* again. And every day he's on that ship, he is in danger. There's no telling whether he could survive that long."

"You could go without her." Maeve's hands were on her hips as she stared her husband down.

"No!" Fionola slammed her hand down on the table. She looked around at her friends and family, her gaze coming to rest on Charles. "I will be there when we rescue Liam. We head for

Winchelsea."

Charles sat down hard on the bench across from her and rested his face in his hands. He couldn't go back to Winchelsea. But could he let Fionola go without him? Absolutely not, given her condition. He had to be by her side. But in Winchelsea, someone was bound to recognize him. And thanks to Black Stephen's lies, he would be risking death setting foot in his old home.

"I've had word from Winchelsea as well," said Thomas. Charles's head snapped up. "I put out feelers as soon as we came back to Gan Ainm. I thought you might want word of your family and what story Black Stephen might have told to explain your disappearance. The locals think you died in a shipwreck."

Hope blossomed in Charles's heart. Did he dare go back? How would they react after all this time? Would they recognize him? Would he even be able to gain access to them? No one would believe he returned from the dead. And even if they did, he had changed too much from the son they remembered. His mind was too unsteady to be the heir once again.

And if by some miracle they accepted him back, they were not going to approve of Fionola. No one who met her would believe she was a high-born lady, despite her being the granddaughter of a king. The only time he'd ever seen her in a dress was on their wedding day. And God help them both if his father learned they were pirates.

Then there was the matter of how much he had changed. It would be good to see them, but it was inevitable that they would be disappointed and distressed by what he had become. Did he dare take his precious new family there with all the uncertainty?

Still, they were his family, and they loved him. A well of emotion swelled in his chest at the thought of seeing them again. He didn't want to spend his whole life hiding from his past, nor did he want to deprive his child of his birthright. While Charles could never inherit, his son could, but only if his parents knew about their grandchild.

Charles cleared his throat. "I'm not sure they'll recognize me. I've changed a lot since I set sail for Ireland. It may be difficult to get an audience with my father, but—"

Pausing, Charles looked his wife in the eyes. "I believe they will welcome us once they are convinced that I am their son." *Hopefully.* "And they won't let any harm come to their grandchild. But Fionola, this means playing the part of a noblewoman. Are you sure?"

"I'm the granddaughter of a king. I was raised for this. You don't think I can pull this off?"

Maeve raised a skeptical brow. "Are you sure you're ready to wear dresses and curtsey and hold your tongue unless you are spoken to? You hated all of that as a girl. Do you even remember how to curtsey?"

Fionola gave her a sharp look. "You think Mother taught me nothing?"

Maeve raised her hands in a conciliatory gesture.

Charles closed his eyes. This plan was full of holes, but he couldn't come up with a better one. They needed to catch the *Gorgon* and get away from Gan Ainm. But did it have to be Winchelsea? "I hadn't planned to return. I wanted to live as a simple sailor."

Opening his eyes, he looked over at his wife.

Something softened in her gaze, as she said, "We don't need to stay there long. I want a better life for our child than we can offer aboard the *Draconis*. And you yourself said we'll need to go away to keep my secret. Who knows how the rest of Gan Ainm would react to learning I'm a woman? They might burn me at the stake for witchcraft. We head to Winchelsea, rescue my brother, then as soon as we have him, we find somewhere safe to stay in France until the baby is born."

"Where will we go?" he asked slowly.

"Anywhere. I don't care, but this is the safest and best option until the child arrives, and it gives us a chance to rescue Liam. We can figure the rest out once we've got my brother safely in our hands."

Everyone else looked on in silence. He fervently wished she'd brought this up when they were alone before bringing it to the group.

He looked around at them and then at her. "Fine. We go to Winchelsea." Their friends nodded discreetly. Whatever doubts he had, everyone else seemed to think this was the right course of action. "But we still need to figure out how we get there. Either we need a very convincing story, or we need to tell the crew."

Thomas cleared his throat. "Captain, I think it's time for you to shed the disguise at least with a select few."

Fionola shook her head. "They won't follow a woman. God only knows what they'll do when they find out."

"We follow you," Ronan said. "It takes more than a beard and balls to make a captain. You're a leader. It shows in everything you do. That will still be true when they find out the beard is fake, and nothing dangles between your legs."

Maeve made a disapproving noise and glared at Ronan. He reddened and stared at his feet.

Taking a deep breath, Fionola said, "What if it goes wrong when we tell them? We need fifteen men in addition to ourselves. Seamus can't join. He still isn't fully healed. Fifteen men is still enough to overwhelm us."

"Then we tell them one by one," Thomas said. "Any that react poorly, we can hold in the great hall until dawn and then send them off with the *Athena*. The rest must swear an oath of secrecy."

Colm nodded and stroked his beard. "Yes, that could work."

Maeve shrugged. "At least you could stop wearing that ridiculous beard."

"Fionola?" Charles asked. This was her decision to make.

"Fine. Draw up a list and start bringing them in one by one. The willing go to Aunt Maeve in the kitchen for food and drink, the unwilling go to the great hall with Uncle Colm. Once we have fifteen willing, we stop. Charles, Ronan, and Thomas, you're with me. Colm, you'll fetch the men and bring them to us one at a time. I need to go take a walk somewhere with no food smells. We regroup and review the list at noon. Agreed?"

She stood up, gritting her teeth and looking pale.

"Aye, Captain," they all said at the same time.

AT THE AGREED upon hour that afternoon, Charles stood behind Fionola, who was wearing her beard, and tried to keep his face blank as their first potential crew member walked through the door. Ronan and Thomas stood to the side, armed and ready should things go badly awry.

Henri was the first to enter.

"What is this, Captain? Did I do something wrong? I thought I was supposed to be preparing for our departure tomorrow," he said, looking around nervously.

"No, you've done nothing wrong," Fionola reassured. "There's something I need to tell you."

Here it comes.

Thomas and Ronan stiffened slightly and rested their hands on their hilts.

"Or really, it's something I need to show you," Fionola said, pulling down her scarf and taking off her beard.

Henri gasped and stared. "You're a woman?"

"I am."

"Jesus. How many times have I taken a piss in front of you?"

Ronan stifled a chuckle.

Fionola laughed aloud. "More times than either of us can count. But I need to know whether you are willing to continue to serve under me, knowing the truth of who I am. My name is Fionola MacMurrough. I'm King Dermott MacMurrough of Leinster's granddaughter, and I'm hunting Black Stephen to rescue my brother, Liam, who my grandfather gave away as a hostage."

For a long moment, Henri stared silently. Brow furrowed.

After what felt like an eternity, Henri shrugged. "You got me out of Black Stephen's ship, and you're making me rich. Why would I care if you have a dick? Though I may be more careful now about where and when I piss…"

"There are two more things you should know." She looked up at Charles who gave her a reassuring nod. "I married Charles, and I'm expecting his child."

Henri smiled broadly. "Hey, congratulations, Captain!"

"Thanks, Henri. That means a lot." She got up, and they clapped each other on the shoulder in a manly half hug.

As they released each other, Fionola said, "Would you mind waiting for me in the kitchen? There's food and ale in there. I have to speak with more men. Once I have a full crew. I want to talk to you together."

Rubbing his hands together, Henri said, "Ooh, free food. I'm in."

Thomas led him out of the room.

"That went well," Charles said, squeezing Fionola's shoulder. "We're off to a good start."

Thomas returned, and moments later, Colm knocked and led in Aidan. They repeated the reveal, and Aidan's eyes went wide. Then he dropped into a deep bow.

"My lady, you are a warrior, and I am your humble servant."

"Aidan, stand up," Fionola said. "I'm your captain, that's all." She shifted in her seat and cleared her throat.

Rising, Aidan said, "You saved my life. So many you have rescued! We owe you everything. I honor you, my la—excuse me, my captain."

Fionola smiled. "So you are willing to continue to serve on my crew?"

"Of course, Captain. I am at your service always."

Nodding, Fionola said, "Thank you, Aidan. I should also let you know…" She took a deep breath, then forged ahead. "I married Charles, and I am now with child."

Aidan beamed and clapped his hands together. "A thousand blessings on you both!"

"Thank you," she said, bowing her head in acknowledgment. "Can you wait with Henri in the great hall? I have more men to meet. I'll join you in a bit to talk about our upcoming voyage."

"Of course, Captain."

Thomas showed him out, and Ronan ushered in the next one.

Over and over, the conversation repeated. In the end, they only needed to meet with sixteen to get a crew of fifteen. Only one raised an objection to continuing to serve Fionola, and his concern was for her safety and that of her child. He didn't think he could be party to putting her in harm's way, though he agreed to keep her secret. Colm sent him on his way, confident he would not tell.

Every one of those men owed their lives to her, some several times over. As Charles suspected, they were too deeply indebted to her and in awe of her abilities to raise objections. Granted, these were the sixteen men they all thought were most likely to respond positively. If her secret got out to the two hundred or so people that lived on the island, the response might have been very different, but for now, she was safe and had a loyal crew. That was all that mattered.

At long last, they joined the group in the kitchen, gathered around the table. Maeve kept bustling about with more food, obviously delighted to have so many to feed. Fionola stood on a crate, and Charles moved to the back of the room. This was her moment.

"Friends. Brothers," she began in her captain's voice. "It means more than I can say to have you here with me tonight, to know that you all accept me as I am. My given name may not be O'Bannon, but I am and always shall be Captain of the *Draconis!*"

Charles joined the rest, banging his tankard of ale against the table and stomping in loud approval.

"Tomorrow, we set sail for Winchelsea. There, I hope to free my brother, Liam, from the *Gorgon*. He's been in Black Stephen's clutches for five years. He started on the *Midas*, then was transferred to the *Xerxes*. You were on the *Xerxes*, weren't you

Henri?"

"I was," Henri said, raising his tankard. "And I wouldn't be alive today if you hadn't freed me."

"Well, the *Midas* took him back before we got to him, and he was sent to the *Gorgon* about a month ago. Here's to catching the *Gorgon* and finding my brother at long last!" They all drank to that.

"My friends, I am going to need to leave you for a while. A pirate ship is no place to give birth. After Winchelsea, Charles, my brother, and I will make a home in France until the baby and I are ready to travel. Once we rescue Liam, I am asking that you leave me and return to Gan Ainm. We will rejoin you here when we are ready. Ronan will be your captain back to Gan Ainm, and Seamus will take over from there. You will carry on our sacred mission to end Black Stephen's tyranny. You will maraud and capture treasures untold from thieves who don't deserve them. You will continue to build Gan Ainm into an island paradise that welcomes one and all. Because you are the crew of the *Draconis*," she said in a loud voice.

The hall burst into cheers and banging.

"*Draconis*," she called out. The noise increased.

"*Draconis*," she bellowed louder. The noise became deafening.

"*Draconis!*" she roared, and they were thunder itself.

Charles knew the men were hers and always would be. They were the family she'd never had, and they would go to the ends of the earth for her.

CHAPTER TWENTY-TWO

H ALF AN HOUR later, when she had sent her crew away to prepare for tomorrow's journey, she led Charles back to their room, where the late afternoon sun slanted through the window. As soon as the door closed, she pushed him up against it, reaching beneath his tunic and stroking him through his hose.

"I am Captain Fionola MacMurrough. Say it."

"You are Captain Fionola MacMurrough," he whispered, barely able to form the words. Ever since the accidental loss of control on the beach, she had kept her distance, sharing a bed but hardly touching him. The sudden return of her interest left him breathless with gratitude and longing.

She kissed him without relenting with her hand. She opened her lips and running her tongue across his so that he opened to her. He moaned as her tongue twisted around his.

Too soon, she backed away. Grabbing the front of his tunic, she pulled him toward the bed. She was radiant in the golden light, all traces of the morning's troubles gone. An impish sideways smile spread across her face, and her green eyes sparkled and flashed.

She pushed him down onto the bed. Above him on her hands and knees, she said, "Do you serve your captain?"

He gulped. "Always and in all things."

She lowered herself, her face so close their breath mingled.

He thought she was going to kiss him, but she pulled away at the last moment.

"Take off your clothes," she ordered, standing to remove her own clothes, which were nearly identical to his own. He noticed idly as she pulled off her cotte that her shoulder's range of motion was improving. She could lift her arm perpendicular to her body now. It was a relief to see her healing so quickly. But there were more important matters at hand, like her gorgeous naked body and his own desperate need for her.

Sitting on the bed, she spread her legs for him. "Kneel," she ordered, and he obeyed, knowing what she wanted without further instruction, the spicy aroma of her arousal drawing him in. He couldn't help moaning as he tasted her. It was pure heaven after nearly a month without. She trembled beneath him as he brought her to her peak. Sweet Jesus, he had missed this so much.

She shuddered beneath his ministrations, shaken by the first waves of her release. Her back arched off the bed, and she cried out his name, clutching his hair and pressing herself against his tongue.

When he pulled away, leaving her spent and content, at least for the moment, she sat up and whispered in his ear, "Do you want to make love to me?"

With a swift intake of breath, he answered, "Yes."

"Yes what?"

He smiled slowly as he understood. "Yes, I do, but only with your permission, Captain Fionola MacMurrough."

She smiled wickedly. "Very well. You'll have to wait and see if I give it. I may need convincing."

"Yes, Captain." He kissed her inner thigh, then grazed it lightly with his teeth. "Fionola." He kissed her belly then traced his tongue up to her breast, suckling her nipple until she moaned. "MacMurrough." Backing away, he hovered over her without touching. It was agony to wait, but captain's orders were captain's orders.

"May I?" he asked, breathing hard.

"God yes," she said, arching towards him.

He claimed her mouth with his own and thrust into her at the same moment.

She cried out, and it was the most beautiful sound he'd ever heard. They rocked together in a tantalizing dance until he could hold back no more.

Closing his eyes and gritting his teeth, he pressed forward until he was embedded to the hilt. He reached between them to find her swollen bud, and he stroked it with his finger, as he continued to move within her. Almost immediately, the telltale pulsation began. She was as close as he was.

Not long now, he told himself as wave after wave of release rocked her. Each reverberation squeezed and pulled him deeper. He was barely hanging on. At last, he let go. He had followed orders to the extent he could. All he could do was ride the tide of sensation as it took him and obliterated all thought and intention.

Afterward, as they lay in each other's arms, recovering and deliciously sated, his mind couldn't help going back to the end point of this journey. Home. Or at least what he once considered home. How would he be received now? How would they treat Fionola?

"It's going to be fine," Fionola murmured against his chest. Had she guessed what he was thinking? "The family that raised a man like you can't be too terrible."

He kissed her head. "They're good people but set in their ways. I don't know how they will react to you or to me. I can't see them turning us away, but it won't be the welcome I dreamed of when I was in captivity."

She gave him a squeeze. "Nothing is ever the way we dream it will be, but that doesn't mean it can't be good. I never dreamed I would meet you, but look at us."

"You don't hate me for getting you pregnant?"

She turned to look him in the eyes. "It was my fault too. I wouldn't let you go. You tried to warn me, but I ignored you."

"I still shouldn't have—"

"I don't hate you. I love you."

"What?" He was silent for a long moment, trying to take in what she said. Was it possible this miraculous woman felt for him what he felt for her?

"I said, 'I love you.'"

Tears formed in his eyes. His heart beat like thunder within his chest. "I love you too."

"I know. You told me so even before you knew who I was."

She propped her head up on her hands.

"Yes, but then I loved a dream. Now I love *you*—Captain Fionola MacMurrough, pirate captain, liberator, devoted sister, magnificent lover, octopus catcher, horse avoider... You are my captain, my wife, and the mother of our child, and I love you more with each day that passes."

She reached up and kissed him tenderly.

⟶⟫⟪⟵

BEFORE DINNER THAT evening, Fionola had a moment alone with Maeve. "Have you seen Deirdre? I haven't seen her since yesterday. I wanted to say goodbye."

"I don't know where she went," Maeve said, grinding something fragrant with a mortar and pestle. "She's been very secretive these last few days. I'm starting to wonder if she's going to surprise us with a husband too, though I have no idea who it would be. You girls are going to be the death of me, I swear."

Fionola put an arm on Maeve's shoulder. "I'm sorry for any pain I've caused you. Can I help with anything?"

Maeve pointed her to a bowl of rising bread dough that had to be kneaded and put back in for a second rise before baking. "You have nice strong arms," Maeve said, as Fionola began kneading. "And it's not the pain you've caused me. It's the pain you're about to cause. Do you have to go away for the birth of your baby? I know how to care for a laboring mother. When my sister gave birth to her twins, I attended her. It pains me no end to think I won't be there for you when your time comes."

"Auntie," Fionola took a deep breath. "Everyone here thinks I'm a man. I can't stay."

Maeve sighed and shook her head. "It breaks my heart."

"I'm sorry. I love you, Auntie," Fionola said, pausing in her kneading to hug Maeve.

"I love you too."

"I didn't mean to make you cry."

Maeve wiped her tears and waved Fionola away. "It's just the onions I was chopping earlier."

DINNER THAT EVENING was a solemn affair. Deirdre showed up late and was uncharacteristically silent, and Maeve could hardly keep her composure at the prospect of losing Fionola for nearly a year. Colm would be back in a month or so, but Fionola…

There were hugs and more than a few tears as everyone went their separate ways that night. They would be setting sail before dawn in the morning, so now was their last chance for goodbyes.

"I love you like my own. You know that don't you?" Maeve asked, holding Fionola in a tight grasp. For some reason Deirdre had tears in her eyes as she looked on. Deirdre never cried before when they left. What was different this time?"

"You're family now too," she said, turning to Charles. "My blessings on you both, and make sure you bring her back as soon as you can. I want to see your beautiful baby before he or she learns to walk."

Charles nodded and squeezed Maeve's shoulder. "I'll bring them back, I promise."

IT WAS FOGGY and unseasonably cool as they left port at the crack of dawn. Fionola's heart ached at saying goodbye to Maeve, Deirdre, Molly, and Seamus, but it was good to be at sea again. And for once she was at sea as herself, no need for a disguise. She was surrounded by loyal men who accepted her as she was. It made her almost giddy.

The day passed without incident, but as the sun was setting, Ronan came storming out of the hatching with a slim boy she didn't recognize in tow. "Captain, we have a stowaway, and you're not going to believe who it is."

Fionola peered at the face and gasped. "Deirdre, what do you think you're doing? Maeve will have my head."

"Please don't send me back," Deirdre said, fists clenched, and brow furrowed. "I left a letter for Mum so that she'd know where I was and that I was safe. I told her I did this on my own. You had nothing to do with it." She paused and gave Fionola a pleading look. "You've sailed across the entire Atlantic. I've seen Wexford and Gan Ainm, and that's all. You were far younger than me when you started sailing disguised as a man, and this is so much safer because I have you and Da to look out for me."

"Does your father know?"

Deirdre shook her head. "I thought I'd wait until we were at sea to tell him."

Auntie Maeve really was going to have her head and Uncle Colm might well tell them to turn the ship around, but Fionola could hardly deny Deirdre the chance to do what she herself had done. Deirdre was an adult. If she could prove herself useful, then as captain, she couldn't come up with a reason to turn her away.

"First, go talk to your father. You can't keep this a secret, and I won't keep you here against his will."

Deirdre hung her head. "I will," she said, staring at her toes.

"After that," Fionola continued, "you'll need to prove you are a worthy member of the crew. Climb up the rigging—those are the rope ladders—and tell Finnegan he can come down. You're keeping watch for the next two hours. Show me you have the courage to do this."

Deirdre blanched. "You know I'm not good with heights."

"Every member of my crew takes a turn keeping watch. If you can't do it, you don't belong on this ship." It was harsh but true. She remembered well when she learned this particular lesson. She'd shaken like a leaf the whole time.

"It's a test."

"Yes. If you pass, there are other tests. If you fail, I send you home with your father. Are we clear?"

"Yes, Captain."

Fionola smiled at the deadly serious look on Deirdre's face. "Then go. I know you can do it."

Ten minutes later, Charles came striding over to her. "Captain, is that Deirdre in the crow's nest?"

"It is. She stowed away to join the crew. I told her I'd give her a chance if she proved herself. So far, she's doing well." Fionola peered up at the crow's nest, shading her eyes. Deirdre had a death grip on the mast but otherwise seemed to be managing.

"Your aunt won't be happy, but as captain, it's your decision."

She nodded. "It is. Don't forget it." Was he questioning her decisions? "I am the captain, married or not, and my word on this ship is law."

"Yes, Captain." He lowered his head in deference. Good. He understood his position.

"When we are alone, we are equals, but not out here. Do you understand?"

Charles took a deep breath and let it out slowly. "Yes, Captain. I am yours to command."

"Good." She gave him a stern look and murmured under her breath, "I'm going to my cabin. Go check our progress with Uncle Colm then meet me there." Without waiting for his response, she went below.

THE MAN WAS punctual. She appreciated that. Soon after she

headed below decks, he followed, and shortly after that, they were naked, and he was driving her out of her mind with pleasure. It was delightful to be able to do this without fear, not that they weren't being quiet and discreet, but if someone found out, at worst a crew member might be irritated. It was strange to let go of the constant tension and vigilance that governed her life at sea up to that point.

As they cleaned themselves up and dressed to resume their work, Charles couldn't stop grinning. "You have to stop smiling or they'll all know what we were doing."

"Sorry, Captain. I'll try to look less like a man who has been well and thoroughly fucked." He toned down the smile. She was almost sorry he obeyed.

She took a deep fortifying breath. "We should get back on deck. Let's sail to Winchelsea, shall we?"

CHAPTER TWENTY-THREE

THE TWO-WEEK VOYAGE passed quickly, despite the monotony of life at sea. Charles couldn't have been happier, sailing by day and making love to Fionola by night. And also, sometimes during the day. They were newlyweds, after all. Fortunately, Fionola's morning sickness abated somewhat. Being at sea agreed with her, and her cheeks took on a new bloom in the sea breeze. He didn't mind the traveling time at all. It was the destination that made him anxious.

They had decided to dock in Rye rather than Winchelsea so as not to alert the *Gorgon* to their presence. It was a mere three miles up the coast from his home, but even that short distance would afford them some cover.

As the *Draconis* sailed past the port of Winchelsea just past dawn, Charles's heart thundered in his chest. His sister, Carenza, had always thought that Winchelsea and the Saint Mary's Abbey were like a cavalier and his lady, looking longingly at each other across the bay. Winchelsea's cloak of gray stone buildings clustered around the castle, his onetime home, and his eyes stung with unshed tears.

As they passed, the outlines of the other ships docked there came into sharp relief, and a jolt ran through him at the sight of the *Gorgon*. They'd caught up to her again at last.

"Liam is on that ship," Fionola said, coming up beside him

and surveying the scene with grim determination. "This time we won't fail."

"No, we won't." Charles squeezed her hand.

"Are you ready to see your family?" She turned to meet his gaze.

He took a deep breath and let it out. How could he put in words the roiling emotions within him? He loved his family and could not wait to see them, but what would they think of him? At the same time, he knew, he had to do this. For his wife. For himself.

"I'm ready," he said, hoping it was true.

It was still early in the day when they docked and paid their fees at the custom house. Charles donned his wedding clothes, and Fionola went below to change into a green silk gown with a gold necklace and gold belt she'd found amongst the booty captured from the *Rosemary*. Deirdre had tailored it to fit her, and when she climbed onto deck in her finery, Charles could hardly believe the transformation.

"Captain, you take my breath away."

She narrowed her eyes. "That's Lady Fionola to you," she said with a smirk. "No more 'captain' until we've rescued my brother. And you lot," she said, turning to the crew who were all staring at her slack-jawed, "I don't want to hear a word. I'm still the captain here, no matter what I'm wearing, and I will string you up by your bleedin' thumbs if you so much as look at me wrong. You all know the plan, so get to work."

She held out her hand with regal poise and took his arm. Together, they descended the gangplank, flanked by Ronan and Deirdre. Thomas and Colm followed close behind. Aidan stood by with horses for the six of them. The rest of the men would follow on foot, led by Ronan, except for the skeleton crew left behind to guard the *Draconis*.

Fionola eyed her horse suspiciously, and the gentle palfrey took one look at her and tried to back away. His wife wasn't joking about not getting along with horses. Charles had to hold the reins so that she could mount. But the horse quickly gave up its fight and followed the other horses in docile compliance for the duration of the brief trip.

After that, the ride to Winchelsea went by all too quickly, and before Charles knew it, they were riding through the northern city gate onto Fish Street, familiar sights, sounds, and smells assaulting his senses.

As they turned up the winding road toward the castle, it was strange the things that caught Charles's attention. A patch of cobblestones that had been repaired and replaced gave him a jolt, diverging from the template in his memory. A cloth merchant now sold his wares out of the little shop where he used to buy perfect, buttery, flaky pastries. The Seagull Tavern had replaced the old, peeling sign he remembered, and their shutters were now painted blue instead of brown. How was it possible he still remembered the color of tavern shutters? And yet he did.

Each tiny difference was jarring, a sour note in a familiar tune. But the thing that had changed the most in the last five years was him. It was only a matter of time before his family noticed. In the meantime, he wore the mask of the man he used to be and hoped it would be sufficient to convince them of who he was.

There was an empty, hollow feeling in the pit of his stomach. His family would be happy to see him. But he knew there were difficult conversations ahead. He felt a guilty itch to turn right around and head back out to sea. It would be good to see his family again, but the prospect only sharpened the sense that this was no longer his world. He could visit but never again belong.

They arrived at the castle gates, and Charles spoke with an unfamiliar guard. "I'm here to see the baron. Tell him Lord Charles and Lady Fionola came from Wexford on the king's business." Charles hoped the combination of Wexford and his name would be sufficient to gain him an audience with his father. After all, Wexford was his last known location.

The guard gave a perfunctory bow and invited them to follow.

Walking through the enormous wooden doors to the main entry hall, a thousand memories flooded back to him. How often had he chased his sisters around the arches that supported the second-floor gallery? He'd had his first kiss in that corner right over there. It was the most awkward kiss imaginable, and he would never forget it or Jeannine, a scullery maid his own age who was as curious as he to learn what all the fuss was about.

He was forced to set aside his reverie as a tall man with blond hair, an eyepatch, and a scar across his face approached.

"Lord Charles and Lady Fionola, welcome to Winchelsea. My name is Sir Victor. I serve the earl. I understand you traveled all the way from Wexford to see Lord Martin?"

Charles wondered who this earl might be. Perhaps a visitor like himself? But then, why would his man be greeting guests?

"Thank you for your welcome, Sir Victor. We have journeyed far to speak with the baron. We are most anxious to see him. Can you take us to him?"

At that moment, a burly man in plain but well-made clothes came through the door with wood shavings caught in his dark beard. "My lord, can you spare a moment?" Sir Victor asked the man.

"Of course. What is it?"

"Lord Charles and Lady Fionola, may I introduce you to Daniel Rossignol, Earl of Winchelsea." The man before him was definitely not an earl. Nonetheless, there were bows all around. Fionola forgot she was supposed to curtsey, remembered halfway through her bow, and barely remained standing as she tried to do a proper obeisance. The strangers looked on, only showing their amusement in a twinkle of their eyes. "My lord, these visitors were sent on the king's business from Wexford to see Lord Martin."

"The king's business?" the so-called earl asked. "That's an odd coincidence. We're already playing host to an envoy from the king."

Fionola tensed beside him. They needed a distraction and fast as their cover story fell apart.

"M-my lord Daniel is it?" Charles asked, trying to project calm. "I'm afraid I'm not familiar with that name. Winchelsea has always been a vassal of Hastings. Has something changed in the last five years? It's been some time since I was last here."

The two men laughed. "Many things have changed," Sir Victor said. "For one thing, Winchelsea no longer owes fealty to the Hastings. Lord Daniel has been Winchelsea's liege lord for two years now. His wife, Lady Carenza, is the baron's daughter."

"Carenza," Charles whispered. The expression on the so-called earl's face hardened.

"That's *Lady* Carenza to you," the man said.

Charles had slipped, and he knew it. "My apologies, my lord. She and I were acquainted as children. You might say I am a ghost from the past."

"A ghost?" asked Sir Victor.

"She likely thinks me dead."

"Who are you?" the maybe-earl asked, suspicion written all over his face. "You aren't Irish. You seem to know a lot about the de Vere family for someone who has been living abroad. What did you say your name was?"

"Charles," he answered carefully.

"Your story doesn't add up, Charles, if that's really your name. If it isn't, you made a poor choice. That name brings only grief to this household. I think you had better leave. Victor, see them out. I don't know what they are after, but they have no business here."

Sir Victor nodded and gestured forcefully toward the door. "Wait. I need to see the baron," Charles pleaded. "It's very important. He wouldn't want you to keep me away. Please."

Sir Victor drew his sword, and before Charles realized what was happening, Fionola had stolen it and was pointing it at Sir Victor's throat.

"We'll see the baron," Fionola said in a commanding voice

that brooked no dissent.

Lord Not-an-Earl drew his sword and pointed it at Fionola. If it was anyone besides Fionola, Charles would be alarmed for her safety. As it was, he feared for Lord Not-an-Earl. This wasn't at all how this was supposed to go. While he appreciated Fionola's loyalty, this was not the best way to reintroduce himself to his family.

At that moment, a familiar voice rang through the hall. Carenza stood on the upper gallery at the top of the stairs looking down, her intelligent eyes and ink black hair the same as ever. "Daniel, what is going on here? Why are you pointing a sword at that woman, and why does she have a sword in the first place?"

"Carenza, stay back. It's dangerous," Lord Definitely-Not-an-Earl yelled.

Charles saw his chance, and he took it. "Carenza, it's Charles. I taught you how to swim and how to sail. On your tenth birthday we snuck out in the middle of the night with a pile of honey cakes and went sailing. You made up a song about a manta ray. It went like this." Everyone stood frozen and staring as Charles cleared his throat and sang,

"When we sail on the open sea,
I grab a lute and sing for thee.
What shall I sing for thee today?
Go ask a manta ray."

As he started on the second verse, he heard a familiar alto voice as Carenza started to sing along in a choked-up voice.

"I asked a sailor how to swim.
He looked at me. His face was grim.
He said, 'I'll not risk life and limb!
Go ask a manta ray.'"

As she was singing, she walked down the stairs, and when she reached the bottom, he could see she was large with child.

"Fionola, lower the sword, please, and give it back to Sir Victor," he said, glancing at her and giving her a reassuring nod. She immediately did so. Sir Victor gave her a look of grudging respect as he took it back. Lord Maybe-Actually-an-Earl lowered his sword hesitantly.

"You're lucky I didn't kill you," said Lord Probably-an-Earl.

"Death can come at any time, and life should not be wasted," Charles answered, touching the skull on a string around his neck, and the blood drained from the earl's face. Apparently, Charles finally said the right thing.

"Why didn't you simply tell the truth?" the earl asked.

"Would you have believed me?"

Carenza pushed her husband aside and wrapped Charles in a crushing hug, her enormous belly pressing against him. His cheek grew damp with her tears. "I've missed you so much," he whispered.

A wracking sob came from Carenza. "I thought you were dead."

"I'm so sorry. If I could have come back, I would have," he said, wiping his own tears away.

"Where were you that you couldn't come back?" she asked, her face still buried in his shoulder.

He pulled her up and wiped her tears. "I'll tell you, but I'd rather do it once, with everyone."

"Carenza, who is that?" asked another familiar voice. *Alais.* "Why are you crying?"

As Alais approached, it was clear she was also large with child. Her face was the same, but she had matured significantly since he'd last saw her at age sixteen. Now she looked a lot like Carenza, except with brown hair. The teasing look in her eye hadn't changed one bit, though.

"Alais, it's Charles," Carenza said. "He's alive."

"What?" Alais demanded, rushing over as fast as her large belly would let her. "How can you be sure it's him? Did he offer proof?"

Alais peered at him with an odd mix of hope and skepticism on her face.

"I let you ride my destrier, Valor, when you were a little girl—maybe nine or ten?" Charles said. "Mother was furious when she found out, even though you always came back safe and sound. She made me swear I'd never let you near him again, but of course I let you sneak out with him every time we could be sure she was otherwise occupied."

Throwing her arms around Charles, Alais nearly knocked him over. Sir Victor looked on warily, his hand glued to his pommel. Fionola was watching with equal focus.

"Alais, is that you?" came a voice that he could swear was his youngest sister, Iselda. "Can I borrow your blue cape? Wait, why is everyone standing around out here?"

Iselda looked the same as when he left but about six inches taller. *She must be…what…eighteen now?* She was still slim as a stick and appeared not to have given up her preference for unflattering, high-necked gowns.

"It's Charles," said Alais. "He's alive and standing right here."

"Charles?" Iselda asked, approaching warily. She looked deeply into his eyes for far longer than was comfortable, then she nodded. "I'm so happy you're home, Charles. We never stopped missing you." She took his hands and smiled kindly. He pulled her into a brief hug, and she turned bright red and fled to the back of the group. Iselda had always been shy. It shouldn't be surprising that she felt that way around him after so long. Still, it made him a little bit sad.

Lord Daniel stepped forward. "My apologies, Charles. I feel we got off on the wrong foot. You must be tired from your journey. Come join us in the great hall while we prepare a room for you. We'll get you some food, and you can tell us all your tale. Victor, go find Martin and Isabella, would you? I'm certain they will want to see him as soon as possible. My wife's maid, Elaine, will help your maid settle in," he said, turning to Fionola and Deirdre. Deirdre squeezed Fionola's hand and followed Elaine upstairs and away.

As they all settled into the great hall, his sisters' attention shifted to Fionola. "Who is this that you've brought with you, Charles?" Carenza asked.

"My wife, Lady Fionola of Wexford." They had agreed on this as her title. It was all true, in a sense.

"You're *married?*" Carenza asked, eyes wide. "I never thought you'd settle down. You had that ridiculous octopus test to scare the marriageable ladies away."

"Octopus test?" Fionola asked in her lovely Wexford lilt, a grin spreading across her face.

"Your husband didn't think much of noblewomen. Every time my parents tried to make a match, he insisted he would only marry a woman who could bring him a live octopus. Of course, none of them ever did. I'm so glad he's seen sense and settled down."

Charles squeezed Fionola's hand under the table. Turning to look into her mesmerizing eyes, he said, "Actually, Carenza, she passed the test, even though I never said a word about it."

"You brought him a live octopus?" Alais asked, wide eyed.

"I did, though it was after we were married. I wondered at the time why he reacted the way he did. Now I know."

Charles's cheeks heated at the memory of that afternoon.

Then the doors opened, and his parents came rushing in with Victor trailing behind.

His mother pulled him from his seat and hugged him as if she was pulling him out of a shipwreck. "Charles? Can it be? Oh. My baby boy, I love you so much," she said, eyes brimming. "When we heard your ship went down, I couldn't help regretting that I hadn't said it enough. I always swore if by some miracle you ever came back to us that I'd tell you first thing."

"I love you too, Mama," he said, giving her an affectionate look as his mind clambered with years of unspoken words. "And you, Papa," he said turning to his father. "I missed you every day, and I prayed for your health and safety every night."

"I love you too, Son," his father said in a hoarse voice, pulling him into a brief, strong hug. "I never thought I'd see you again, but some part of me always held out hope."

His mother gave his father an I-told-you-so look. "I insisted on keeping your things instead of giving them away," she said. "They've been in a trunk in the cellar for five years, so they might be a bit musty, and moth eaten, but I'm sure it's enough to get by until we can have new clothing made." Then her fingers tightened on his arm, and she looked up with alarm. "You are staying, aren't you? Please tell me you're staying."

"I don't know how long we can stay. We'll need to return to Fionola's home well before the baby's born." He didn't want to overpromise.

"Baby?" his mother gasped, looking like she might pass out from joy.

Charles smiled. "Mother, Father, I'd like you to meet my wife, Fionola. She's expecting, though not quite so far along as my sisters, it seems."

Charles was interrupted by a commotion at the door. He turned to see what had caused it, and there, to his horror, stood Lord Stephen de Burgh, clad in his customary black finery. He raked Charles up and down with narrowed eyes. "Can it be? Am I seeing a ghost?"

CHAPTER TWENTY-FOUR

I T TOOK ALL Fionola's willpower to resist the urge to pull her knives from her sleeves and carve Black Stephen to pieces where he stood. If she'd had her sword, she would have run him through without a second thought, despite the audience. Perhaps she could steal one again?

No, Sir Victor was keeping a watchful eye on her. Though she had fooled him once, she didn't think it would work a second time. She knew a seasoned swordsman when she saw one.

Black Stephen's eyes flashed as they turned from Charles to her. "Fionola MacMurrough?" he asked, disbelief written on his face.

She was caught. All those years ago she had fled, and now she stood before him, exposed. But she was not the same girl who ran away from her betrothed all those years ago. She was Captain O'Bannon, not that he would have any suspicion she was the infamous pirate attacking his ships. The shiver of dread that washed through her on hearing her name on his lips was quashed by welling rage. Her hand twitched as one violent urge after another ran through her overheated mind.

"Two ghosts I see before me. What a curious coincidence," Black Stephen said quietly, his beady eyes shifting from one of them to the other.

She needed a plan. It wouldn't do to attack him with so many witnesses. She needed to get him alone. Then she would make him suffer for all he had done to her family.

Charles grabbed her hand, tearing her from her plotting. She glanced at him. He had turned white as a sheet. His jaw clenched, and a shiver shook him head to toe. She had to do something, or Charles would have a fit right there in front of everyone.

"Lord Charles, Lady Fionola," said Lord Daniel, breaking the tense silence. "It seems you know our guest, Lord Stephen de Burgh."

Fionola squeezed Charles's hand with all her might, praying it would be enough to help him keep his head until she got him out of here so that they could form a plan.

Charles cleared his throat and looked Black Stephen in the eye. "We're acquainted." His voice was rough and low. The gleam in Charles's eye told her that her husband's thoughts were as murderous as her own.

"Yes, indeed," said Black Stephen, all innocence. "Charles sailed to Ireland under my command two years ago, and his ship was lost at sea. I had no idea he had survived. I'm pleased to see you alive and well, my lord." Then the snake turned to her. "And how, might I ask, do you know this lovely lady?"

"My wife," Charles ground out. It was a good thing Fionola's hand was strong. Otherwise, Charles might have crushed it in his grip.

Black Stephen's eyes narrowed at that news and took on a malevolent gleam. "Your wife. How interesting."

She needed to draw attention away from Charles, who was trembling more and more with each moment.

"My lord," she said, putting on her most winning and feminine smile. "What a pleasant surprise to see you again." She curtsied deeply while picturing the man being drawn and quartered. This time, she didn't lose her balance.

Today will be your last, you demon.

Lord Stephen's gaze turned lecherous, and he licked his lips as he looked at her. "The pleasure is all mine, my lady."

Charles jerked beside her, and she darted a glance at his face. *Oh no.* He was about to tear Black Stephen limb from limb in front of his entire family. Much as the evil man deserved it, she needed to get Charles out of here before he did something desperate. Black Stephen needed to die a long, painful death, and to accomplish that, they needed to bide their time.

"My lords and ladies," she said in the most obsequious voice she could manage. "We are tired from our journey. Might we retire to refresh ourselves for a bit?"

"Of course," said Charles's mother, still beaming at her long-lost son. "Where are my manners? Come with me."

Fionola dragged Charles behind her as she followed Lady Isabella up the grand stone staircase to the second floor.

"How long has Lord Stephen been your guest?" Fionola asked her mother-in-law to distract attention from Charles's deteriorating state.

"He arrived yesterday on the *Gorgon*, saying he had business to attend to with my husband. Something to do with shipping investments. He's been a regular guest ever since we lost—or thought we did—our dear Charles at sea. Always brought me flowers for my loss. Such a kind and thoughtful man!"

Such a conniving fiend more like. Oh, how Black Stephen must have been gloating at the solicitousness of the de Veres while he held their son captive and stole their ship out from under them!

"I'll put you in your old room, Charles," Lady Isabella de Vere said, leading them along a hall to the easternmost room. Opening the door, she beckoned them to enter the generously proportioned bedroom with its two tall, slender windows with pointed tops, that faced the sea. An elaborately carved canopy bed draped in deep blue damask dominated the room, despite its size. Otherwise, the furnishings were sparse—a heavy, wooden sea chest, a simple desk and stool, a small table with a pitcher and ewer. The floor was freshly strewn with rushes and herbs. Despite its spare furnishings, it was the most opulent room

Fionola had ever stayed in.

"We've put your things in storage, dear," Lady Isabella said to Charles, who swallowed and nodded. "But I hope you'll be comfortable nonetheless."

"Thank you, Mother," he answered in a strained voice.

His mother's brow furrowed. "Are you well my dear? You look a bit off color. Shall I send for a healer?"

"I'm fine," he said quickly with a forced smile. "I just need a moment to myself. I'll be downstairs again shortly."

She nodded and turned to go. At the door, she paused. "I love you so much, my baby boy. I can't tell you how happy I am to have you back."

"I love you too, Mama," Charles answered, a genuine smile peeking through.

With a satisfied grin, his mother left the room and closed the heavy wooden door behind her.

As soon as the door closed, Charles sat heavily on the bed, head in hands, and whispered, "He's here."

Fionola slipped off her shoes and climbed onto the bed behind him, massaging his rigid shoulders. Another shudder wracked his body.

"Yes, he is," she whispered back. "Until we kill him."

Charles's spine stiffened. "There is no 'we,' Fionola. You're carrying our child. I'll deal with him."

Like hell he would. He could barely hold himself upright. Besides, weren't the wounds Black Stephen had inflicted on her and her family even more severe than what he had done to Charles?

"No, you will not. He's mine. I will tear his beating heart out and make him eat it for what he's done to my brother."

He shook his head and curled up in a ball on the bed. "I can't talk about this now. I need a moment." His eyes were squeezed shut, and he shook like a luffing sail.

Taking deep breaths, Fionola set aside the rage that roiled within her so that she could care for her husband in his moment of distress. She curled her body around him like a protective shell and took his hand. He needed her right now, and she wouldn't fail him like she'd failed Liam. There was nothing she wouldn't do for this beloved man who lay trembling in her arms.

In time, his shaking subsided, and his heartbeat slowed to a more regular rhythm. He brought her hand to his lips and kissed it. "I don't deserve you," he said quietly.

She laughed. "No one deserves me."

He rolled on his back and looked her in the eye, the ghost of a smile flitting across his lips. She pinned his hands above his head. There was one sure way to bring him back to himself quickly, and she needed his full attention. She straddled him. "But," she murmured in his ear before nipping it, "do you want me?"

His breathing grew ragged for an entirely different reason.

"I always want you," he answered as he hardened beneath her.

Good. It was working.

She pulled up his cotte and untied his breeches, caressing the hard evidence of his need, and he groaned at her touch.

Grasping him firmly, she took him into her mouth. He cried out and tried to push her away. "Fionola…too much…" he said, straining to form words as she licked and sucked, feeling him convulse beneath her. She was beginning to understand why he enjoyed doing this to her so much. It was a heady sensation to give someone so much pleasure and have them so absolutely at your mercy.

Ignoring his protests, she let go her hand so that she could take him in deeper, letting his tip slide along the back of her throat, as she tickled and fondled his balls.

"Christ on the cross," he swore as he thrust into her, unable to stop himself. "Oh sweet Jesus. I want to be inside you. Please. Now." His voice shook in his desperation, she noticed with a smile as she wrangled her skirts so that she could climb on top of him. He touched her as she straddled him and gasped.

With no preamble, she slid down his slick shaft, still moist from her ministrations, and she momentarily lost the ability to form thoughts as pleasure bloomed through every part of her spreading out from her core.

"Thank you," he whispered as she began to move.

She bent down and kissed him as he raised himself up on his arms to meet her. There was too much fabric between them, so she pulled off his cotte and shirt, touching and kissing every part of him she could reach as they continued their slow, tantalizing dance.

Loosening the ties on her dress, he slid it down her shoulders until her breasts spilled out, her taut nipples grazing against the smooth skin of his chiseled chest. Their pace quickened, as she strove to exorcize his demons and bring him back to himself. With each movement, his eyes became more focused until his gaze burned hot. Yes, now she had him back. Soon pleasure overtook her like a wave on the beach—swelling, crashing, and then subsiding. As she peaked, he convulsed against her in his own release.

At last, they collapsed side by side, sated and exhausted.

"I'll never know why you married me," he murmured when he recovered sufficiently to speak, "but I'll never stop being grateful that you did." He pulled her body against his own so that they were spooned together.

It was so tempting to remain cocooned in this room with him and forget all the troubles on her doorstep. But she couldn't. She had to rescue her brother and take her revenge on Black Stephen.

As if he could sense her thoughts, he murmured, "What is our plan now, Captain?" into her hair.

Good. He hadn't forgotten who was in charge.

"I can't stop you from going after him. I know that," he said quietly. "But I'm begging you not to. Rescuing Liam is dangerous enough, and I could never live with myself if something happened to you or the baby."

She had to answer carefully. His heart was in the right place, but did he truly understand the depth of her vengeful fury?

"We stick to the plan to rescue Liam tonight," she said. "I'll deal with Black Stephen after I know my brother is safe."

He stilled. "Are you sure? Black Stephen's presence makes everything all the riskier. Shouldn't we regroup and revisit the plan?"

"I've waited five bleedin' years for this. My brother is not rotting in that brig another night."

Holding his gaze, she narrowed her eyes. He opened his mouth to object, then closed it, probably realizing there was nothing he could say to dissuade her from her set course.

"Yes, Captain," he said at last. "And Black Stephen?"

What that course was, she wasn't so sure. But it didn't matter. She wasn't going to back down. The time to strike was now. "I'll let you know as soon as I've come up with a plan."

That was a lie. She was going to seek him out and slit his throat as soon as Liam was free of his grasp, but she didn't want Charles to know that. He wouldn't like it one bit.

"We should clean ourselves up and go see my family. It's nearly time for lunch," he said, stroking her side.

"So we should." It was so hard to make herself move.

"We wouldn't want to waste that elaborate story we concocted." He kissed her bare shoulder.

She turned to face him, grinning. "About how I saved your life and you fell prey to my feminine wiles?"

"You did save my life, and I certainly fell prey to your feminine wiles."

That earned a laugh. "I don't have any feminine wiles."

"You're wrong, Captain. You most certainly do." He leaned in and kissed her so deeply, she moaned against him. "See?" he said, pulling away. "You have me utterly bewitched."

"Then hopefully we can convince your family." She tapped his nose with her finger, and he caught it and kissed it. But his face fell. "What's wrong?"

He looked at her in silence then turned to lie on his back and gaze to the blue canopy. "I wish I didn't have to lie to them. I know it's necessary, but it feels wrong."

She nestled into the crook of his shoulder, her favorite place to be. "They seem like good people, and they clearly love you. I'm sorry it's necessary, but we can't exactly tell them you were accused of treason and married a pirate."

"Of course not." He kissed the top of her head. "I know that. I just wish that things were different."

If only the world were a better place… But there was nothing to be gained from such thoughts. Pulling herself together, she rolled away from Charles and got out of bed.

"You remember the story we agreed on?" They had to focus on practicalities, not on wishing things were otherwise.

"I do. And you?" he asked, sitting up so that the sheets fell away from his lovely form.

She averted her eyes quickly, ignoring the warmth that spread through her at the sight, and picked up her gown, which had landed in a puddle on the floor.

"Of course, I do. Come on, Sailor. Let's get this over with." She pulled on her dress, tightening the laces and straightening the skirts, to make herself as presentable as she could manage.

"Aye, Captain," he said, getting up with a groan.

It really was a shame that they had to put clothes on again, but if they succeeded tonight, they could run away to France and live in happy anonymity until the child was born. And then…? Well, that was a question for another day.

She placed her hand in the crook of Charles's arm, and together, they strode out toward whatever fate might bring.

CHAPTER TWENTY-FIVE

FIONOLA LOOKED STUNNING in her green silk gown, not that Charles should have been focused on his beautiful wife at a moment like this. There was more than enough to occupy his spinning mind, but focusing on her helped ground him as he descended the familiar stone staircase to the main entrance hall with its arching ceilings. A few more steps brought them to the heavy double doors of the great hall where he would face his family. And Black Stephen. He couldn't think about that without breaking out in a cold sweat, so he refocused on his wife.

With Fionola by his side, he could do anything, and he would do absolutely anything for her. Pausing before pushing the doors open, he gave her one last lingering look, taking in her glorious red curls, the glow of her skin, the flash of her sparkling green eyes, her lovely feminine curves accentuated by the gown she wore. God had blessed him beyond measure with such a wife.

Pulling the creaking doors open, he stepped forward, and the performance began in earnest. The familiar space seemed smaller than he remembered. Slanted light poured in through the tall, slender windows on the southern wall, the open shutters allowing in a hint of a breeze. The long wooden table had three heavy candelabras, none of which were lit, as the summer evening sunlight was still strong. The enormous hearth carved with mythical monsters stood empty, the weather being far too hot for a fire. As always, twenty seats carved with the House de Vere coat of arms surrounded the head table, and the places were set with gleaming silver plates and his mother's treasured filigreed silver goblets. The tapestries of picnicking ladies on the northern wall were new, but everything else looked exactly as he had left it.

He heaved a sigh of relief to see that Black Stephen wasn't here yet. At present, it was only his parents, Carenza, and Lord Daniel.

His mother came bustling over in a blue brocade gown with bell sleeves that dipped to the floor. A heavy gold-braided necklace with a large, sapphire cross glinted in the evening light. Her penchant for dramatic attire hadn't changed, he could see.

"Come over here so that I can look at you," his mother said, taking his hand and guiding him to a place at the table beside Carenza, who was wearing a color other than black for once. Perhaps marriage had changed her ascetic tastes. The deep maroon of her gown suited her complexion, and she looked positively rosy with her enormous belly.

"Not dressing like a nun anymore?" he asked quietly, leaning toward his sister.

She laughed. "It would hardly do for me to dress in black as a married woman. Everyone would think I was in mourning. My husband is alive and well, thank you very much." Her eyes strayed to the earl, who had just paused in an animated conversation with Charles's father. The look of adoration on her face made Charles grin.

"I'm glad to see your earl makes you happy."

"And I'm glad to see you've found happiness yourself," Carenza said, glancing at Fionola. "You've met your match at last, I see."

"She's more than my match," he said, glancing at his lovely, fearsome bride and taking her hand. "She is my sovereign, and I am merely her humble servant."

Carenza winked at Fionola. "I think you and I are going to get along very well. Anyone who could tame Charles must be a force to be reckoned with."

Fionola smiled back at his sister. "I've looked forward to meeting you. Charles has told me so much about you."

"Son," said Charles's father, drawing their attention away. "We are anxious to learn where you have been these last five years. What kept you away?"

His father seated himself across from Carenza rather than in his customary seat at the head of the table. Lord Daniel had precedence, Charles supposed, though it rubbed him the wrong way to see his father displaced. His father didn't seem to mind, though, so Charles took a deep breath and did his best to accept the new status quo.

"Shall I tell my tale now or wait until the rest are here?" Alais would want to hear every word, and Charles suspected Black Stephen would take an avid interest as well. Would their lies align, or would some stray detail give him away? The temptation to tell the truth and unmask Black Stephen's villainy was strong, but he had no proof. Lord Chester, who had been with him that fateful night, had never come forward with what he knew, or else Lord Stephen would not have been walking free.

Accusing Black Stephen now would only anger the man and make him all the more dangerous. Liam was still in the man's clutches, and Charles wouldn't risk his friend. It was safer by far to reveal the extent of Black Stephen's crimes after he was dead.

"Here come Alais and Victor now, and your sister, Iselda," his father said as the heavy wooden doors scraped open, admitting them. "And Lord Stephen and Lord Cuthbert, the king's envoy." Charles stiffened. "I'm sure they're as curious as I am to hear your story."

What should he say in front of Lord Cuthbert? The man was a stranger to Charles. His incisive, ice blue eyes examined Charles minutely. There was something sharp and unyielding about this thin fellow. Was he in league with Lord Stephen? Charles watched him closely, as the envoy seated himself beside his father. Then his attention turned to his nemesis.

To Charles's horror, Black Stephen took the chair beside Fionola, his coal-black eyes sweeping down her figure greedily. His wife's right hand swept to her left sleeve, feeling for the knife hidden there. Charles pulled her hand away, though his own murderous impulses were hardly better contained. It would be a wonder if they all made it out of this room without bloodshed.

"I am indeed most curious." Black Stephen turned his cold gaze on Charles as he seated himself. "Pray tell us how you survived that terrible accident at sea and what kept you away from your family for so long."

Blood thundered in Charles's ears, but he breathed deeply to keep his madness at bay. It helped that he still held Fionola's hand in his own. She was his tether in the midst of this storm, and for her, he had to keep his head and navigate these deadly waters.

Sitting, along with the rest of his family, Charles turned to his father, deliberately ignoring Lord Stephen and Lord Cuthbert. He needed a friendly face to focus on as he spun his tale.

"As you know," Charles began, "I sailed for Wexford on the *Wind Song* five years ago in the service of the king and was placed under Lord Stephen's command. For months, I fought to bring peace to the good people of Ireland."

The truth so far. He could look his father in the eye without guilt. The next bit would be harder. Turning to his nemesis, he continued, "As Lord Stephen told you, the *Wind Song* got caught in a squall and was lost at sea."

Black Stephen's cruel mouth twisted into a mockery of a sympathetic smile, making Charles's stomach churn. Lord Cuthbert's eyes narrowed. Fionola squeezed Charles's hand, bringing him back to himself.

"I don't know how I survived," Charles said, turning back to his father. "Or rather, I wouldn't have, if it weren't for my lovely wife." Thank goodness his shaking left hand was hidden beneath the table where no one could see. The lie tasted like gall in the back of his throat, and it was all he could do to meet his father's eye and continue.

"I washed up on shore, and she rescued me. I received a blow to the head and though I knew my name, I could not remember where I came from or how I came to be there. For two years, I lived beneath her father's roof. Though I grew to care for her deeply, I didn't dare speak up. For all I knew, I was a lowly sailor with nothing to offer this proud, beautiful granddaughter of the King of Leinster."

Fionola gazed adoringly at him, helping him sell the lie, but he didn't miss that her hand strayed once again to her sleeve. Black Stephen was leaning in, far too close to her shoulder, in the guise of listening attentively. Lord Cuthbert's gaze darted to Lord Stephen and then back to Charles. Did he suspect this story was a lie?

"Then one day a man was playing a tune on the viol that I recognized, and my memories came flooding back. Remembering that I was the son of a baron, I dared to follow my heart. I declared myself to Fionola's father and asked for permission to court her while I looked for a ship to take me back to Winchelsea. Fortunately, I was not alone in my feelings, and it wasn't long before we married. I came here as soon as I could find a ship to take us. I want our child to know his or her family, and if we have a son, I want him to be able to claim his birthright."

There. It was done. His innards twisted at the lie, but it couldn't be helped. His mother's eyes welled with tears, and even his father looked a bit misty-eyed. There was no trace of doubt in their faces, though Lord Cuthbert looked distinctly skeptical.

Servants arrived with the first course, a thick chicken pottage served with fresh baked bread and herbed soft cheese. Steaming crockery bowls were placed in front of each guest in unison. Charles paused in his story to breathe deeply. It was the smell of home. If only he belonged here.

"What a touching tale," said a deep, oily voice behind him. Charles turned to Black Stephen and met his malicious gaze. "How lucky you are to have been taken in by such kind strangers.

Your parents were so distraught when they thought they'd lost you. But now you are safe as can be back here in Winchelsea. Not that life is ever certain. Illness and accidents can happen us anywhere. But I would think your father's house is as safe a place as any."

Fionola stiffened between them. The not-so-veiled threat in the blackguard's words wasn't lost on her either.

"A fascinating tale indeed," said Lord Cuthbert, his cunning face alight with suspicion. Whatever the king's envoy might think, he clearly didn't believe Charles's tale.

"My lovely lady," Black Stephen said, turning his eyes to Fionola and then glancing none-too-subtly at her chest. "As I have heard your husband say on more than one occasion, 'Death can come at any time, and life should not be wasted.' Is that not so, Lord Charles?"

"So it is," Charles said, mentally dismembering his enemy. "Any day could be your last."

And you, sir, will not live to see another dawn.

Lord Cuthbert's sharp eyes darted back and forth between them. Lord Daniel cleared his throat. What he must think of the tension in the room, Charles couldn't begin to guess. "Lord Stephen," said Lord Daniel, "you mentioned that there was something you wished to speak to Martin and me about."

Martin? Lord Daniel called Father by his given name?

Not that it mattered. Charles had far larger problems than the apparent closeness between Lord Daniel and his father. Still, it should have been Charles by his father's side, his right hand in all things. How much had changed in his absence!

"My men tell me a ship docked in Rye Harbor this morning," Black Stephen said, causing Charles's head to whip around. "The *Draconis.*"

Fionola gripped Charles's wrist with bruising force.

"It's a pirate vessel that has been plaguing my fleet for five years," Black Stephen continued.

"Pirates?" Lord Cuthbert's eyebrows rose nearly to his hairline. "They must be dealt with swiftly and harshly. The king will not tolerate such brigands in his waters." A scrawny hand pounded down on the table.

"I quite agree, my lord," Lord Stephen answered. "But despite the price I've placed on the captain's head, none have been able to capture him. Captain O'Bannon has proved as elusive as he has troublesome. He attacked the ship I arrived on a little over a month ago off the coast of Honfleur. I was hoping you might lend me some of your men-at-arms to comb the area in search of him and his crew and send your boats to patrol in case he tries to escape. I swear O'Bannon will hang at the end of a gibbet if it's the last thing I do."

Not if she slits your throat first.

Charles placed his hand over Fionola's to keep her from lashing out in the middle of the great hall. Fortunately, she kept her face a careful blank. Only her nails digging into his wrist told him how close she was to losing control. They would have to act quickly and get the *Draconis* out to sea. Lord Cuthbert would surely order Charles's father to send every ship he had after the *Draconis*, and he would encourage the Baron of Rye to do the same. Somehow, Charles and Fionola had to get word to the crew, but they were stuck playing lord and lady at a fancy dinner.

As Charles racked his brain for some excuse that would allow them to leave, Fionola put one hand to her stomach and the other to her lips. She puffed out her cheeks and convulsed as if she was about to vomit and mumbled, "Excuse me," right before running out of the room. Clever. No one would question the sensitive stomach of a lady in her early months of pregnancy.

"Poor dear," his mother exclaimed. "I remember those days. I couldn't abide the smell of meat either when I was with child."

Black Stephen's eyebrows shot up at the words "with child."

Charles forced himself to smile. "She only wants fish. Everything else seems to upset her delicate stomach. I should go check on her. She doesn't know the castle and may get lost looking for the garderobe."

"Such an attentive husband," his mother said with a pleased-sounding sigh. "Go and take care of your wife, my dear. We'll have Cook keep your food warm."

Charles sprang out of his seat and practically ran from the room, heading straight back to their bedroom. If he knew anything about his wife, she would have headed straight for her trunk where her sword was stowed.

He flung the bedroom doors open, but he was too late. The trunk with her belongings lay open with clothes spilling out. A quick examination revealed the sword was gone. And so was Fionola.

CHAPTER TWENTY-SIX

FIONOLA KNEW THE first place Charles would look for her was their bedchamber, so instead of lingering there, she had retrieved her sword, wrapped it in a gown, and gone in search of Deirdre. After asking a servant, she found her cousin leaving the kitchens where she had shared a repast with the other servants.

"Thank God I found you," Fionola said, pulling Deirdre aside into a quiet alcove. "I need your help." She quickly explained the situation with Black Stephen and how she needed to get out to the crew in disguise. "Do you think you could help me find something to wear that would help me slip out unnoticed?"

Deirdre grinned widely. "Of course, you tickle-brained dewberry. What do you think I've been doing while you've been flouncing about in fancy dresses?"

Fionola narrowed her eyes. "Your job, I hope."

Deirdre's smile grew crafty. "I've done just as we discussed. I've explored every corner of this castle and grounds while you've been mincing and prancing about, playing the lady."

Ignoring her cousin's teasing jibes, she adjusted her grip on her bundle of cloth and steel. "Then lead the way," she said in her most commanding captain's voice.

Snapping to attention, Deirdre led her out to a small outbuilding behind the castle where the laundresses did their work. It was mercifully empty at this hour. As quickly as she could, Fionola stripped off her silk gown and exchanged it for a rough-spun linen dress in the pile that looked approximately the right size.

As soon as she was clothed, she said to her cousin, "Go back inside now, and don't say a word to anyone, not even Charles. If he asks, you haven't seen me. Do you understand?"

"Yes, Captain," Deirdre answered with a little nod of her head.

"If all goes well, I'll be back before nightfall."

"Godspeed," Deirdre said, pulling her into a quick hug. "Be safe."

For a moment, Fionola forgot she was captain, and she hugged her cousin back with all her might.

"Just don't forget you're mortal like the rest of us," Deirdre whispered, then pulled away and disappeared out the door.

Fionola needed a moment to compose herself after her cousin's embrace, but it wouldn't do to get maudlin at a time like this. She needed all her wits about her.

Dressed as a servant, her sword hidden in a bundle of laundry, Fionola sauntered out the castle gate without attracting a second glance. Once she was out of sight of the guards, she quickened her pace and headed straight toward the Sailor's Rest, the inn where her men had taken rooms. She had to find Ronan and tell him of the change in plans.

And what exactly was the new plan? Well, she'd have to think of one in the next two minutes. If she didn't act swiftly, all would be lost.

The original plan had been to infiltrate the ship by stealth that night, but they could no longer wait for cover of darkness to act. Nor could they afford to make the trip back to Rye to the *Draconis* to make their escape. The *Draconis* was likely now crawling with soldiers intent on bringing down an infamous pirate. Return was out of the question. Unless…

A mad idea came to her. Could she? No one sane would consider it, but did they have any choice?

She rounded a corner and hurried along the bustling cobblestone street, maneuvering past a donkey cart loaded with barrels and two men carrying an enormous tree trunk into a nearby warehouse. Men in rough clothes milled about outside the heavy wood double doors of the half-timbered building that was the Sailor's Rest. This was where she belonged, not in some fine castle, she thought as she made for the door, but she was stopped by two leering drunkards.

"Where are you off to in such a rush, sweetheart?" one of them asked, a dangerous look in his eye. Thank heavens she was well armed, though it would hardly do to run a man through in the street when she was trying to keep a low profile. It was so inconvenient, the attention she attracted as a woman. She thought with longing of the false beard wrapped in her bundle of clothes. As soon as she could find Ronan, she was going to his room to change back into her captain's garb. Being a woman among sailors was far too much trouble.

"None of your concern, you pox bottle," she said, shoving past the man. She didn't have time for this.

"Ooh. Feisty," said the man's friend, standing in her way. "You know what they say about redheads." He reached out and tried to grab her. His friend laughed. She dodged the man's grasp and swept his feet out from under him with her foot. He landed on his ass with a look of astonishment as she stepped neatly around him. His friend stared at her wide-eyed, swaying where he stood.

"Try it again, you feckin' swine, and you'll be singing like a girl for the next week," she said, glaring. Both men stepped back under the force of her gaze. "Now if you'll excuse me," she said, hurrying through the door into the dim, boisterous common room.

She spotted Ronan immediately, which was fortunate because several men at the nearest table wolf whistled as she entered, one making a grab at her skirts. *Ugh.* As Captain O'Bannon, she'd had the luxury of forgetting what pigs men could be.

"Ronan, you big oaf, get your lazy bones over here this instant, or I'll cut off your balls and add them to this evening's stew," she yelled, hoping to gain his attention through the din. His head snapped around, and he came running. "You bloody drunkard. How is a wife to love a man who drinks more than he fecks?"

"My apologies, my love," he said loudly. Fortunately, he understood her ruse immediately. Wrapping an arm around her, he grinned sheepishly. "I was only having a drink with the boys. Let's go up to my room where we'll have a bit more privacy, and you can tell me what's got you so upset."

"Aye, I'll go up to your room and give you the tongue lashing of a lifetime. If you think to lay a hand on me after what you did, you are sorely mistaken."

The men around them laughed and turned back to their drinks as Ronan said, "Please, Mary, just come upstairs with me, and I'll explain everything, I swear."

She let him whisk her upstairs to the small sparsely furnished room he shared with Thomas. As soon as the door was closed, she dropped her bundle and said, "Black Stephen is here, and he knows the *Draconis* is in harbor at Rye. We can't go back to it, or we'll be caught like fish in his net. Our only chance is to steal another ship and take to sea."

Ronan sat down hard on the spindly cot behind him. His lips pressed together in a thin line, and he stared at the wall. After a few moments, he nodded. "Tonight, we'll—"

"We can't wait for tonight. We have to act now."

"In broad daylight?" He pulled his head back and stared at her.

"I'm afraid so. But I have a plan."

He raised an eyebrow. "Aye, Captain?" he asked warily.

"You steal the *Gorgon* and leave harbor before anyone notices."

"We steal the—"

"Aye. I've thought it through, and it's the only way to save

Liam and all of you."

His brow furrowed. "You say that as if you aren't coming with us."

"I'm not. For this to work, I must lead them astray."

Shaking his head slowly, his visage darkened. "No, Captain. We're not leaving you behind."

She stepped toward him, staring him down. "You'll do as I order, Sailor."

He held her gaze for a long moment, then dropped it to the floor, running his hands through his dark hair. "I don't like it, and neither will the men," he said to her feet.

Softening, she added, "I'll meet up with you at Calais before the week is out. You don't think I mean to let myself get caught, do you?" Ronan looked back up at her, disapproval written on every line of his face. "Just get Liam and the men to safety. That's all that matters."

Ronan let out a long, slow breath. "What of your husband? What does Charles think of this mad plan? Surely, he can't have agreed to this."

At the mention of Charles's name, her heart clenched. Was it wrong to leave him behind? It was for his own good. He was safest if he stayed with his family and kept out of what was about to unfold.

"I haven't told him," she admitted. "He thinks I'm back at the castle, taking a rest because of my delicate condition."

"That man loves you to pieces, Captain. It will destroy him to lose you."

She shook her head slowly. "He won't lose me. If everything goes according to plan, I'll be back in his arms tonight," she said, hoping it was true.

Ronan stared at her long and hard. "And what exactly is the plan, Captain?"

"I'm going to let Captain O'Bannon be seen in town. Thomas will go to the *Gorgon* and claim to be a messenger from Lord Stephen, ordering them to join the manhunt for me. I'll ride right past the ship and take off toward Rye, leading them north. That should largely empty out the ship." She hoped.

"But Captain, you're a terrible rider. What if they catch you?" It was a serious risk but one she'd have to take. As many men as possible needed to join the chase to leave the *Gorgon* as vulnerable as possible.

"They won't," she said with more confidence than she felt. "While I'm leading them on a merry chase, you and the crew will pose as the Town Watch with intelligence that one of O'Bannon's men has snuck aboard. Let someone else do the talking, and don't show your face, since they've seen you before. You and the men will conduct a thorough search, subduing any of the skeleton crew that remains behind as quietly as possible. As soon as you have control of the ship, set sail for Calais. Charles and I will meet you there. If we're not there within a week, set sail to Gan Ainm, and don't look back."

This plan was as full of holes as a sieve, but it was the best she could come up with on short notice. She didn't doubt her own ability to create a distraction or her men's ability to take a ship. But could they do it without drawing attention? And could she ride a horse well enough to escape?

"What about Black Stephen?" he asked. Damn it all, he knew her too well.

"When I escape my pursuers, I'll circle back to Winchelsea. I'll sneak back into the castle tonight. Posing as a laundress got me out. I expect it will get me back in. That gobshite won't survive the night. Once the deed is done, I'll return to Charles. No one will suspect Lady Fionola."

When the alarm was raised, they could always point the finger at Captain O'Bannon, who would have disappeared into the mist, never to be seen again.

"This is a terrible plan, Captain," Ronan said, shaking his head.

"Do you have a better one?"

He wiped his hands down his face. "No, I don't."

She nodded brusquely. "Go downstairs and gather the men in a private room. I need to change. I'll join you shortly."

Ronan left, shoulders bowed and shaking his head. It didn't matter what he thought as long as he followed orders. God willing, her brother would be free before the day was out, safely on his way to Calais with the crew.

As soon as he stepped out, Fionola bolted the door and rummaged through the pile of clothes she'd brought with her. Laying aside the sword, she pulled out Captain O'Bannon's rough cotte, shirt, and hose. Moments later, her maid's costume puddled on the floor, discarded. Relief flooded her as she pulled on the familiar garb. After five years spent as a man, being a woman was such a strain. Even with the danger that came along with becoming Captain O'Bannon one last time, there was comfort in her old disguise.

She looped the strings of her false beard over her ears and tied a scarf around her face. Letting her hair down, she tied it back in a simple queue.

Smiling beneath her scarf, she gave her beard an affectionate tug to make sure it was secure. This was the last ride of Captain O'Bannon, she knew. There would be no going back to this particular identity after a stunt like this. Well, if it was the last time, she was going to make it count.

She slipped her knives up her sleeves and fastened her sword belt around her waist. It was time to go put on a show.

Unlatching the door, she swaggered out, ready to meet her fate.

CHAPTER TWENTY-SEVEN

CHARLES STRODE TO the door of his bedroom then stopped short. He couldn't run straight to the Sailor's Rest. Black Stephen would be sure to have Charles followed, and that would lead him straight to the crew of the *Draconis*. And Fionola. And there was Lord Cuthbert to worry about too.

He was going to have to keep up Fionola's ruse and pretend she was resting because of her delicate condition. But then, how would he get to her? The idea of her wandering around Winchelsea with Black Stephen at her heels filled him with dread. Going to her was out of the question. It would only put her in further danger. The best thing he could do right now was distract attention.

He pulled open the door and strode down the familiar stone staircase. The torch-lit entrance hall was filled with shadows and shafts of light from the high narrow windows as he turned toward the great hall. Hopefully, everyone would still be assembled there.

Forcing his face into a placid expression, he entered the great hall. Fortunately, Black Stephen and Lord Cuthbert were still there. They were in animated discussion with his father as he entered.

"I've sent riders to Rye," said his father. "The *Draconis* will not be allowed to leave port, and anyone who approaches it will be arrested."

Charles's heart sank to his stomach. He could only pray that the handful of men left behind to watch the ship escaped before the Baron of Rye's men closed in.

"Good," said Charles a little too heartily. "We can't have pirates on these shores."

Black Stephen turned his calculating gaze on him. Did he suspect? But no, that would be impossible. No one but the crew of the *Draconis* knew that Charles had turned pirate. Still, the look in Black Stephen's eyes disconcerted him.

"Pirates are a scourge upon this earth," Charles continued, holding Black Stephen's gaze. "Little better than traitors, wouldn't you say, Lord Stephen?"

The effect of the word "traitor" was immediate. Black Stephen's eyes bulged, and his lips thinned to a line. For a moment, the mask of gentility slipped completely, revealing a serpent ready to strike. But that was what Charles wanted. As long as Black Stephen's full attention was on him, it wasn't on Captain O'Bannon.

"Treachery comes in many forms," Black Stephen said, re-composing his face. "But I've always known what to do with a traitor. The wages of sin are death, as the Lord says. And I know how to make a man's final moments long and slow, eking out every scream he has in him before delivering his quivering soul to Satan."

"I couldn't agree with you more, Lord Stephen," said Lord Cuthbert, steepling his long, thin fingers.

The sadistic smile now spreading across Black Stephen's face was likely the last sight a man saw when delivered to the tender mercies of the king's dismemberer of malefactors. Charles's heart beat faster at the threat, but so far, goading his enemy was producing exactly the effect he hoped for. No one had asked about Fionola.

"The pirates will be weeded out and dealt with, my lord," said Lord Daniel, his brow furrowed as he looked between

Charles and Lord Stephen. "Captain O'Bannon will trouble you no more. Victor," he said, turning to Alais's husband, "organize the Watch into a search party, and join the hunt for O'Bannon and his men."

"Yes, my lord." Sir Victor rose and bowed, then exited the room.

"I'll join," said Lord Cuthbert, rising. "I want to see justice served."

For a moment, Charles thought about joining them to lead them astray, but he decided not to. Fionola had bested Victor once. Surely, she could do so again. And Lord Cuthbert looked like more of a thinker and plotter than a fighter.

"And I must rest," said Alais, stifling a yawn. "Carrying a baby makes me ever so tired. Charles, do forgive me. I promise to spend lots of time with you later this afternoon. It's so good to have you back." She rose and curtsied before waddling out the door.

"And I have some correspondence to attend to," said Carenza. Her husband helped her rise, holding her elbow. "Not that this baby is going to let me focus. The little devil takes pleasure in dancing a jig on my ribcage every time I sit down to get something done." She smiled and patted her belly. Lord Daniel put his hand over hers, and they exchanged a loving look. Charles was glad to see his sister so happy. Perhaps this Lord Daniel wasn't so bad after all. If only Charles could settle down and enjoy the same domestic bliss with Fionola. But that could never be if Captain O'Bannon was caught.

"There are things I must attend to as well," said his mother, coming round the table and cupping his cheek in her hand. "Please forgive me, but I must take my leave for a short while. Know I love you, and I'll see you in in a few hours." She patted his cheek and turned to leave.

Charles's heart broke with the sweetness of the gesture. He'd dreamed of coming home for so long in the belly of the ship. If only he could settle back in as Lord Charles and be the son and brother they all wished. But he was too changed and had too many secrets.

Black Stephen watched the scene with a calculating gaze, his presence marring the moment and bringing Charles back to his objective. The Charles who belonged here was dead and gone. Only Fionola could heal his soul. Without her, he was nothing. So he had to save her, at all costs.

Only the men remained now—his father, Lord Daniel, and Black Stephen. "I saw the *Draconis* when I docked," Charles said, turning to his father. "The ship I was on took a nearby berth. I wondered at the time if it was a pirate vessel. It looks like a Viking nightmare come to life."

"What ship did you come in on?" Black Stephen asked with a malevolent grin. "And why did you dock in Rye rather than coming straight to Winchelsea?"

Thank heaven they checked which ships were in port before heading to Winchelsea. "Fionola and I traveled aboard the *North Star*, which did not stop at Winchelsea. Since Rye is so close, it was easy to hire horses to take us the final few miles." He knew the *North Star* and its captain from before he went to Ireland, so he could make his lie convincing if need be.

At that moment, the door opened, and a servant came rushing in. "My Lords, Captain O'Bannon has been sighted here in Winchelsea. They say he was at the Sailor's Rest Inn."

The words hit Charles with the force of a blow. He couldn't breathe. He felt lightheaded. Everything vanished except for the pit of terror in his stomach. His heart thundered in his ears, drowning out most sound as he fought to draw in breath and avert another attack.

And so he barely heard Lord Daniel say, "Summon my knights. We must defend the port. At all costs, we must protect Winchelsea."

Dear God. Armored knights against his loving, pregnant wife? He tried to think of her as the captain, master swordsman and leader of men, but all he could recall was the tender look on her face as they'd made love a short while ago. To all the world, she put on a brave and fearless face, but he knew behind it all, she was only human, mere flesh and blood. He'd seen her injured, heard her cry, and knew her vulnerabilities. He had to do something to save her.

"Let me lead the defense," he heard himself say. "I'll bring O'Bannon to justice." If he was leading the knights, he could find a way to leave an opening for her escape.

"Let me join you, my lord," said Black Stephen, his lips curling into a malevolent smile. "I've been chasing this rogue for years. I'd like to see to it that he's brought to justice."

It would be much harder to let Fionola escape with Black Stephen dogging his every step, but how could he refuse with his father and brother-in-law looking on?

"As you wish," Charles said quietly.

"You must make haste," his father said. "Who knows what O'Bannon plans to do? The town is in danger until the man is caught."

Charles nodded and rose, hurrying out of the great hall, down the corridor, and through the back door that opened on the rear courtyard. He strode across the cobblestones with Black Stephen close on his heels, reaching the armory moments later. Maybe once they were alone, Charles could end the nightmare and rid the world of this evil man.

But no sooner did the door close behind them than Black Stephen reached out, grabbed his shoulder and shoved him against the stone wall, bringing an ugly dagger to his throat. "I should have killed you years ago."

Was this it? Was Black Stephen finally going to dispatch him? Cold sweat dripped down Charles's back beneath his armor.

"You still need my secret. It's still eating at you who was with me that night. And you wouldn't dare kill me in my father's own home."

Black Stephen's eyes narrowed. "Perhaps not, but mistakes happen in the heat of battle. Tell me who it was, you dog. I'll spare your life and let you return to your pretty little wife. Set one foot out of line, and I'll have my revenge on you. And her."

"Don't you dare touch her, you filth," Charles ground out through clenched teeth.

Black Stephen smiled. "Good. Then we understand each other. And don't you dare think of letting your friend O'Bannon get away. Don't think it's escaped my notice that you and he are in league somehow."

"That's ridiculous. He's a pirate." God's blood. Had his reactions made it that obvious?

"And you conveniently arrive from Rye exactly the same time the *Draconis* docked there. My suspicions were confirmed when I saw the look on your face when it was announced O'Bannon had been spotted. Don't try to deny it."

Charles growled.

Black Stephen pressed the blade harder against his neck. "Tell me who it was, and let me capture O'Bannon, or I slit your throat and take your lovely wife. Do we understand each other?"

"I didn't tell you for two years. What makes you think I'll tell you now?"

"Because," Black Stephen said, leaning closer, "before you had nothing to lose except your life. Now you have a wife and a child on the way. There's nothing you wouldn't do to keep them safe. Am I right?"

Damn it all, he was. Somehow, Charles had to get out of this room so that he could save her. How could he get out of this?

"All right. You have me," Charles said, and Black Stephen's eyebrows shot up, his gaze sharpening. "It was Lord Ashford."

"Lord Ashford died in battle a month after I captured you."

That was exactly why Charles had picked him. Black Stephen couldn't harm the dead.

"Why should I believe you?" Black Stephen asked, pressing harder with the blade.

"What choice do you have?"

After a long moment, Black Stephen said, "I'll spare your life today, dog. But only because I don't want to make an enemy of your father. I owe him too much money. But know this. If you ever breathe a word to anyone, I will cut your throat and make your wife's life a living hell."

Black Stephen stepped back, blade now aimed at Charles's heart. "Now we go capture that bastard who has been stealing from my ships. And if he gets away, you know what will happen."

"You'll cut my throat and make my wife's life a living hell."

"Precisely. I'm glad we understand each other. Now put on your armor, and go out in the courtyard. I don't trust you not to try to stab me in the back while I'm putting on my chainmail."

With very little choice, Charles complied. Lord Stephen might have won this round, but Charles was going to see to it the man didn't survive the night.

CHAPTER TWENTY-EIGHT

FIONOLA EYED THE horse in front of her with trepidation. This was a serious flaw in her plan, and she knew it. Horses never liked her, and this one looked more skittish than any other she'd tried to ride. But he was the fastest horse they could procure on short notice.

All she had to do was gallop through town at high speed and lead her pursuers toward Rye. Then she would turn off into the woods north of town and disappear. Simple, right?

Ronan cocked his head as he held the reins of her mount. "Are you ready, Captain? You should go now. I've already started a rumor about your presence, and Michael has alerted the crew of the *Gorgon* about Black Stephen's order to hunt you down."

"Take the ship, and sail for Calais. Give Liam my love. I'll see him soon."

"I will. I'll see you soon, Captain."

Fionola clapped him on the shoulder and squeezed. "I'll see you soon." Ronan was a good man. She could only pray that her words were true.

Taking the reins, she stepped into the stirrup and, after a few tries, managed to pull herself into the saddle and get her foot into the opposite stirrup, scowling the whole time at Ronan for trying to help. Point realized he kept his distance. It was time. The mid-afternoon sun shone down on her as she steered the horse with some difficulty from the stables at the Sailor's Rest down to the docks until she saw the first guards marching along, questioning passersby. The creature was tossing its head and fighting the reins at every step, trying to turn around and go back to the stable. Finally arriving at the quay, she dug her heel into the horse's side, and the unruly beast took off like a boulder launched from a trebuchet, nearly throwing her off.

She only just managed to steer her mount to charge along Fish Street, gripping mane and gritting her teeth until she found her balance. The *Gorgon* passed in a blur. She could only just hear Ronan yell, "It's Captain O'Bannon! Get him!" over the pounding of hooves. Good. He was following the plan. The horse still fought her, but she managed to direct him around carts and only just avoid men carrying cargo to warehouses; she headed for the city gate, and the din of yells grew behind her.

Guards at the city's northern gate tried to bar her way, but at the last moment gave way as her horse's trampling hooves showed no sign of slowing. One of them managed to nick her leg with a blade. No matter. She'd suffered far worse.

Thundering along the ancient packed-dirt road to Rye, she dared a glance back. She'd certainly succeeded in drawing attention. Over a dozen men on horseback were in hot pursuit. She prayed that the crew of the *Gorgon* were among them. Even now, Liam might be getting his first taste of freedom in years. If only she could have been there with him! But no. She had to concoct this foolish plan to make herself the red stag in a town-wide hunt. There was nothing for it but to run.

The earthy scent of horse sweat filled her nose, and the thudding of hooves rolled like thunder, nearly blocking out the sounds of men yelling behind her. Wind blew in her face, doing little to cool the hot blood coursing through her.

An arrow whizzed by her ear, and she dug her heels in harder. She cursed under her breath. There was a horse archer among them. Knights from the castle must have joined the chase. She hugged the horse as close as she could, practically laying on its back with her cheek pressed to his neck to offer the lowest profile possible.

Another arrow whistled by, and it was all she could do to cling to her mount and not get jounced off as the frustrated horse increased its speed, still trying to go back to the stable. This horse might be fast, but it was no war horse trained to do its owner's bidding no matter what chaos reigned around it.

Saint Jude, intercede for me and send help so that I can get off this feckin' horse alive.

Her pursuers were closing in. She had to turn off the road into the woods soon to lose them, or all would be lost. She tried steering the horse with the reins, but it tossed its head, ears pressed flat and foam flying from its mouth, and continued to pound down the straightaway.

Hell and damnation. I should never have trusted a horse.

Her pursuers were getting closer and closer. A mere horse's length separated them now. Fionola dug in her heels, but the horse couldn't go any faster.

Christ on the cross. If I make it out of this alive, I swear by every saint in heaven and every demon in hell, I am never getting on a horse again.

Somewhere above the din, the twang and snap of a loosed arrow reached her ears, and a second later, her horse reared and screamed. Fionola's heart stopped beating as the world went sideways. Losing her grip, she careened out of control through the air, tossed like a rag doll.

With a bone-shattering jolt, the world righted itself, and somehow, she was still clinging to the rampaging animal as branches tore at her. By some miracle, they had turned into the woods at last.

Fionola turned her head for a quick glance back. An arrow was lodged in the horse's flank. She needed to get off this wounded creature before it lost all control, but her pursuers were still close behind. Better riders than she, they navigated the twists and turns around trees with ease while her horse scraped against every tree it passed. She tried to steer toward denser thickets of trees, but the beast was too spooked to pay any mind.

Dear God, please get me off of here.

As if listening, the horse bucked, making her lose her stirrups. Then it raced straight toward a tree, and especially the low branch she couldn't duck beneath. *Thwack!* The breath was knocked from her lungs as the branch struck her chest, and she tumbled backward. Her vision swam as she landed on her back on tufts of grass, the ground, thankfully, still soft from a recent rain. The thunder of the wretched creature's hoofbeats vibrated through her as it raced away.

A knight in chainmail and wearing a helm that covered his face rode straight toward her. She couldn't move and lay there, still stunned, and helpless. She was doomed.

"Do you see him?" shouted someone in the distance.

"No," said the knight staring straight at her. There was something familiar about his voice that she couldn't place. "He went that way," he said, pointing away from her.

The knight galloped off into the trees, and the other riders followed, the thudding of hooves fading as Fionola struggled to pull in breath.

Why did that knight let her go? Had he somehow missed her directly in front of him? No, it wasn't possible. He deliberately chose to let her escape. Did she have an unexpected ally? There was no time to puzzle it out. They could be back any moment.

She rolled over onto her belly and crawled into a nearby thicket, brambles tearing at her clothes. It was far from a perfect hiding place, but it would have to do for the moment. Every part of her body ached, but nothing was broken so far as she could tell.

Would a fall like that make her lose the baby? She prayed not. In the short time since she'd conceived, she'd grown attached to the person growing inside of her. Grumble as she might, she loved the idea of a child with Charles and couldn't wait to meet him or her, provided she got out of this alive. But it was no good to let her mind go down that path. She needed to keep her wits, and to do that, she needed hope.

At least she was off that demonic horse. A small blessing, to be sure, but a blessing, nonetheless.

A rumble in the distance told her that her pursuers were circling back around. Did she have time to climb a tree? More importantly, did she have the strength after that fall?

No time. As the thudding hooves approached, she made herself as small as possible in the bushes and stayed absolutely still.

The hooves came to a halt nearby, and Fionola held her breath.

"She's nearby," said a voice that haunted her nightmares. Black Stephen was here. "I followed the tracks of that runaway horse back here, and over there, the grass is crushed as if someone fell on it."

"I told you I checked here and found nothing." Now she knew who her savior knight was. That voice could only be Charles. Bless him a thousand times for trying to mislead them!

Boots hit the ground. Oh no. They were dismounting to look.

"I see blood on this leaf over here," said Black Stephen. "He's here."

Damn it all! Her leg wound.

More horses arrived.

"Sir Victor, tell your men to spread out and look for him," called out a voice she didn't recognize. "He can't have gone far."

It was a good thing they didn't have hounds with them, or she'd have been exposed immediately.

Boots approached her hiding place. There was nowhere for her to go. She would have to fight her way out. Ever so carefully, she slid one of her daggers from her sleeve.

"My lord, I think I see something," said the man closest to her as he chopped at the brush with his sword.

He was too close. There were men all around her. Fleeing was out of the question. The only thing she could do was fight.

With a silent apology to the man in front of her, she jabbed her knife into his unarmored calf. As the man fell backward, howling, she leapt to her feet and drew her sword. Pain shot through her side. Had she broken a rib in her fall? No matter. There was nothing she could do about it now.

Time slowed as she breathed in painfully, assessing her situation. She counted ten men that she could see. There were likely others in the vicinity. The odds weren't good, but when were they ever?

Three men charged at her, and she dodged at the last moment, a smile playing on her lips as two of them collided. The third thundered past where she had been a moment before, cursing. Two more came forward, and she spun, disarming one before he knew what hit him and hitting the other with the flat of her blade behind his knees to send him sprawling. These men had done nothing wrong. She only needed to escape, not dismember.

"Back off," Black Stephen yelled. "He's mine."

She turned around and saw the man who was the focus of all her loathing. He wore a mail shirt, boiled leather gloves, and metal grieves. The helm he wore was simple, protecting his skull and guarding his nose. His neck was vulnerable, she noted, as were the backs of his legs.

"No, he's not," said Charles, coming forward and breaking her concentration. "I'm in charge here. The man is *mine*."

She loved her husband for stepping up, but he had too much to lose if he was seen taking her side. She had gotten herself into this mess. She would get herself out of it without his help, despite the odds.

The rest of the men closed in around the three of them in a tight circle, blades drawn. Good. Circles could be broken. One only had to find the weakest link and push through. But damn it all, if she succeeded, she'd have to get on another godforsaken horse to escape.

Black Stephen advanced, sword raised. "Not a chance, Lord Charles. This man has been a boil on my arse for years now, and I mean to lance him."

"Then fight me, you lily-livered flesh-monger," she said as stepped forward to attack. "I have a bone to pick with you." Turning her face to Charles without taking her eyes off her enemy, she said, "Stand back. This is not your fight."

Without waiting for his response, she attacked Black Stephen, raining down blows from every angle. But Black Stephen met every blow, fending her off with remarkable skill. She'd never engaged this man in swordplay before. Perhaps she was in for more of a challenge than she expected.

Red tinged the corners of her vision as battle lust coursed through her. Her injuries forgotten, she charged at him like an angry boar, determined to gore the man.

He stepped aside lightly, and as she swept past him, she was close enough to smell the costly scented oils he bathed in. But they could not disguise the underlying rot at the heart of him. This wasn't a man. This was a midden heap wielding a sword.

As she passed, she swept out her foot, making him stumble, but he didn't fall.

He turned on her and swung his blade with furious force. As metal clanged against metal, pain shot up her arm. Her opponent had strength and skill. It was going to be no easy feat to take him down. But then, this was Black Stephen. She didn't want it to be easy. She wanted to stretch it out and make it long, painful, and humiliating for him.

He needed to pay for every scar on Charles's back as well as the ones that no doubt covered her brother's. He needed to pay for every day she and her brother had been apart, every moment of his captivity.

Whipping around, she struck at his exposed neck, drawing a thin red line as he dodged the deadly blow. First blood. She could practically taste it.

Black Stephen growled as he narrowly missed her shoulder with his counterblow. He was fighting well, but he hadn't spent a lifetime preparing for this fight. She would take him. She *had* to take him.

Striking again and again, she drove him back. With one of her blows, she sliced through the heavy leather of his glove to nick his sword hand, but he pulled away before she could relieve him of a finger or three.

Victory was in sight. She only had to keep up this barrage long enough for him to tire and make a mistake. Never mind that her own body was tired and aching, that each twist of her torso made her wince in pain. She was willing to give everything she had to destroy this man.

He stepped back and back again, swinging his blade wildly.

Then, suddenly, his gaze sharpened, and he smiled. That was all the warning she had before pain exploded from her chest, and she stumbled back.

CHAPTER TWENTY-NINE

"No," CHARLES CRIED out as Fionola fell to the ground. He ran toward her, and Black Stephen turned on him with narrowed eyes and a wide smile, raising his sword. Charles lashed out with his blade.

"I knew you were in league with him," the devil said as he easily deflected Charles. "And now I have my proof."

The men around them shifted uneasily, looking from Charles to Fionola, some stepping forward to join Lord Stephen. But it didn't matter. Not with his wife lying wounded on the forest floor. Blood bloomed from the wound in her chest, and he could hardly breathe, as if the injury was his own.

For a moment, panic gripped him, and he trembled with the effort to hold back the onset of his madness. But he couldn't give in. He had to keep his head or lose everything.

The path to Fionola lay through Black Stephen. Until he killed his foe, he could not reach her, tend to her, whisper words of love to tie her to this life. Without her, his life was empty, meaningless. Each minute that passed, her blood seeped out, and hope faded. She needed a healer. She needed *him*, imperfect as he was.

Fury overtook fear, flooding through his veins—a new kind of madness, one he welcomed. His vision turned red as he attacked again. It was time to take a stand against his enemy and expose him for what he was. "I've kept your secrets for too long, Lord Stephen," he yelled so all could hear. "But I will live in fear no more. I name you a traitor to the crown, and I mean to mete out the justice you so richly deserve."

The men around them stepped back, now staring at Black Stephen. Lord Cuthbert's gaze sharpened.

His foe turned bright red, and his lip twitched in an ugly sneer as he swung his blade with deadly force. "How dare you speak such lies! You're the traitor!"

Blocking, Charles stepped forward, swinging upward. Tension thrummed in every corner of his body. "He's plotting to make himself high king of Ireland, then to challenge King Henry for the throne of England," Charles bellowed, blocking another punishing blow. "I overhead him plotting, and that's why he imprisoned me and kept me from my family for two long years. And now he's wounded my wife."

"Your *wife*?" Lord Stephen's brow furrowed, and his sneer deepened. His blade missed Charles by an inch. As the it flew past, Charles could see Fionola's blood on its tip, and his heart stuttered.

"That is my wife, Fionola, beneath that scarf and beard, and you've killed her, you whoreson." Charles thrust with all his might, his blade hitting Black Stephen in the chest and knocking him back, but the blow glanced off the chainmail.

His enemy grunted and staggered back, momentarily knocked off balance. He nearly tripped over Fionola where she lay.

One of the men in the circle knelt beside her and pulled off the scarf and false beard. As one, the gathered men gasped.

Black Stephen coughed and raised his sword again. "So," he said in a wheezy voice. Charles must have knocked the breath out of him. "Fionola MacMurrough is Captain O'Bannon, and you are her accomplice. Not only are you a traitor but a pirate too."

"I am loyal to King Henry, which is more than I can say for you." Charles struck, but Black Stephen knocked his blade aside.

"What do we do?" one of the men asked. "Which of them speaks the truth?"

"Tend to the woman, guard her, and let them fight," said Lord Cuthbert, eyeing them closely. "Let God decide who is in the right."

Charles said a silent prayer. While his cause was just, his skill with a blade could not match his wife's, and even she had been bested by Black Stephen's hand. But what he lacked in skill he made up for in fury and fierce determination.

Steeling himself, he breathed deeply, remembering his captain's advice during a certain practice sword fight. *There are no rules. There is only your body and your sword. Use them well.*

He had to find his enemy's weakness, provoking him to reveal it. It took everything in him to do as his wife had once done and lower his sword. Every instinct screamed to keep it raised. Murmurs broke out amongst the men surrounding them. What was he doing? Was he giving up?

"Surrendering so soon?" Lord Stephen asked with an arched eyebrow.

"Not at all. Merely waiting for you to engage." Charles smiled grimly.

"Very well. Let us end this." Black Stephen struck out in a long arc meant to slice Charles in half diagonally.

Focused on evading and observing rather than fighting back, Charles stepped to the side, and his opponent's sword sliced air, and then grass.

Cursing, Black Stephen tried again, this time aiming for his neck. Charles ducked. The blade shaved a curl from the top of his head.

That was close. Too close.

But Black Stephen was off kilter. Encountering air when he had meant to cleave flesh and bone, his foe staggered.

Charles could use that. Swiping out with one foot, he kicked his enemy's unsteady feet from under him, and Black Stephen nearly fell backward before catching himself.

His opponent let out a low growl. "Raise your sword and fight like a man, you cur."

On the next pass, could he steal Black Stephen's blade? How exactly had Fionola done that?

As Lord Stephen slashed, Charles danced close to his foe, turning, and plucking at the sword as it neared the end of its arc. The pommel slid in the heavy leather glove, and Charles almost had it.

Then Black Stephen's grip tightened. Now behind Charles, he raised his sword arm, pulling Charles close and trapping him. His other hand grasped for the dagger at Charles's belt. But Charles wrenched free before he could raise it.

As he spun away, his enemy's sword slid against his leg, leaving a long, shallow cut. The sting of it made him hiss through his teeth. The iron scent of blood filled his nostrils as he retreated. Sweat trickled down his back. All was silent except for their panting. Dappled afternoon light filtered through leaves, making shifting patterns on the forest floor as a summer breeze failed to alleviate the heat.

Turning to face his foe once again, Charles glanced at his wife, lying behind him. Her eyes flickered open. She lived! All was not lost. Their eyes met, and her gaze sharpened, then grew wide as Black Stephen's boots thudded closer. Wrenching his attention away, he concentrated on his enemy, who stalked forward, a wild, deadly look in his eyes.

"Enough of your tricks," Lord Stephen said, raising his sword for another blow.

Charles needed new way to throw his opponent off. Perhaps words would work where his pitiful attempts to use his wife's tactics had failed.

"Enough of your treachery," Charles said, raising his own sword at last and slicing at his foe's exposed neck. "How do you think the king would feel about your attempts to assassinate your liege lord?"

Lord Cuthbert's eyes widened.

The tip of Charles's blade nicked Black Stephen's skin, as his enemy raised his defense a moment too late. Good. His distraction was working.

"At the Battle of Thurles," Charles continued, pressing his advantage, "that wasn't an enemy arrow that struck him. Nor was it an imbalance of humors that left him sick and weakened for weeks two winters ago. Lord only knows how many times you've tried since."

Their swords clashed with jarring force. Lord Stephen was forced to step back. Charles's strategy was working. Veins throbbed in his enemy's already bright-red neck, as a trickle of blood dripped down his collar.

"And you tried to marry the former King of Leinster's granddaughter to legitimize your claims." Charles's gaze flicked to Fionola before he pivoted and swung low, aiming for the unarmored back of his opponent's knee. If he could hamstring him, the fight would be over. "Fortunately, Fionola ran away and escaped your grasp."

His enemy stepped out of reach at the last second, countering with a rib-cracking blow to Charles's side. Fortunately, his mail shirt held. His side would ache, but no blood was drawn.

"You'll never touch her again, you beast," Charles ground out through gritted teeth. Pain radiating all through his side. He staggered back, sword raised in defense.

"You are a liar, a traitor, and a thief. No one will believe a word of these wild inventions." His foe's sword came down again and again, driving Charles back.

Chancing a quick glance at Lord Cuthbert, though, it appeared his words were sinking in.

"You even made an attempt on the life of the king when he was visiting Ireland."

"What is this?" Lord Cuthbert demanded.

"Fortunately for the king, it was only his poor taster that perished," Charles continued, driving his enemy back. "The poisoned wine was blamed on the King of Connacht, but I know it was you."

Lord Stephen tripped over a root, and Charles took advantage of the moment to try again for the back of his knees.

Once again, he failed, catching the man's calf instead. With a hiss, Black Stephen righted himself.

Charles spared another glance at his wife. Her eyes were glassy with pain, but they followed his every movement. He needed to go to her, cradle her in his arms.

Fionola, my love...

Black Stephen jabbed at his heart, but instead hit Charles's left shoulder. The blade found a weakness in the chainmail and slipped in. Searing pain radiated from the wound, as Charles swung up and sliced his enemy's thigh.

Relentless, Black Stephen struck at his right arm. Metal against chain mail. A crack. Charles's sword dropped from nerveless fingers, his arm broken by the blow.

A wide grin spread across his enemy's face.

No. It couldn't end like this.

Black Stephen stepped forward, raising his sword for the final blow.

He stopped short, eyes wide. The blood drained from his face. His sword fell to the ground. He collapsed to his knees then fell face first in the dirt.

What in heaven's name?

Then Charles saw it. One of Fionola's throwing knives protruded from Black Stephen's neck.

Taking his dagger from its sheath with his left hand, Charles approached his nemesis. Black Stephen's eyes were fixed on Fionola as his life blood seeped into the grass. "I could have been king, you bitch."

"Never," she groaned, then closed her eyes.

Kneeling down, Charles drew his dagger across the dying man's throat. Black Stephen's eyes clouded over, and his breathing came to a halt. It was over. The snake lay dead in the grass, his reign of terror at an end.

Charles shivered despite the heat. Even the vindication of this final triumph could not undo all the damage this man had done.

"God has decided," Lord Cuthbert declared. "Justice has been done, though the pirates must still answer for crimes against the crown. Guard them."

Charles ignored Lord Cuthbert. Dropping his dagger, Charles crawled to his wife. "My love," he whispered, kissing her cheek gently. "Can you hear me?"

"Yes," came a raspy but clear whisper.

"You saved my life."

"I couldn't…let him kill you." She wheezed as she spoke, her breathing shallow and ragged.

He kissed her precious forehead. "Thank you." He grazed her cheek again with his lips.

Sitting up on his knees, he turned to Sir Victor. "She needs a healer. We must bring her back to the castle."

"Under guard," Lord Cuthbert added.

But Sir Victor nodded. "We need a litter," he said to the man next to him. "She can't ride in this state. Go as quickly as you can."

The man ran to his horse, mounted, and was gone.

Charles turned back to his wife. "Stay with me, Captain. Don't you dare leave me." He took the blood-soaked cloth staunching her wound from the man who held it.

"I'm hard to kill," she whispered with a wan smile. "At least this time, there's no arrowhead to remove."

"No, there isn't." Charles smiled and blinked back tears.

Her eyelid fluttered closed. "Thank God."

A wave of tenderness flooded Charles at the memory of the last time he tended to his wounded captain. So much joy had been born of so much pain that night.

"Charles." Her eyes didn't open, but her hand clasped his arm. Her breathing grew more labored. Charles's heart broke at the sound. He willed her to keep breathing, in and out. In and out. "Liam," she whispered but trailed off.

"As soon as we get you to a healer, I'll find out, love." He cradled her hand in his and kissed it. She'd sacrificed so much for her brother. He could only pray her plan had been successful, whatever it was.

Hoof beats approached, and Sir Victor's man returned with a litter and the ancient castle healer in his voluminous robes, his bag clinking with potions.

Charles could hardly breathe as the healer examined her.

"It's a deep wound, but it appears to have missed any vital organs," the man said at last.

Relief trickled through Charles like sweet wine.

"We must transport her carefully. She has lost a lot of blood. But if we can get her back to the castle safely, she should make a full recovery."

"You four," said Sir Victor, directing his men. "Take the litter."

They immediately obeyed, and Charles was forced to relinquish his wife as they carefully transferred her and picked up the four poles.

"You need a healer too, my lord," said the old man, looking him over.

"Care for my wife first. I can wait."

"Yes, my lord."

With difficulty, Charles mounted his horse and followed the slow procession back to the castle, surrounded by guards. His family would have questions. There was no escaping it. He'd turned pirate and brought a pirate bride beneath their roof. But he prayed they would give him peace until Fionola had been tended to. Fortunately, his parents let him be as soon as they saw the severity of her injury.

"We'll talk later," his father said, giving him a meaningful look as they climbed the stairs to his bedchamber. "I'll fend off Lord Cuthbert for now."

The healer sewed and bandaged Fionola's wound then tended to Charles.

When the healer left, Fionola's eyes fluttered open. Once again, he was struck by how vulnerable she looked, lying in the enormous bed with her chest stitched and bandaged, though a spark of the captain still lingered in her gaze.

Charles sat beside her, taking her hand. They sat quietly for a long moment.

"You fought bravely today," she said, breaking the silence. "I wasn't sure you would be able to face him the way you did, given how he's affected you in the past."

The madness. Was it any wonder she doubted him? It had nearly taken him when he first faced his foe, but knowing her life depended on his defeating the blackguard helped him keep his head.

"You were hurt. You needed me, and the way to you was through him."

She squeezed his hand weakly. "You faced your demons and triumphed. You are stronger than you think, my love."

Something in his heart broke open at her words. He'd been so convinced he was irrevocably broken by his years of imprisonment, but love had given him strength in his darkest hour, healing him when he needed it most. For her, he could overcome anything, even the failings of his own mind.

He had to take her away from here. After everything they'd been through, he couldn't bear the thought of her facing punishment at the hands of Lord Cuthbert. There had to be a way out.

"As soon as you're well enough, we'll find a way to escape. I won't have you face the king's justice."

She closed her eyes for a long moment, then opened them. "I'm not sure I'll recover quickly enough, and I don't wish to make an enemy of the King of England. My family swore fealty to him, and I wouldn't have him think that oath has been broken. If he thinks the MacMurroughs have turned against him, it could have consequences for all of Leinster. I choose to stay and face judgment, though I do have one request."

His heart clenched at her words. "Yes, captain of my heart? What can I do? If it is in my power, I will see it done." He would move heaven and earth for her, undertake any quest she might ask of him.

She looked him in the eye and squeezed his hand. "Find out what happened to the *Gorgon* and my brother, and bring him here if you can. If I must face judgment, I want to see his face and hold him in my arms one last time. Will you go? I'm not fit for travel at the moment."

Of course. Liam. Closing his eyes, he wracked his brain for ideas on how to retrieve his friend. Could he escape to Calais and come back? It would be difficult without assistance. They were too well guarded. That meant turning to his family. "I'll need to enlist my father's help. But I think I can get him to agree."

She pulled his hand to her lips and kissed it. "Thank you. With you and my brother by my side, I can face anything at all, even the King of England."

She closed her eyes and drifted off to sleep. Now that she was safe and resting soundly in their feather bed, it was time to tell his family the truth and face the consequences.

CHAPTER THIRTY

C HARLES WALKED DOWN the stone steps to his father's study, shadowed by guards as if he were walking to the gallows. It reminded him of being a little boy, forced by his conscience to confess his mischief. But this time, he had gone too far, and he knew even his kind and just father would find it hard to forgive piracy. He'd broken the law, and he was prepared to face the consequences. How he was going to convince his father to let him go to Calais, he did not know.

He knocked on the door of his father's study, and his father invited him in and closed the door. The guards remained outside. Little had changed in this room in the last five years. It was still filled with simple furnishings, an absurd number of books and scrolls, and this one ridiculous, ostentatious table. The familiar round table with the pedestal in the shape of sea creatures stood just where he'd last seen it. Heaven only knew what his father saw in it.

Charles sat down in a heavy wooden chair across from his father, unable to find the words to begin.

"Well?" his father prompted when a minute had passed, and he still hadn't spoken.

Charles let out a long sigh. This had to be done. There was no avoiding it.

"It all began when I was in Lord Stephen's camp one night

and went to deliver a message to him."

He related to tale of how he overheard de Burgh's plotting along with Lord Chester.

"Black Stephen took the *Wind Song* and rechristened it the *Midas*, spreading the word that I had perished and holding me prisoner aboard the ship."

"Black Stephen," his father mused. "An apt name. Victor told me of your fight and of Lord Stephen's final words. That villain's treachery knew no bounds. I am ashamed I ever let the man into my house."

Taking a deep, shuddering breath, Charles reminded himself that the snake lived no more. His poison could not reach them now.

"For two years, he kept me aboard that ship as a prisoner and a slave. I will not tell you what life was like or what suffering he made me endure, but I will bear the scars to my dying day."

"Show me, Son. I need to know what this man did to you."

Hesitantly, he took off his cotte, pulled off his shirt, and showed his back.

His father gasped.

"I don't know what it looks like, but I can guess," Charles said. "I can't feel it when someone touches my back."

"Oh, Son. If he weren't dead, I would kill him for this," his father said in a quiet voice tinged with steel.

"I had given up all hope of rescue when one day Fionola, disguised as Captain O'Bannon, liberated my ship. I joined her crew, not knowing who she truly was. I had nothing, and I was very sick when she found me. I did what I had to in order to survive."

His father looked deep into his eyes and then nodded. "I can't pretend I'm not deeply disappointed that my son turned pirate. But as you say, you did what you had to. I would rather you be rescued by pirates than not at all. But why did you stay?"

Charles looked into his father's eyes and told him the truth. "I stayed for her."

His father's face was stern as Charles recounted the night that he saved her life and pledged his troth.

Staring at Charles long and hard after he finished, his father burst into laughter. He laughed so hard tears formed in the corners of his eyes, and he was gasping for breath.

"Why are you laughing? Is it the idea of Fionola being O'Bannon? Because I assure you she is."

"No, no, no," he said, waving his hand dismissively. "You think I could live with your mother and sisters all these years and not know women are quite capable of just about anything? No. I'm laughing at *you*. Because of course, you married a lady pirate. I should have known. You've been in love with stories of pirates and smugglers since you were a boy. And you never were going to settle down with a nice noblewoman. You and your ridiculous octopus test. Well, I hope you're happy." He chuckled again. Then his expression turned serious. "But even if the king grants you clemency, you know you can't become baron after this."

Charles swallowed. He'd expected this, hoped for it even. After everything, he didn't want the title and all that came with it. Nonetheless, his father's words left him momentarily speechless. "Yes, I know," he said at last. "There are other reasons I'm unsuited."

His father nodded. "I imagine going through what you have left many scars, not all of them visible."

"More than you know. I just hope that if we have a son, you'll let him inherit. I know Winchelsea's future is safe with Carenza and her earl having a son, but I wouldn't want my child to lose his birthright because of me." His head dropped to his hands. He could only pray that his family never saw him in the grips of one of his fits. They might call an exorcist.

But the baron merely nodded. "Your son will inherit my title, provided the king spares your lives. Lord Cuthbert has already announced his plan to escort us all to Dover, where the king is visiting for the next month, as soon as your wife can travel. King Henry himself will judge your case."

No. They were trapped. Charles's stomach clenched. Perhaps if she healed enough they could attempt escape? But there was no chance of moving her now, wounded as she was.

"It has not gone unnoticed," his father said, giving him a sharp look, "that the *Gorgon* disappeared in the midst of the dramatic chase for Captain O'Bannon. I'm sure that is merely a coincidence."

They got away! Praise the Lord!

His relief must have shown on his face because his father shook his head and pursed his lips. "The crew of the *Draconis* can never return to these shores. Do you understand me? The penalty for piracy is death, and Lord Cuthbert will not hesitate to uphold the law should they come back to England."

"I understand." Charles stared at his hands as he attempted to school his face into an appropriately somber and apologetic expression. Taking a deep breath, he looked up at his father again. "But I have a favor to ask you, even though I know I don't deserve it. Fionola wants to see her brother, Liam, one last time before facing the king's judgment. He was a prisoner on the *Gorgon*. Help me find him and bring him back."

There was a long, tense silence.

Steepling his hands, her father said, "You're asking me to help you escape."

Charles shook his head. "I would never leave Fionola behind. I only ask for your assistance bringing back her brother. The journey will only take me a few days."

"Where are they?"

Should he answer? His father could tell Lord Cuthbert, then all hope would be lost. But he'd already made his choice. He would have to trust that his father would not betray him.

Meeting his father's gaze, he said, "Calais."

The baron looked at him long and hard, then nodded. "The *Gorgon* is rightful property of the crown, now that Lord Stephen has been unmasked. I might need my pirate son to help me recover that property from the brigands who have captured it. I'll speak to Lord Cuthbert. I'm certain he'll agree, as long as I guarantee you will return to face justice. Your wife stays as a guarantee of your good behavior. We'll sail for Calais at first light tomorrow."

An interesting proposition. But what would his father's men do to his friends when he found them? "I won't betray my friends."

"Your pirate friends?" his father asked sharply. "They stole a ship. Should they not face justice?"

"They stole from a traitor and a thief. They only ever attacked Black Stephen's ships, never anyone else's. I swear it. And I am certain I can convince them to give the *Gorgon* up to you without bloodshed if you let me go to them alone. If you try to capture it through force, it will cost lives on both sides. Please, Papa, let me try."

His father gave him a wary look and sighed. "All right. You may try. But I must have your solemn oath that you will not try to escape with them."

"How could I escape when the woman I love more than life itself lies wounded in Winchelsea? You could not stop me from returning if you tried. But if you insist—"

"I do," his father said with furrowed brow.

Charles looked his father squarely in the eye and said, "I solemnly swear that I will not attempt to escape in Calais and that I will return with you to Winchelsea to face the king's justice."

The baron nodded solemnly. Then his gaze softened, and he reached out to squeeze Charles's shoulder. "Thank you. I'm sorry it has to be this way. We'll leave at dawn. Now go see to that pirate wife of yours. I must speak to Lord Cuthbert."

Charles rose and took his leave, praying that he could make good on his word once they reached Calais.

CHAPTER THIRTY-ONE

FIONOLA WAS TIRED of being cooped up in her bedchamber, comfortable and spacious as it was. She was ill suited to being an invalid, and Charles could not return soon enough with her brother.

There was a knock on her door. Could it be Charles and Liam? For a moment, hope blossomed in her heart. Then she remembered that Charles wouldn't knock.

Swallowing her disappointment, she said, "Come in."

Expecting a servant, she was surprised when Lady Carenza walked in, wearing a voluminous blue gown with sleeves that dripped to the floor and carrying a lute.

"My lady, I hope you'll forgive me if I don't curtsey," Fionola said, wondering what exactly she was in for.

"Don't be ridiculous. Call me Carenza. You're family now. There's no need for all that nonsense between us, even if there weren't a hole in your chest."

Carenza crossed the room and seated herself on the elaborately carved wooden chair that sat beside the equally elaborate writing desk.

"I thought you might need some distraction as you heal from your wounds and wait for your husband to return," Carenza said, settling her lute against her pregnant belly. "And I've been composing something I could use your help with." She turned the pegs of the lute, tuning it carefully.

"My help? What could I do to help you, helpless as I am in my current state?"

Carenza laughed, her voice rich and low. "Somehow, I don't think you're ever helpless, no matter what your state. I heard about how you killed Lord Stephen. How did you manage it?"

Fionola shrugged, then winced. Movement was a terrible idea, no matter how much she yearned to leave her bed.

"I'm very good with throwing knives." She felt for her sleeve reflexively then remembered that Lord Cuthbert had her searched and had taken away her blades. "As long as Charles was winning, I let him fight. He needed to bring that bastard down as much as I did, and I would not have begrudged him dealing the final blow. But when the outcome looked uncertain, I had to act."

"But your guard—"

"Was too absorbed in watching the fight to notice."

Leaning in, Carenza asked, "But didn't it hurt?"

"It did, but I would endure any pain to save Charles."

Her sister-in-law smiled at that. "I'm so happy the two of you found love. Charles would have been miserable in an arranged marriage. Also, a love story will add extra interest to the epic ballad I'm composing about you." She absently strummed a few chords. "Would you like to hear it?"

"You wrote a ballad about Charles and me?" Never had Fionola dreamed anyone would do such a thing. She had always loved to listen to the minstrels in her grandfather's court, singing epic tales of valor. The idea of one about her was absolutely delightful.

"I did. It's still a work in progress, but I hope you'll enjoy it. It goes like this."

Lady Carenza began to strum brisk chords, building an air of excitement even before singing the first word.

> "*Lord Charles, a nobleman, set sail upon the sea,*
> *And led brave men who left in search of victory.*

To Ireland they went, commanded by their king
To end a bloody war and—"

The song was interrupted when the door opened, and in walked Charles, leading the person she most longed to see. So many emotions flowed through her she could hardly breathe. Her twin at long last! Tears of joy formed in the corners of her eyes even as outrage coursed through her at the years they'd lost.

Her brother came straight to her side and sat on the bed next to her. For a long moment, she lay silent as she looked him up and down, drinking him in. He was thin as a rail but wearing clothes of good make. His bright red hair was cropped so short, you couldn't tell it was curly. There was no trace of a beard on his chin. The bones in his cheeks and jaw made stark angles beneath his sunken flesh, and his green eyes had a haunted look to them, even as he smiled at the sight of her. She wished she could kill Black Stephen all over again for his ill treatment of her beloved brother.

"Liam," she said, gasping. As she tried to get up to go to him, pain lanced through her, and she was forced to lie back down.

"Fionola, what have you done now?" Liam asked, shaking his head, and smiling at her.

"I ended the nightmare. I killed Lord Stephen and rescued you at long last." A tear streaked down her face.

Liam reached out and brushed it away with his thumb. "Mother would never approve, you know."

She guffawed then winced at the radiating pain it caused her. "Then it's a good thing she'll never know," she said, attempting a jaunty wink.

"Your secret is safe with me." He grinned, and for a moment he was back to the brother she remembered, full of joy and kindness, his sadness wiped away. Then it returned, and his face fell, and moisture gathered in the corners of his eyes. "Thank you, Fi. I never thought I would get out of there alive."

Carenza cleared her throat. "Charles, I think we'd better leave them." She rose and headed for the door, and Charles started to follow.

"Wait," Fionola called out. "Charles, please stay. I want you here. Come sit with us. You're family now."

"Are you sure?" Her beloved's brow furrowed.

"Yes," she and Liam said at the same time.

"Come sit by my side." She patted the bed on the opposite side from where Liam sat.

Carenza closed the door quietly behind her as Charles slipped off his shoes and climbed onto the bed beside her.

"Are you comfortable, my love? Would you like to sit up?" he asked as soon as he was settled.

"Yes, I would, very much."

With tender care, he raised her to sitting and arranged pillows behind her to prop her up.

"Thank you," she said, taking his hand and kissing it. His skin still tasted of sea salt and was warm from the sun. How she longed to return to the sea with him! But that would have to wait. She had a long recovery ahead of her, to be followed by a long confinement as her belly grew. That is, if she kept the child after all that had happened. So far, she hadn't bled down below, and that gave her tenuous hope.

But her two favorite people were here by her side. This was not a moment for worry and sadness.

"Fi," Liam said, breaking her revery. "Thank you. I know those words are entirely inadequate compared to what I owe you. It was a living hell. The less that's said about it, the better. And you helped me escape! I can't tell you how my heart swelled at the sight of Thomas coming to unlock us."

Fionola smiled. "Tell me the whole story. I was too busy causing a distraction to see how they took the ship. I want to hear every detail."

"Of course, sister, though a lot of it I only know second hand. I was locked up in the dark through most of it, unaware that anything was afoot until I saw Thomas. But they all regaled me with the story at length and repeatedly. I think your crew was a bit smug after pulling this off. Aidan even started making up a song about it."

Of course, he did. She couldn't wait to get back to Gan Ainm to hear it. If the king granted her clemency, that was. "They should be proud. It was no small feat. Tell me everything."

"They told me about your wild ride through the streets of Winchelsea dressed as Captain O'Bannon, dread pirate of the Atlantic. Someday, you'll have to show me your pirate get-up. I still can't believe you pulled off pretending to be a man for years on end."

She chuckled. "I think I was better at being Captain O'Bannon than I am at being Fionola MacMurrough. The good Lord knows, mother was never able to make a proper lady of me."

"You were very convincing," Charles said and then kissed her hand. "I can't deny I love the way you look in a dress, but no matter what you wear, you will always be my captain."

She took a moment to gaze adoringly into her husband's eyes before turning back to her brother. "So tell me what happened after I rode by."

"Thomas ran to the *Draconis* and told the first mate that Lord Stephen had ordered them to join the chase for O'Bannon. The ship emptied of all but four crew left to guard it. Then Aidan came aboard with Godric and Bartholomew, just as you planned, and he told the guards they were part of the Winchelsea Watch and had heard a stowaway from O'Bannon's crew might be on board. He lured one below decks to help him search, where he easily subdued the man and tied him up. Then he called for help, saying he'd found the stowaway, and another man went down only to be captured by Aidan. Godric and Bartholomew were able to subdue the remaining two with a minimum of noise. The rest of your crew boarded, and before anyone in the port knew what happened, we set sail. No one suspected a thing. They were all too busy hunting for you."

Holy Mother of God, it worked. All the saints in heaven must have been looking after them for such a scheme to succeed. But here was the proof before her. Liam, in the flesh. There was an ache in her chest that had nothing to do with her wound. She squeezed her brother's hand.

"I knew they could pull it off," she said, turning to her husband with a wink, ignoring the well of love that threatened to overpower her every time she looked at Liam. "I have an excellent crew." She blinked back the irritating moisture that had gathered in the corners of her eyes.

"That you do," her brother agreed. How she loved the sound of his soft and gentle voice! "I'm afraid my retelling doesn't do it full justice. When Aidan sings it, he embellishes it with feats of strength, thrilling sword fights, near misses, making it all sound so grand it's hardly to be believed. The best part is his telling of the ride of Captain O'Bannon, bravely charging through scores of enemies on a demonic horse—"

"Well, he got the demonic horse right. The bloody creature threw me off! It's a wonder I survived that ride, and not because of my many pursuers. I swear to you both, I am never getting on a horse again."

Charles and Liam both burst out laughing. "You always did hate riding," Liam said, still chuckling. "Is that why you took to the sea? To avoid horses? And here I thought you were coming to rescue me."

He caught her gaze and held it, his eyes full of brotherly affection.

She swallowed to clear a lump in her throat.

"I was. The lack of horses on board a ship was merely a side benefit."

Liam smiled at her as if he understood all the earnest, heartfelt words she couldn't find. "I missed you, Fi," he said simply.

Tears welled up, and she couldn't stop them. "I missed you too," she said in a wobbly voice she hardly recognized as her own.

"It's all right, Captain," her husband murmured, bringing her hand to his lips again. "You're with us. There's nothing but love here."

She wasn't sure how long they sat and talked together, but it was late in the night when Liam left for bed.

"Thank you for bringing him back to me," she murmured as Charles snuggled beside her. "With you and him, I feel whole again, despite the hole in my chest. I feel ready to face anything, even the King of England."

He kissed her ever so gently and carefully. "It was the least I could do after all you've done for me. Whatever the future holds, we'll face it together."

In the soothing circle of his arms, she let herself drift off to sleep as contented as she'd ever been, despite the judgment that loomed before them.

CHAPTER THIRTY-TWO

CHARLES HELD FIONOLA close in the wee hours of the morning, unable to sleep despite the comforts of the inn where they were staying. A month had passed since they dispatched Black Stephen. Fionola had been bedridden for the first few weeks as her wound began to heal. They had both remained confined in Winchelsea Castle until it was time to travel to Dover. It was a bittersweet time, alternating between tending to Fionola and reacquainting himself with his family. One bright spot was the quiet ceremony to renew their vows before a proper priest and his gathered family. Charles was glad to be her husband twice over, he thought to himself as he ran his hand over the growing swell of her belly.

Dover Castle was full to bursting with the king's retinue, and the Lord Warden was unable to house them. Fortunately, they found a place to stay not far from the castle. Lord Cuthbert stationed a guard outside their door to make sure they didn't attempt to flee, but his father had pleaded to allow them to stay together this final night before facing the king. His parents were in a room down the hall, bless them. Liam was here too. They were determined to come along and plead for them if the king's judgment turned against them.

Running away was no use. Fionola was still too weak from her injury. And even if they did manage to escape, justice would find them eventually, one way or another. The king's reach was too great. It was best to face this head-on while Lord Stephen's perfidy was fresh in the king's mind and pray that he would be sympathetic.

Fionola moved and murmured, "You're not asleep."

"No, love, I'm not."

"You need distraction before battle." She reached down and started to stroke him. "Fortunately, I know just how to do it."

Tendrils of pleasure spread through him, unraveling his tension. He surrendered to her tender ministrations. This could be their last chance before facing an uncertain doom.

God, he loved his wife. He could still hardly believe his luck after years of captivity, deprived of every joy and comfort. In his darkest hours, the dream of her kept him alive, even before he knew her. And here she was, in his bed, driving him wild with bliss, a dream made flesh.

Settling between her thighs, he was carried away by a wave of pure bliss. If only he could stay here forever, surrounded by the ocean of her love. The winds of fate could bellow all they wanted and do nothing but ruffle the surface of the fathomless bond they shared.

Too soon, it was at an end. He collapsed beside her, both of them sated and exhausted. They slept fitfully until dawn when the cock in the yard behind the inn crowed to wake them.

"Are you sure you want to do this?" Charles asked, one final time. If she said no, they would try to fight their way to the port and leave everything behind, no matter the risk.

"There's no escaping now, love, and you know it. We must face the king's justice and pray he has mercy."

"Even if he does, you realize this means you can never be Captain O'Bannon again."

A sly smile spread across her face. "I much prefer to be Captain Fionola MacMurrough, an honest trader. It's the sea I love, not the piracy. I only did what I had to in order to reunite my family. Now that Liam is safe, I want peace. And I want my child to know his or her family. I firmly believe God is on our side and that justice will prevail today."

With grim determination, Charles rode through the imposing gates of Dover Castle with Fionola by his side, their guard riding behind them. The fortress was still under construction, and masons scurried along the curtain wall, hammering away as they added layer after layer of gray stone to build up its battlements. The imposing front gate was dwarfed by the scale of the walls around it, and it opened like a dark maw, ready to swallow them. A sense of foreboding settled over him as he rode beneath the portcullis, his wife at his side. His parents and Liam followed, bolstering his will.

They dismounted and let stable hands lead their horses away. As they entered the great hall, they found themselves in line behind dozens of petitioners waiting their turn for an audience with the king. He could see His Majesty at the opposite end of the hall, sitting on a throne on a dais, but from this distance, he could only make out the royal purple of his attire and the gold of his crown.

Charles had only ever seen the king from afar. When he was growing up, Queen Eleanor visited Winchelsea on several occasions to see his mother who had been her lady in waiting, but the king had never accompanied her. His father had once taken him to Windsor Castle where he only caught the briefest glimpses of the sovereign of all England, greeting throngs of subjects on the day of the Assumption of the Virgin Mary.

King Henry II was known as a fair and just ruler, having brought peace to England after years of civil war between his mother, Empress Mathilda, and his cousin, King Stephen. But which way would his justice lean today? Surely, he would be glad to be rid of an enemy in Lord Stephen. But would he forgive attacks against English ships, even if they were justified?

Knights stood on either side of the sovereign, motionless and impassive in their armor. A woman sat beside him, wearing a red dress trimmed with gold. Charles couldn't make out her features, but he could see the flash of her jewels in the morning sunlight that slanted through the narrow windows of the hall. It must have been one of the king's mistresses. Everyone knew his fiery queen was imprisoned and that the two of them were estranged. Would Charles's mother's long connection to the queen work for or against them?

As they approached, Charles studied the king's features, looking for some hint at his mood, some indication of what their fate might be. The king's face was somber and serious as he listened to petitioner after petitioner, passing judgment brusquely and sending them on their way. He had intelligent eyes, a long nose, and a pointed beard. His brows were perpetually furrowed, the only indication of emotion the occasional rise of one brow.

Lord Cuthbert stood to the side, looking on with sharp eyes and glancing down every so often at the scribe who was recording the proceedings, pointing, and offering corrections. He caught Charles's eye for a moment as he surveyed the line, and his eyes narrowed before he turned back to his work.

Fionola grasped Charles's hand, and whispered in his ear, "God will be with us today. We will prevail." The squeeze of her hand belied the certainty in her voice.

He squeezed back and turned to whisper back, "Aye, Captain." He winked and smiled at her, projecting a confidence he did not feel.

A young page whose voice had not yet broken asked them to step forward and state their business with the king. Charles bowed deeply, and Fionola curtsied.

"Your Majesty," Charles began, glad that his voice remained even and clear, despite the sudden dryness in his throat. "I am Charles de Vere, son of Martin de Vere, Baron of Winchelsea and this is my wife, Lady Fionola. We come to recount a tale of treachery and woe and to seek your clemency for acts we committed in defeating an enemy of yours, Lord Stephen de Burgh."

The furrow between the king's brows deepened at the mention of Black Stephen. "That overweening snake. Word of his plots and crimes against me has reached me, and Lord Chester came forward to confirm his treachery." The king glanced at Lord Cuthbert. "I've heard a wild rumor that he was killed by a lady pirate, though I hardly gave that credence." Nonetheless, he paused and gave Fionola an appraising look. "Tell me your tale, and be succinct. As you can see, I have many petitioners today."

Charles told their wild tale, starting with the night he overheard Lord Stephen plotting and finishing with the man's death at Fionola's hands. The king's eyebrow raised several times during the telling, and by the end, he was leaning forward, eyes narrowed and staring at Fionola. "And so, Your Majesty," Charles said, holding his wife's hand tightly, "we beg for your clemency for the acts we committed in the name of bringing your enemy down and ending a threat to your rule."

Charles bowed, and Fionola curtsied beside him, as they awaited their doom. This could be the end. His heart hammered in his chest, and the silence thundered in his ears.

Lord Cuthbert cleared his throat, and the stone-faced king turned to him. "Your Majesty, as I told you, these two are guilty of piracy against English ships. You heard it from their own lips just now. God may have allowed them to prevail against the traitor, Lord Stephen, but I recommend you punish them to the fullest extent of the law." He bowed and stepped back.

After a long silence, Charles dared to look up at the man who held their fate in his hands and saw the slightest hint of a smile curling his lips.

"Young man," the king said at last, "many years ago, a fiery red head with a thirst for battle demanded that I marry her. Like you, I said yes. I cannot say it has been easy to have such a wife, but it has certainly been…interesting."

The woman beside the king bristled and cleared her throat.

Turning to her, the king arched an eyebrow. "Someone bring Lady Rosamund a flagon of wine. Her throat is dry," he ordered, and a servant went scurrying to obey.

"Young lady," the king said, turning to Fionola, "your family has been loyal to me, and you have done me a great favor dispensing with an enemy whose treachery went undiscovered for far too long. Nonetheless, piracy is a serious crime."

The king straightened and looked out at the hall. Lord Cuthbert glared at them. All of the courtiers and supplicants in attendance hushed beneath his sharp gaze. Turning back to Charles and Fionola, he announced in a booming voice that carried the length of the hall. "Lord Charles de Vere and Lady Fionola de Vere, hear my judgment. God granted you victory against Lord Stephen de Burgh, a traitor to the crown. You are absolved of any wrongdoing as it relates to his killing. However..." The king paused and looked back and forth between Charles and Fionola.

Charles's heart stuttered, and he held his breath, dreading what might come next.

"Piracy will not be tolerated in my waters," the king continued. "If you both take a solemn oath today before God and your king never to engage in an act of piracy again, I will allow you to return to Ireland, and I will grant you permission to visit your family in Winchelsea on the condition that they guarantee your good behavior," he said, giving a pointed look to Charles's father.

Turning back to Charles and Fionola, he continued, "However, Winchelsea is the only place in England where you are permitted. If you ever set foot in England anywhere outside of Winchelsea, your lives are forfeit. If you ever engage in an act of piracy again, your lives are forfeit. This is my judgment. Do you accept my conditions?"

Lord Cuthbert turned bright red, gritting his teeth.

Relief flooded Charles as he took a deep breath and responded, "I do, Your Majesty."

"And you, Lady Fionola?"

"I do, Your Majesty."

Charles took a quick glance at his wife. This was the end of Captain O'Bannon and the *Draconis*—a life she had taken on of necessity but that he knew she loved. Nonetheless, he did not read any regret in her expression, only dignity and determination.

"Good," said the king. "Then kneel and repeat after me."

They obeyed, kneeling on the flagstone floor of the hall.

"I solemnly swear before God, my king, and all assembled here that I will never engage in an act of piracy again."

They repeated the words, projecting their voices for all to hear.

"Furthermore," the king continued, "I swear never to return to England except to visit Winchelsea, on pain of death."

Charles swore the oath with Fionola by his side, and his heart lightened as he spoke the words. They were exiled, but they were free. And he could still see his family. He wanted to get up and dance a jig, but he fought to keep his expression solemn as befitted the occasion.

"Rise and go forth. I hope never to see you two again," the king said, dismissing them, but a hint of a smile played on his lips.

Charles immediately obeyed, offering an arm to help Fionola up. She still wasn't entirely accustomed to navigating skirts. They bowed and curtsied one last time and hurried from the hall, followed by his parents and Liam.

As they walked through the castle gates and back into the morning's bright sunlight, Charles's heart was full to bursting. Not caring what anyone thought, he took Fionola in his arms and kissed her then twirled her around.

"We're free, my love. The nightmare is at an end," he said, letting her up for breath at last. "What shall we do to celebrate?"

A sly grin spread across her face. "Let's go sailing."

EPILOGUE

Gan Ainm

CHARLES WAS GOING easy on her, Fionola was certain. Not that it was easy to sword fight when one's body felt like an overripe gourd ready to drop off the vine. He'd won more than he'd lost, despite holding back. Her center of gravity was all wrong, and everything ached. Nonetheless, she fought every day, much to Maeve's consternation. Though maybe, going forward, she should stick to fighting Deirdre, whose swordsmanship was improving by the day but who still lacked the skill and stamina to push as hard as Charles.

"Will you stop this nonsense and come inside?" Maeve said, barging out the kitchen door and into the castle courtyard between them. "You're due any day now. I would think you'd be more careful with yourself," she said, nudging Fionola inside. "And you," she said, rounding on Charles. "I'm surprised at you, endangering your wife like that."

Charles laughed. "Do you really think she gave me a choice? She may be a bit slower with a sword these days, but she still has her throwing knives up her sleeves."

And she would use them, too, if he didn't cooperate and give her what she wanted—not to hurt him, only to scare him. But he was right to be cautious.

"How much longer is this baby going to be inside me, Auntie? I'm tired of being pregnant."

"Any day now, as I've told you."

Fionola had been feeling little cramps all morning, but she was accustomed to ignoring pain. So she thought nothing of them. Labor, when it came, would be big waves of pain, as she understood it. She was ready when the time came. Pain didn't scare her.

"Has Liam been by this morning? Did I miss him?"

"Not yet," said Maeve. "Why he didn't move in here, I will never understand. We have the room."

Poor Liam. Maeve would never give up.

"He's very happy living with Thomas and Ronan," Charles said, picking up a freshly baked pastry from the tray Maeve set out on the table.

"Do you have any fish?" Fionola asked, looking at the pastries with suspicion.

Maeve put a bowl in front of her with barley, chunks of fish, and a green sauce.

"Thank you!"

As she was about to dig in, Liam came through the door with Ronan.

"Still pregnant, Captain?" Ronan teased. "You're delinquent in your childbearing duties. You'd better get to work."

A sharp pain seized her belly, but it was gone in a moment, so she ignored it.

"Never mind him," said Liam. "How are you feeling?"

"Too big," she answered. This had to end soon. She couldn't possibly grow any bigger.

"Is there anything you need?"

"Not unless you know of a magic potion to make the baby come. How is the village?" she asked, turning to Ronan.

"We've sent the last of the troublemakers on their way."

Fionola nodded. Most of the town took the news that Captain O'Bannon was a woman in stride after the initial shock wore off, but some refused to come around. Ronan and her loyal crew saw to it that those who refused to accept her moved on from Gan Ainm.

"They're still calling you the Queen of Gan Ainm, though," Ronan continued with a smirk.

Furrowing her brown, Fionola said, "Just wait until I've got this baby out of me. Then I dare anyone to say it to my face."

Another sharp pain seized her belly, and she rubbed it unconsciously. Must have been something she ate. Or the thought of being called queen. That was enough to turn anyone's stomach.

Suddenly, liquid dripped down her legs. She gasped as realization dawned. All the morning's minor pains now added up to something larger. "Maeve, I think it's time for battle."

Everyone stared at her, frozen for a moment.

"You mean—?" Maeve said, shaking off the shock and moving into action.

"My water just broke."

Charles's face lit up with delight. He kissed her forehead, and ran out of the room, returning moments later with her sword. He knelt before her, offering her the hilt.

"What in the name of all that's holy are you doing?" Maeve objected.

"You heard her," he said. "She's going into battle. She needs her sword."

Fionola knew there was a reason she loved this man.

"Ridiculous. That thing had better not get anywhere near me," Maeve scolded. "Upstairs. Now, young lady."

Following someone else's orders for once, Fionola made her way up to her chamber with Maeve right behind her. She settled in on the bed, her sword clutched beside her.

"Now what happens?" Fionola asked, even though Maeve had talked her through the process many times.

"You will have more pains and they will get worse and closer together until the baby comes out."

"I am ready."

For hours, she breathed deeply through the pain. At first it was manageable. She gritted her teeth through the contractions and reminisced with Maeve about her childhood back in Wexford. Then the pains became harder to shrug off, and she got quieter, clutching the hilt of her sword until her knuckles were white but refusing to let herself cry out.

She was Captain O'Bannon, scourge of the Atlantic. No mere labor pains could defeat her. This was a battle in which she must emerge victorious, using all her strength and determination to birth this child whom she had grown to love over the last nine months. The babe would be her scion, her heir, just as much as Charles's. He or she would grow into a fearsome and brave warrior, leader of men, and master of the seas. Everything she had learned over the years she would impart to this child. Her dreams for the baby's future were boundless.

A pain assailed her. She welcomed it with a low growl. Maeve took a step back as Fionola's sword twitched by her side. The pain seized her belly and turned it hard as a rock.

I will defeat the pain. I will pass through it undaunted.

Showing her teeth, she gave a battle yell.

"It's time for you to push," said Maeve from between her legs. "Don't take my head off."

"I would never hurt you," Fionola grunted as she bore down.

"I know, my sweet girl. But you may be sorely tempted during these final pains."

The pain passed, and she had a moment's respite.

"My sheath is over there," Fionola said, pointing. "Quickly, put it on the sword so that I can't do any real harm. I want you to feel safe."

Fionola would never use her sword against Maeve, but she could see the worried look in her auntie's eyes.

Maeve ran to comply before the next contraction hit. She also wrapped a sheet tightly around the sheathed sword to make extra certain.

Another pain seized Fionola, making her snarl.

"Push," Maeve ordered.

Fionola did with all her strength. She felt herself stretching and opening as her body worked to push the baby out.

There was barely a moment to breathe before another pain hit.

"Push!"

Grasping her sword with all her strength, Fionola faced down the pain with her most murderous, ferocious cry—a cry that would strike terror into the heart of her enemies. It was her moment of triumph, she was certain.

"Here comes the baby's head. Just one more push!"

With the next contraction, every muscle in Fionola's body tensed.

A moment later, she heard a baby's cry.

Success!

Her grip relaxed on her sword, and tears streamed down her face.

The battle was won.

"It's a boy," Maeve said as she handed a sweet, squalling bundle to Fionola.

"Hello, little Thomas," Fionola murmured, bringing the baby to her breast.

"Thomas?" Maeve asked.

"Who else has done so much and sacrificed so much for me? He is my dearest friend and the bravest, kindest man I know. Aside from Charles, of course. But Charles agreed to the name. Speaking of Charles, you should go get him so that he can meet his son."

Maeve scurried out. Fionola looked down at the baby in her arms.

"Hello, little warrior. You did well today, coming out into the big world. Your mama and papa love you very much, and we can't wait to show you everything. There's so much in this wide world to see."

Charles came barreling through the door and came to an

abrupt halt beside her. "Are you all right? How is the baby? How do you feel, my love?"

"We're both fine," she said with a smile. "We were victorious in battle."

Charles smiled and looked over at the sword wrapped in sheets. "I see Maeve took precautions. Very wise of her."

Fionola laughed.

"I love you, Captain," he said, kissing her forehead.

"I love you too," she said, reaching up and touching her lips to his. "Would you like to hold our son?"

"Very much."

She lifted little Thomas from her breast and handed him to Charles. Unhappy at being removed from his cozy spot, Thomas screamed. Fionola's eyes immediately darted to Charles. Would he be able to withstand the baby's cries? As she watched, Charles stuffed bee's wax into his ears and took several deep breaths, then held out his hands.

"I'm fine with a little help. You see?" he said as he took the infant in his arms, beaming. "Hello, little Thomas. Your papa loves you very much. We're going to have such fun together!"

Little Thomas instantly settled into his father's arms, staring up at him with wide eyes. Fionola smiled. She knew Charles would be an excellent father.

She reached out and took Charles's hand and watched their tiny child, unable to recall when she'd been so content.

There was a knock at the door. Fionola covered herself up.

"Come in," she called, and Liam poked his head in.

"Can I see him?"

"Of course."

"What's his name?"

"Thomas."

Liam grinned as Charles brought little Thomas over. "I've never seen a more beautiful baby."

Fionola laughed. "And how many babies have you seen?"

"Not many," Liam admitted. "But with parents like you two,

I know he'll be extraordinary."

Little Thomas grabbed Liam's pinky in his tiny grip. Fionola's heart melted to see the three people she loved most in the world so happy together.

"You'll be his godfather, of course," Charles said, a little too loudly.

"Of course, you must be," she agreed.

Liam blinked and blinked again. A tear rolled down his cheek. "I'd be honored."

Fionola looked around the room at the two men she loved. Here on Gan Ainm she had everything she wanted—her beloved family, her friends, her sword, a ship to sail. She had found her true home at last.

About the Author

Leslie Vollard has a longstanding passion for the Middle Ages. Her obsession with all things medieval dates back to college when she dug through archives at the Bibliothèque Nationale in Paris to study the 12th century troubadour, Arnaut Daniel. In her work, she brings courtly love, chivalry, and the troubadour tradition to life. Romance reigns supreme in her steamy novels about how love conquers all.

Leslie lives in Long Island with her delightfully nerdy husband and two cats. She loves gardening, baking, and reading love poems in dead languages.